I0601910

Seducing the
Dragon Knight

A Dragon Protectors Novel

Michelle Miles

This is a work of fiction. All characters, organizations and events portrayed in this novel are either products of the author's imagination or used fictitiously.

SEDUCING THE DRAGON KNIGHT

Cover Design by Erin Dameron-Hill

ISBN: 978-1-7333887-3-3

Seducing the Dragon Knight

A Dragon Protectors Novel

"From the start this book has danger and a bit of mystery."
—*4 stars, Amazon Reviewer*

"I love this author and this genre. A must read."
—*5 stars, Booksprout Reviewer*

"I was half in love with Rafe when we met him in *Desiring the Dragon Lord*, but oh get me a fan and a cool drink, because his hot factor increased 100-fold in the second installment."
—*4 stars, Amazon Reviewer*

He'll risk his freedom to keep her safe.

Dragon Knight Rafe has lived in lonely exile in New York City for years. Banished from his ancient clan, all he wants is to redeem himself and return to the Hidden Lands. In order to clear his name, he must find the rare cold-drake dragon shifter who holds the key to activate the fabled Blood Stone. When the exotic and lovely Princess Mia falls into his arms in need of protection from a dangerous group of dragon hunters, Rafe finds his goal within reach. If only Mia's kiss wasn't too powerful for him to resist.

Princess Mia is one of the last of the cold-drake dragon shifters. Under the guise of an ambassadorial visit to the United States, the fiercely independent royal is on a secret, risky mission to retrieve her stolen family jewels, including the fabled Blood Stone. When her security detail is ambushed, she's nearly kidnapped, but lands in the arms of the oh-so-sexy Rafe.

Rafe needs Mia to redeem himself and return to his kingdom. Mia needs Rafe to help her secure the Blood Stone and return it to her family. As they become a bonded pair, needing each other more than life itself, will he trade everything he's worked hard for to save her, or will he risk losing her—and his freedom—forever?

❧ 1 ❧

A frosty winter held New York City in its grip when Princess Mia Draynor stepped off the plane at JFK Airport and descended the stairs to the tarmac. It would take some adjustment to adapt to the climate change—warmer here compared to her home. Andonia winters could be long and harsh but that was normal to her. As a cold-drake dragon-shifter, she rarely noticed the cold.

She hated having to wear a coat since, to her, the temperatures were downright balmy. In her suitcase, she packed a light jacket for other diplomatic occasions, knowing that would be all she really needed. But, because humans didn't know her kind existed, she wore a red peacoat for appearance sake only.

The press waited with cameras at the ready for her as she descended the stairs behind her security detail. Her personal bodyguard, Helmut, had been with her since the day she was born and likely knew her better than anyone. Even her parents. But Helmut was aging and nearing retirement so he brought along his protégé, Armond. He was a young dragon and eager to please and generally annoying when it came to her personal safety. He insisted on sticking as close to her as possible claiming it was his duty to protect her no matter what.

It was, of course. She understood that. But Helmut gave her space to breathe. Armond didn't.

Security had been tightened as she and her small entourage of seven made their way off the airplane. She detested flying commercial—even in first class. Her parents were off on their own diplomatic tour of Australia and claimed the use of the private jet.

She took the last step onto the tarmac. Her assistant, Freya, appeared at her side armed with her tablet and open calendar. They paused to wave at the crowd.

"We're headed directly to the Plaza for a quick change and then you have dinner scheduled with the ambassador, the mayor, and his wife at the ambassador's private residence on Park Avenue. Tomorrow morning you'll be opening the stock exchange as well as visiting Ground Zero. Then on to the Statue of Liberty—"

"That's enough. I don't need all the details." Already Mia's head throbbed. "All I need you to do is tell me when, where and what to wear. And tell Louisa I need her to fix my hair." She tucked a wayward lock of silver hair behind her ear that came loose from her chignon.

"Yes, your highness."

At the girls' dejected tone, guilt swept through her for snapping. Freya could be overwhelming with her enthusiasm for her schedule, though. Armond moved to her left side and gripped her elbow, steering her to the motorcade waiting to transport her and the group to the hotel. She traveled with Freya, her hairdresser, Helmut, Armond and two more bodyguards. Her parents had wanted more security, but Mia talked them out of it. The smaller the group, the easier it would be to accomplish what she came to do.

"I don't need your escort, you know," she said to Armond behind the fake smile. She waved to the press and the crowd of gawkers who all wanted a look at a royal.

"Just doing my job, your highness."

She huffed annoyance. He never called her anything other than that. Helmut, at least, called her by her first name.

Armond, though, was all about rules and regulations. As he walked her through the airport, he was stiff and unmoving as his gaze flickered over the crowd. He kept everyone under surveillance no matter where they were even if he was escorting her through the palace.

Helmut fell in step on her other side and lowered his voice so only she could hear. "Are you sure about this, Mia?"

"Yes. Absolutely."

There was more to her trip to the States than a diplomatic mission. She came to reclaim what belonged to her family for centuries—the Blood Stone. The family heirloom was stolen a few months ago. The international officer they hired to find it tracked the stone to New York City to Bar Inferno in Hell's Kitchen. The thief sold it to a man named Mario Anderson. Mia used the scheduled tour of New England as an opportunity to search for it.

She only had a few days in the city, so she had to work fast.

Only Helmut knew her plan. She'd made him promise to keep it from Armond. While she appreciated the younger man's tenacity, she needed to be able to slip away to search for the stone. Armond would insist on following her and she couldn't have that.

"Sure about what?" Armond never turned to look at either of them. His gaze focused on the crowd as they headed toward the cars. The two other bodyguards retrieved the luggage and loaded everything in the second car.

"Coming to the U.S.," Mia said, before Helmut could answer. "My parents were concerned about me traveling alone but I convinced them it would be fine since I was in such good hands." She smiled, hoping her explanation would stave off any more questions.

Helmut leaned in close and whispered, "Just remember what I told you."

She nodded and reached up to touch the necklace with the pale blue teardrop stone. Helmut had given it to her before the trip. He made her promise she wouldn't take it off, which made her wonder if there was something magical about it. Knowing Helmut, he managed to put some type of tracking device in it so he could find her if anything went wrong.

As they halted at the car door, Armond looked her over. Though she couldn't see anything behind his dark sunglasses, she could feel the glare he had in place for her. Almost as though he knew she lied. Almost as though he could sense there was more to the story.

So be it. She didn't owe him an explanation.

He held the car door open for her and she slid inside the back. Helmut took the passenger seat in the front. One of the bodyguards who had accompanied them on the plane tried to get into the car, too, but Armond put a hand on the guy's chest and gave him a push.

"You ride in the other car with the rest of the team."

"But his majesty requested—"

"The other car."

Tension filled the air. The two of them stared each other down before the guy relented. He and the other man headed for the second car. Louisa and Freya also headed for the second car. Armond made sure they were inside before getting in the back with Mia.

"That was a bit rude, don't you think?"

"You are my responsibility so no, I don't think."

"I'm yours and *Helmut's* responsibility. Helmut's first. Never forget that."

"And never forget I will soon be taking over for Helmut, your highness."

She huffed out a breath. After settling in the backseat, she shucked the coat and crossed her legs, wishing she didn't have to wear the skirt and stockings. The heels weren't so comfortable either but she was a princess. Her parents would never let her forget it if she stepped into public in anything other than proper attire. She much preferred a pair of faded jeans and a soft cotton shirt to heels and hose and skirts.

Next to her, Armond pulled off the shades and did a quick scan of the area through the dark tint of the windows, his keen eyes taking in everyone and everything. He shifted in his seat getting a little close to her and glanced down. That's when she suddenly realized he looked at her legs.

Mia wasn't sure why she was shocked he had looked at her legs.

Should she be flattered by it? Or was it merely a male reaction to a pair of long legs? She was far from attracted to him—he certainly wasn't her type. Despite his good looks, he was too stiff and rigid for her. She wanted to say something, to needle him about it but she didn't. She pressed her lips together and remained silent.

She didn't want him to think she encouraged that behavior, after all.

"Something bothering you?" He put the shades back on and leaned back into the leather seat, the material crunching with his movement.

"No." She uncrossed her legs and tucked one foot behind the other. It would, at least, keep her legs out of his line of vision.

In the front seat, Helmut craned his neck to give them a sideways glance but said nothing as the car lurched forward. Sleet and rain fell, making it more difficult to see out the tinted windows.

As they made it out of the airport, Armond checked his watch.

"Got a date?" she asked.

He gave her a sidelong glance as he dropped his hands in his lap. "Just checking the time, your highness."

"Clearly." She lifted an eyebrow but he kept his face impassive as he stared straight ahead.

"We're about thirty minutes out from the hotel," Armond said. "You should use this time to rest."

Something about his tone raked on her nerves. She didn't want to admit the fatigue pounding through her. They had been traveling since the early morning. Even so she detested he told her what to do. Instead, she pulled out her smartphone and opened the calendar, scrolling through appointments.

"I'm fine. I'll just look over the schedule."

She didn't need to look over the schedule. She could recite it from memory but she needed something to distract her from his overbearing presence. He checked his watch again which she thought odd. When he dropped his wrist, she could see the illuminated dial with what appeared to be a countdown. Or perhaps a second hand? She tried to look at it without drawing his attention.

"Is there something you want to say, your highness?" His gaze still locked on the window.

"No."

"You keep looking at me."

"I'm not." She disliked the defensive tone that had crept into her voice.

Helmut turned his head to give them both a glare. "You two getting along?"

As far as she was concerned, Armond could never measure up to Helmut. She nodded. Armond didn't bother to respond. Helmut faced forward, leaning towards the windshield looking out to scan the area.

"Where's the police escort?" he asked.

"Coming, sir. Just there." The driver pointed off to the left.

Mia glanced out the window as the police escort pulled up next to them, flanking the cars as they entered the highway and headed west toward the city. She had committed to memory the map of Manhattan, including the exact route they would take to the Plaza and the exact route she would take to Hell's Kitchen.

She couldn't help but wonder why Armond had chosen to sit in the backseat with her. Why not Helmut? Unless he tried to make the transition between him and Armond easier and positioned the new guy with her. She could respect that but she didn't have to like it.

Mia skimmed her schedule and looked through her notes for her upcoming events. When that failed to entertain her, she put the smartphone on the seat between them and stared out the window. She was tired of sitting. Her legs were stiff and she wanted out of these clothes and in something more comfortable. She shifted in her seat again and stretched her legs. It didn't escape her notice Armond looked at them again.

She turned toward him, throwing him a look full of daggers. "Stop that."

He held up his hands as though he surrendered. "Stop what?"

"Looking at me like that. I mean it." She wagged an accusatory finger at him.

"I would never disrespect her highness by looking at her in a way that displeased her," he said, his voice deadpan.

She scowled and turned back to the window. They had entered the Midtown Tunnel. She sat up straighter in her seat.

"Why are we taking the tunnel?" she asked. "Isn't there another route to the hotel?"

"This is the quickest way, your highness," Armond said.

"Helmut?" she queried.

He nodded. "We'll be there in no time."

As they approached the exit to the tunnel, the hairs on the back of her neck stood at attention. She had no idea why she had a sudden anxiety about the area but something didn't feel right to her. Her gut was never wrong.

The car lurched forward as they came to a sudden halt at the exit for 37th Street. In their lane up ahead, a stalled box truck blocked traffic. Two other large vehicles stopped traffic in the other lanes, sealing off the tunnel. The police halted next to the cars. Mia leaned over to peer through the windshield. The second car with the security detail stopped behind them. They were stuck, unmoving. Something wasn't right.

"I don't like this," she said.

"Somebody get this box truck out of the way," Armond said into his cell phone. She never saw him pull it out of his pocket. "I don't give a shit what the excuse is. Move it out of the way."

She knew he must be talking to the other car behind them. A moment later, one of the security guards walked by at a brisk pace toward the box truck as two men jumped out of the cab.

"See if you can go around the truck on the left," Helmut ordered the driver, pointing to the other lane.

The driver nodded as he tried to maneuver the car into the next lane but they were blocked by the police escort. There was no way they could back up either, since the other car stopped behind them. A flash of cold dread went through her. Something was definitely not right.

"Helmut—" she started.

But was cut off when the men from the box truck pulled out guns and started shooting. Mia ducked as glass shattered around her. Next to her, Armond pulled out his gun and returned fire.

"The driver is dead," Helmut said. "And we're trapped."

The back of the box truck opened and more men came pouring out with guns.

"Get us out of here," Armond shouted.

"The dead man is in the way," Helmut said. "They're heading for us. Take Mia out of here while I cover you."

She popped up. "No! I'm not leaving without you."

"Do as I say, Mia. Go with Armond." Helmut reloaded his pistol. He gave the younger man a nod. "Go."

"Keep your head down," he said to her.

Armond opened the door and then reached for her. He didn't waste a moment as he dragged her from the car. Helmut threw open his door and crouched behind it, using it as a shield to return fire. He managed to hit several of the assailants, killing them. They returned fire, hitting Helmut in the side of the neck. He fell to the ground. Mia shrieked while Armond dragged her toward the front of the car, putting as much distance between them and the motorcade as he could.

"Helmut!"

"It's too late for him," Armond said.

Two policemen intercepted them, both pointing weapons at them.

"Drop the gun or the princess dies."

It took a moment to register the guy pointing the gun at her was not a real police officer. In that moment, she understood what had happened. The box truck was nothing more than a distraction. Nothing more than a stall tactic to get them right where they wanted them—at the end of the tunnel.

Armond complied. She glanced toward the second car and saw Freya and Louisa still inside, a gun pointed at them. At the front of her car, Helmut was not moving and she knew he was dead.

Emotion clogged in her throat. Now was not the time to mourn him. She swallowed back the tears trying to keep her face impassive. Her princess training never prepared her for something like this but she had to remain strong. She erected mental walls to keep herself together, so she wouldn't fall apart.

"We both know you won't kill her. What do you want?" Armond said.

The man who appeared to be the leader gave him a feral smile. "As if you don't know. We're here to make sure you deliver on your promise."

Confusion flickered through her as she looked at Armond. His jaw had tightened, the muscles along the edge working there. The man's gaze flickered from him to her and back again, that same feral smile on his face.

"Armond?" She turned to look at him, trying to understand what that meant.

His face was rock steady, a mask of unreadable emotion. His throat bobbed with the movement, his jaw still tight.

"I intend to deliver what I promised." Armond gripped her elbow. "As long as I get what I was promised."

The man's gaze went to one of the men behind Armond. "Oh, you'll get it all right."

She looked between the man and Armond, trying to make sense of what they were saying. Armond squeezed her elbow and gave her a gentle tug but she refused to move. Panic bubbled up through her, making her dragon magic come alive. She tried her best to tamp it down but with all the other emotions pumping through her, it was difficult to control. Not that she could *ever* control it.

"What is going on here, Armond?" A snowflake drifted off her body, floating in the air between them.

"I thought that obvious," the man chuckled. "You're coming with us. He gets a special prize."

"And what is that?" Armond asked, leery.

"A bullet in the head." He laughed then.

Behind her a gun cocked. Armond squeezed her elbow again as the gun pressed against the base of his skull.

Fear slammed into her, making her skin turn from cool to frigid. She clutched her hands into a fist, trying to keep the dragon magic at bay. Once she released it, there was no stopping it.

"I don't want to hurt you, but I will if I have to." Her breath plumed between them.

He snorted.

"Mia…" Hearing Armond say her name stopped her. She turned her head to look at him. He looked defeated. "It's all right."

What the hell was he saying? He was giving up? He was letting them take her and kill him?

"Ah, isn't that valiant of him. Do it now, Jacob."

Mia inhaled a sharp breath and released the dragon magic building inside her. Her lungs stung as she puffed out a breath of icy air, hitting the leader in the face. Ice crystals formed on his face. His skin turned blue. He was rendered immobile. She sucked in another breath and turned toward the other two men behind them. Their eyes went wide and round.

"Don't. It's dangerous to use your magic here," Armond scolded.

She released her cold breath. He dove out of the way at the last second to avoid getting hit by it. As soon as the breath was out of her, she faltered. Mia pitched forward, the ground rising up in a hurry to meet her. Before she smacked the pavement, though, he caught her.

"Take your damn hands off me, you traitor."

She shoved away from him and regained her footing, stumbling back toward the car. Helmut's lifeless body was face down on the ground, a pool of blood beneath his head. It pained her to think of him abandoned here with none of her kind to make sure he was returned to their homeland for a proper burial.

"He's dead," Armond said, his tone less than sympathetic. As though wanting to make sure she knew he was gone. She hated him all the more. "There's nothing you can do for him."

She fought back the tears as Armond advanced on her.

"Your highness, we have to go."

"You…" She took a step back from him. "Did you orchestrate this?"

She could hear others yelling and thought of the other car. Freya and Louisa and the other bodyguards. The men were frozen statues around them. She spotted the starburst on the wrist of the first man. She glanced back at the one dressed as a police officer and then at the other two. Cold fear trickled through her.

They were Drakana. Why would dragon hunters want her?

Drakana had once hunted the cold-drakes to near extinction. If they had tried to take her, then what of her parents? Would they be under attack, too? She had to get a message to them. She had to find out if they were all right. Her hands shook as she glanced from the men back to Armond.

"I didn't want to do this." He retrieved his gun and now pointed it at her. "But you leave me no choice. I need you to come with me." He reached for her but she jerked away.

"I'm not going anywhere with you."

Nor was she leaving without Freya and Louisa. Before she could take a step, the explosion rocked the entire tunnel. The second car burst into a ball of fiery death and flame. Armond flung his body on top of her and shoved her to the ground. Her hose ripped as her knees scrapped against the concrete and she banged her chin on the ground, clacking her teeth together in a sickening snap. Debris rained down around them. Unbearable heat scorched through the tunnel. Her ears rang with a high-pitched squeal. She could hear nothing but a muffled hum that sounded a million miles away.

Mia couldn't stop the tears as she looked back at the smoldering car. Freya and Louisa were dead. Both of them. Armond shouted something in her ear, then tugging her to her feet. Her clothes were soiled, her knees skinned, her shoes scuffed. He clamped a hand around her wrist and dragged her toward the tunnel exit, the gun still clutched in his other hand. She dug in her heels and pulled him to a stop. He gave her a questioning look.

"What are you doing?" His muffled voice sounded far away even though he stood right in front of her. "You have to come with me."

His desperation to get her out of the tunnel struck her wrong. She didn't like it or him. Maybe it was the stifling heat from the car fire behind her. Or her emotions running high. She didn't know. All she knew was going with him was wrong.

"I don't want to hurt you, your highness." To press his point, he turned the gun on her again.

She shook her head. "No."

The hand around her wrist turned blue. A sheen of ice coated his skin. He sucked in his breath and jerked his hand away, cradling it against his chest. Ice crystals formed on her lashes. More snowflakes floated off her skin, dancing in the air around them.

"Stop." Panic edged his voice.

Ice spread from her feet to his and began a slow crawl up his legs. The build-up of magic inside her burst through her weak control. Ice water with sleet doused the flames and covered Armond, drenching him. He cried out, ducking as sleet pricked his exposed skin.

In that instant, she knew what she had to do. She had to get as far from him as possible and she had to control her dragon magic before she turned the inside of the tunnel into an ice cave. She kicked off her heels and ran toward the box truck, cursing the restrictive movement of the skirt. Mia knew he followed and she suddenly understood what was happening. Armond had to be part of or working for the Drakana.

Before she could make it to the truck, Armond grabbed her. She hadn't accounted for his speed. The years of self-defense training with Helmut flooded her mind and she tried to think what she should do first.

Armond wrapped an arm around her shoulders as he held her tight.

"Don't run. It will make things more difficult for both of us."

He didn't account for her training. She shoved her elbow back into his ribs as hard as she could. He grunted and released her enough for her to spin around and kick him in the shin. When he doubled over, she used the heel of her hand to strike him in the nose.

There was only one way to escape and get her magic under control. She knew it was a risk, but she had to do it. She had to shift. She took off at a run, unzipping her skirt as she went, concentrating on how the change felt when she went from human form to dragon form. She grabbed a fistful of her silk blouse and ripped, popping the delicate buttons. She shrugged out of her clothes and a second later her wings sprouted from her back and, as she sucked in a deep breath, she was airborne. But the small space made it difficult to maneuver around the truck. She didn't let that deter her and swiped it with her massive tail.

She was free from the traitor. She knew exactly where she had to go.

Hell's Kitchen.

❧ 2 ❧

Rafe exhaled an annoyed breath as he stared out the window of his high-rise apartment near Times Square. He was tired of dealing with contractors. If he could use his dragon magic to repair his home in East Hampton he would. But as it was, he relied on humans to make things right again. It had been nearly six months since Logan's flight of destruction through the home. Now his friend was Chief Magistrate of his clan and split his time between the human realm and the Hidden Lands with his new wife and mate, Bree, who was expecting their first child.

Is this what his life had come to? Dealing with contractors and living in a city full of pollution and crime? He was once a dragon knight and protector. And now? Exiled to the human realm for eternity.

Uncountable decades passed since his exile. He built a life for himself by learning how to invest his money better than any investment banker on Wall Street. A long time to be alone in an alien world. But over the years it had become not so alien and not so human. He watched clan after clan move in secret to the human realm. And not just dragon-shifters. Other shifters as well as vampires, Fae, angels, demons. The vamps had been there almost as long as the dragons.

Even so, he longed for the days of auld where chivalry still thrived. Where royalty still ruled. Where he was still a part of the Hidden Lands and not forever banished.

A knock on his door interrupted his brooding. He padded through the apartment to the door and opened it, surprised to see his friend, Logan Blake, on the other side.

He waved him inside. "I thought you were back in the Hidden Lands."

"Bree and I are here for the remainder of her pregnancy." Logan entered the apartment and halted in the middle of the living room.

Not long ago, Rafe gave him refuge here when he was injured and seeking revenge. And yet it seemed it all happened a thousand years ago.

"I hope you don't mind me showing up here, but I need your help," Logan said.

Rafe went to the wet bar and poured two whiskeys. He handed one to his friend. "Haven't I helped you enough?"

Logan grinned. "You have and I appreciate everything you did for me and Bree. I'm not sure I ever thanked you for all you did."

"I don't need thanks." He motioned for Logan to sit on one of the sofas and then sat across from him. "I did what I had to do. What anyone would have done."

He helped Logan recover from a nasty stab wound from an obsidian blade. He also helped get him the undercover job at Bar Inferno where he met Bree.

"What can I do for you?" he asked.

Logan sat back in the cushions and propped an ankle on his knee, holding the glass in his hand and looking him over with consideration lining his face. He knew he was about to ask him to do something he probably didn't want to do.

"I have taken my place as Chief Magistrate in the Hidden Lands," he said. "Bree and I are living in the house that once belonged to my parents."

He knew that already.

Rafe cocked his head to the side, wondering what this had to do with him. "And?"

"I found my father's journals on the Blood Stone and the Hidden Lands."

Rafe sat up a little straighter. "What did you find?"

"He wrote them in the language of the Ancients. It took me some time to translate them. I enlisted the help of one of the clan elders. All this time we thought the Hidden Lands were toxic, that it was a natural phenomenon."

"But it's not?"

Logan shook his head. "It's a curse."

He blinked. "What do you mean a curse?"

"Long ago, when the Hidden Lands were threatened by invaders from the north, the Ancients formed the Whispering Mountains."

Rafe snickered. "I've heard this bedtime story before. Ienir the Great and the other Ancients banded together to use their Dragon's Breath to form the mist around the mountains to hide it from the rest of the realms."

"Not a bedtime story," Logan said with a shake of his head. "A legend that is true. The Ancients' blood runs through my veins as it does yours. The Dragon's Breath is not just a mist. It has become the curse itself. It can no longer hide the Hidden Lands and once it fails, it will reveal our realm to all the other realms, including this one. We will be susceptible to invasion once more. And worse."

"Worse being a human invasion," Rafe said.

He nodded. "I can't allow humans into our world. They've made a mess of theirs. We don't need that."

"How does the Blood Stone figure into all of this?"

"Ienir the Great wanted a failsafe. The clan elder was able to tell me it is possible the Hidden Lands can be saved with the Blood Stone but not by itself," he said. "One of the journals was a book of enchantments."

"Spells?" He lifted a brow in disbelief, scoffing at the idea.

"Yes, and one of the enchantments my father uncovered involved the Blood Stone, a dragon scale and a dragon tooth along with some blood ritual that's supposed to break the curse. Something about certain drops of blood from an elemental mingled together in the Blood Stone," he said. "I haven't finished translating that part yet."

"Do you actually believe all that magic mumbo-jumbo?" he asked.

"I believe it's worth a shot." He paused to take a sip of whiskey. "The enchantment called for scale from a fire-drake and a tooth from a cold-drake."

Rafe stared at his friend in disbelief. He knew of these dragon-shifting clans and most of them were gone from the Hidden Lands. A few had migrated to the human realm. The cold-drakes had been hunted to near extinction by the Drakana before they finally entered the human realm. He didn't know if there were any surviving members of either of those dragons.

"How are you going to get those?" he asked.

"That's where I need your help."

Rafe shook his head. "Forget it. You can leave me out of it."

"Even if it means I can release you from exile?"

That stopped him. When Rafe left the Hidden Lands, he knew he would never be able to return even in death. He was forever a part of the human realm. Now Logan was offering him a chance to right his wrong and get back to his world. His rightful place in the world. He practically salivated at the thought.

"Tell me more." He kept his voice even so he wouldn't seem too eager.

"There's a clan of cold-drakes who have moved into the human realm and positioned themselves as a royal family in the small kingdom of Andonia in Western Europe. They had the Blood Stone with them when they left," Logan said. "Likely they will come looking for it since it was stolen from them."

"And I gather you don't want to give it back."

"I need it to complete the enchantment as well as a tooth from one of the cold-drakes. A royal would make it even better since their blood is pure. A royal who's living in the human realm." Logan let the idea hang in the air between them.

Rafe knew what he wanted. He almost laughed. "You want me to find this cold-drake and get a tooth from him? Wouldn't he have to be in dragon form to do that?"

"He or *she* would," he said with a nod.

His brows knit with question. "What do you want me to do?"

"I was hoping you'd track down a cold-drake and get me that tooth."

Rafe slowly placed his glass the table in front of him, trying to understand what Logan wanted him to do.

"What do you expect me to do? Walk up to the palace, knock on the door and ask them to hand over a royal tooth from the king?" He shook his head. "That's not going to work."

Logan pressed his lips together in a thin line. Annoyance etched along either side of his mouth. "Have you seen the news today?"

"No. Why?"

"Princess Mia of Andonia is arriving at JFK Airport."

Rafe blinked surprise and stared at Logan as though he had grown a second head. "And?"

"She's likely here to recover the Blood Stone, don't you think?"

"Under the guise of an ambassadorial visit?"

"Perhaps."

Fuck. He knew what Logan wanted. "You want me to find her?"

"Yes. Convince her to help us."

"If she won't?"

"Then the Hidden Lands are no more."

"Why would she want to help us? Likely she's never heard of the Hidden Lands. Her life isn't there. It's in Andonia."

"That's where I need your charms to come in." Logan flashed a smile.

Rafe snorted. "Right. Like I could get close to her. She's a *royal*. Surrounded by security guards twenty-four-seven."

"And you were once part of that world. You understand them. You know how to interact with them."

Rafe scowled. "And it sucks you know that."

Logan gave him a conspiratorial smile that scared him. "I know a lot more. I have her schedule. I also made arrangements for you to be at the state dinner tomorrow night. You'll be able to meet her there."

Rafe suppressed a sigh of annoyance. "You've thought of it all. So, if she will help us, then what?"

"Then you are released from exile. You can return to the Hidden Lands and join my clan as Captain of the Guard," Logan said.

He stiffened as he stared at his friend, an eerie feeling pinging through him. That title had meant something to him once when he was a knight in the Hidden Lands. Logan clearly knew the truth about him and that's why he offered it to him once again.

Rafe stared at his friend, wishing he could turn him down. Knowing he couldn't.

"There is war coming," Logan continued. "I received information that proves Lord Herrick is making a move against me. Against all the clans. He means to take over."

Lord Herrick was once a member of Logan's Council of Five who had aligned himself with Lord Archer. Logan defeated Archer in a battle for the title of Chief Magistrate. A battle to the death that Logan won.

"How?" Rafe asked.

"I don't know yet. I need your help to stop him."

Rafe blew out a breath, considering the situation. "Do you even know what I did to get exiled? Are you sure you want me as Captain of the Guard?"

"I do. I found the damning document of what happened in my father's papers. It doesn't matter anymore. I'm sure you've had plenty of time to think about and atone for it."

His friend was right about one thing. Rafe had spent the equivalent of several human lifetimes thinking about what happened and how he should have done things differently. But the past was the past and he couldn't change it no matter how much he wished he could. Logan was giving him an opportunity to fully redeem himself and get out of exile, which was something he had wanted from the day he stepped foot into the human realm. All the thoughts of the past made his long-sleeping dragon perk up and take notice. Rafe shoved it back down into the dark recesses, telling it to chill out.

He ran his hand over his chin, his skin bristling against the stubble.

"Now that you're Chief Magistrate, you have all this power to wield, don't you? You make it sound so easy."

"It is easy. And yes, I do have the power to make those kinds of decisions. So, what do you say? Will you help us?"

Rafe swallowed the lump in his throat and tried to ignore the knot twisting in his gut. The last time he had dealings with a princess, it had ended in tragedy. He should really say no, but it was hard to refuse his friend when he knew so much was at stake. When he knew what Logan had faced to gain his rightful title as Chief Magistrate. When he knew he could help his cursed homeland.

Finally, he sighed and nodded. "All right. I'll see what I can do."

A broad smile broke out on Logan's face. "I knew I could count on you."

"Don't get your hopes up, yet."

Logan downed the drink and placed the crystal glass with a gentle hand on the cocktail table. No doubt he remembered the last glass he cracked when he clutched it too tight in his fist. He got to his feet. "Thanks for your help."

"Don't thank me until I come through," Rafe said.

What Logan asked him to do was impossible. He had to meet the princess and convince her—somehow—to help them save the Hidden Lands. A realm in which she had likely never stepped foot. And why should she? She was a princess of a small European country. How would he talk her into shifting and giving up a tooth?

"If anyone can do it, you can." Logan headed for the door.

"I'm glad you have so much confidence in me."

Rafe bid him farewell. He shut the door and turned back to the living room, looking at the gray and dismal weather outside the floor-to-ceiling windows. Then he noticed a strange shadow in the sky. He moved closer to the windows and caught another glimpse of it.

Not a shadow. A dragon.

A dragon with translucent skin the color of a winter's day with an elegant serpentine body. Iridescent wings caught what little sunlight there was and reflected it against the steel and glass buildings in a display of fantastical luminosity. The elongated head ended in a pointed chin and two horns extended backward from the top of the head. It had large amethyst eyes fringed in dark lashes giving it a decidedly female appearance.

It was the most beautiful dragon he had ever seen.

What the hell was she doing over Manhattan?

She disappeared just overhead. He attuned his dragon senses to his surroundings and felt the slight tremor of the building as she landed on the roof. He snatched a nearby throw and bolted from the apartment, taking the four flights to the top of the building two at a time. If his suspicion was right, the dragon would be in human form and quite naked.

Rafe shoved open the door to the roof with such violence it banged against the wall with a resounding clang. He halted mid-step when he saw the woman cowering on the rooftop in a hunched position, clutching her elbows to hide her breasts. A blue teardrop necklace was the only thing she wore. Her head snapped up and her brilliant purple gaze met his as her long hair the color of moonlight blew across her face. Opalescent skin shimmered in the morning light, giving it a lustrous and luxurious appearance. Could she be real?

"Stay where you are." Her voice was like a melody as she shivered in the breeze. Snowflakes drifted around her head.

Yes, she was definitely real and scared to death. The only thing keeping her from bolting was the fact she was naked.

"I want to help you. I'm not going to hurt you. I brought you this."

He held up the throw and then tossed it to her. It landed a foot from her. Grabbing it on his way out the door had been quick thinking. He held up his hands in surrender to show he meant her no harm.

She glanced from the throw back to him. "Who are you?" Suspicion laced every word.

He couldn't blame her. She didn't know him. "A friend."

Her gaze drifted over him as though assessing him. He could see her visibly swallow. "Turn around."

He complied, knowing she didn't want him to see her naked. He strained his ears and listened as she grabbed the throw followed by a rustle of material.

"Thank you."

Her voice was near. He turned his head to see her standing behind him clutching the blanket around her shoulders. It was just long enough to fall mid-thigh and cover her. Even so, he could see her sleek body underneath the material. Her angular face ended in a pointed chin much like her dragon-self. She had high cheekbones and sparkling violet eyes, an exquisite dainty nose and full kissable lips. But he couldn't ignore the deer-in-headlights look she had.

"Are you all right?" He started to reach for her but she shrank away.

"I...I don't know what to do."

"My apartment is four flights down. You look like you could use a friend and maybe a stiff drink."

She regarded him with a wary look. "Are you a friend?"

"I told you. I'm not going to hurt you. I meant it." He held his hands up, palms out. "I know what you are."

She stiffened. "Do you?"

He nodded. "I'm one, too."

The girl seemed to relax a little as her shoulders dropped. "Then you know why I'm..." She glanced down at the blanket wrapped around her frame. He didn't miss the blush coloring her pale cheeks, staining them a pretty shade of pink.

"I do. Come on. It's cold up here." He waved toward the door.

She followed him down the stairs to his place. Once they were safely inside, he shut the door and locked it. She moved to the center of the living room. Her gaze landed on everything as she took in all the décor and every detail. The two empty whiskey glasses did not escape her notice either. She glanced back at him and then around the room again.

"There's no one else here." He collected the empty glasses and took them to the kitchen, dropping them in the sink. "I'll find you some clothes."

"Thank you."

In the bedroom, he found an old shirt and sweatpants that would likely be way too big for her but at least she would have something to wear until they could find her proper attire. He returned to the living room and found her standing at one of the windows staring down at the street.

"They all look so small," she said.

"That's because they are. They're human."

He handed her the clothes. Her gaze met his and his dragon stirred deep inside him. As though it sensed her, it perked up.

How long had it been since he had a woman? He couldn't remember the last time. *Ka daeko*, the equivalent of puberty in young human males, had long since passed. He managed to miss bonding with a female through the years but something about this particular female clicked all his senses into high gear and made his dragon purr with delight.

He resisted the urge to tuck a wayward tendril of hair behind her ear. His fingers curled into a fist to keep him in check. Her scent washed over him, reminding him of a cold winter's day. She was perfection and beauty in every way.

Pretty girl, it said.

Shut up and go back to sleep, Rafe retorted.

It snarled at him. He ignored it and focused on the girl.

"What happened to you?" he asked, his voice soft.

Her bottom lip quivered for a brief moment. He might have missed it if he hadn't been looking. "Nothing. Thanks for the clothes."

As she moved by him, her body whispered against his in an

unintentional sensual way. He almost went after her, pulled her into his arms and crushed his mouth against hers. But he didn't. He forced his feet to remain rooted in place as he watched her walk away.

Want pretty girl.

He clutched his hands into tight fists. *Not now.*

She was hurting—whoever she was—and too afraid to tell him. He wanted to help her. Needed to help her. It was hard-wired into his DNA. He couldn't suppress all those years of instinct to be the guardian knight.

She didn't shut the door but stayed out of sight. He could hear the whisper of material against her skin and clenched his fists tighter. He turned away to gaze out the window, to keep his mind occupied and off the female in his bedroom. He reminded himself he was a knight. Honorable. Noble. Despite not being part of the Hidden Lands any longer, he had continued to honor the code and would until his dying breath.

With his keen hearing, he heard her pad from the bedroom and turned to face her. The shirt sagged over her thin frame showing a hint of the curve of her breasts. She rolled the top of the sweatpants down as far as they would go to shorten them. The pants clung to her hips showing off her rounded thighs.

The clothes swallowed her and yet there was something attractive about her wearing them. He wanted to fold her into his arms, tell her everything was going to be all right, that he would kill or maim whoever had terrified her. But he didn't. He moved toward the wet bar, suddenly desperate for another shot of whiskey.

"Do you drink?"

"No. Yes. Well...only wine and only sometimes."

He smiled, trying to put her at ease. "Only sometimes?"

"During an occasional important dinner. I thank you, sir, for your help but I really shouldn't impose on you further. I should be going." Her words rushed out of her as she started for the door.

"Wait." The drink forgotten, he hurried after her. "You can't walk around barefoot. What sort of gentleman would I be if I let you leave dressed like that?"

She halted at the door, her hand on the knob. A ring of frost appeared on it as it spread outward. He cocked his head, staring at it, trying to figure out how she managed to do that. She released the knob and clenched her fist. Her shoulders were so stiff they were up near her ears. Her rigid body was pulled taut like a bowstring. She was on edge. Scared.

"I appreciate the offer," she said, her voice thin and reedy.

"But?"

"But I *must* go."

"Go where? At least let me drive you and get you proper clothing. It's cold outside. I have a car downstairs."

She spun toward him, her eyes wide. "No, really, I can walk. And besides the cold doesn't bother me."

He took a tentative step toward her, closing the distance between them and inhaling her crisp winter scent. He lowered his voice and used his best non-accusatory tone. "Why were you flying over the city?"

She didn't flinch. She didn't move. Her face went impassive as she decided how to answer. He was aware of the pulse throbbing in her neck.

"It was wrong. I shouldn't have but I had no choice."

He inched toward her again, closing the gap between them. A chilliness he couldn't explain emanated off her. The urge to lean into her, to warm her, went through him. "Why not?"

Her gaze searched his as she pressed against the door. She no longer had the deer-in-headlights look. Her shoulders dropped a little as she looked at him, the fear gone. When she spoke, her voice was barely above a whisper. "I can't tell you."

"Because you don't trust me." It was a simple statement, not a question.

"Because I don't know you."

"My name is Rafe," he said. "And yours?"

She dragged her lower lip through her teeth before answering.

"Freya."

The corner of his mouth lifted in a smile. "There. Was that so hard?"

"I-I'm scared."

"Of me?"

"No." She shook her head. "There are…men hunting me."

Now they were getting somewhere. "And that's why you shifted?"

"Yes."

"Who are these men?"

Indecision flashed through her violet eyes. He knew she calculated whether or not to tell him more. "Dangerous men."

"Stay here. I'll protect you."

She stared at him for a long quiet moment, her eyes wide. "Why would you do that?"

"Why wouldn't I? You are one of my kind." Meaning a dragon-shifter.

"You don't know me," she whispered.

"I know you're alone and need help. That's good enough for me."

He could see the consideration flicking through her eyes and knew she considered. At last, she gave a little nod.

"I would be grateful for the help."

Who was she? Someone of importance? Her mannerisms appeared refined, almost practiced. Like she had been trained for her perfection all her life. She also mentioned important dinners, which told him she was someone who needed protection.

He suspected she lied about her name. He didn't know how he knew, but he did. One of the things he had learned over the years was how to read people and something about this woman told him she wasn't a common dragon-shifter. He would find out eventually who she was though. It would only be a matter of time.

She gave him a quizzical look, her violet eyes sharp and assessing. "And I can truly trust you?"

"You can."

"Then you should know the men hunting me are Drakana."

Mia didn't know why she lied about her name. For now, she thought it would be better if he didn't know her true identity. She didn't know why Armond had tried to capture her or why the Drakana wanted her. She had a lot of unanswered questions about him and what happened at the tunnel. None of it made sense.

Help from a sexy stranger had been unexpected. It took all her self-control to maintain her calm exterior when she was falling apart inside. Helmut was dead. Poor Freya and Louisa were gone. She knew it had been a risk to shift into dragon form but it was the only choice she had to escape. And when she saw the humans noticing her flying through the sky, she had to land.

It could have caused mass hysteria.

And then Rafe was there, offering her something to cover her nakedness. When he banged out of the door on the rooftop, it had startled her. But then she saw him carrying that blanket. In that moment, despite her vulnerability, she knew she'd be safe. He wouldn't hurt her. She could tell immediately he was one of her kind by the way he smelled. That he wasn't Drakana was a plus.

The vision of his square muscular frame holding that blanket looking at her with eyes the color of steel would forever be emblazoned on her mind. She would never forget it. And she was drawn to him in a way she couldn't explain or deny. He made her feel warm and safe, something she had only felt when Helmut was with her. But it was far different with Rafe. He could make her forget everything. She could pretend her life was normal even though it never would be.

Being near him hinted at his warmth, that it could thaw that ever-present chill she harbored deep inside because she was a cold-drake. She resisted pulling him to her, pressing her body against his to get the full effect of his warmth, to chase away the frost.

"The Drakana?" he repeated.

27

His voice was like molasses on a hot summer day. Deep, dark, slow. She didn't know why that image came to mind when he spoke. Her gaze focused on his lips—perfect lips made for kissing. His cheeks and chin were covered in a three-day growth of tawny-gold stubble that made her wonder how abrasive it would be against her face or the palm of her hand.

This was not the time or the place. She had to keep that in mind. She had to get a grip.

Mia nodded as she forced her gaze back to his. She had to choose her words carefully so she wouldn't give her identity away. "They attacked me but I escaped."

"It was dangerous to shift into dragon form in the city."

She could hear the note of caution in his tone. She pressed her lips together.

"I know I shouldn't have but it was the only way I could get away. I only tell you this because the Drakana will not stop hunting me and I may have put you in danger."

A smirk passed over his face before he managed to hide it. "I'm not afraid of the Drakana."

"You should be," she said. "They're dangerous."

"I know what they are. There's no way they'll find you here."

"But they—"

"I own the building. They aren't getting in here unless I'm dead."

"You sound certain about that."

"I am. You can stay here as long as you want or need to."

"That's very kind of you."

It would give her time to figure out a plan of action. Before Rafe stopped her, her plan was to leave the apartment, find suitable clothes. She had to get to Hell's Kitchen and find Mario Anderson to get back the Blood Stone. Once she had that back, she intended to make her way to the embassy. It would be the only way to get out of the city alive.

She didn't know how she would navigate the city without her phone or a map. She left everything behind. And she was certain

Armond wouldn't give up looking for her. He wanted her for a specific reason. She just didn't know what that reason was yet.

Still she was determined to go through with her plan. Mostly she needed clothes so she could move around the city. Rafe was right. She couldn't very well walk the streets in baggy sweats, barefoot and commando. She needed clothes, shoes. A bra.

"Well, then, if you're going to stay, I better get some provisions."

"You're leaving me alone?"

Dread swept through her. She couldn't recall a time in her life when she was completely alone. She was always surrounded by someone—bodyguards, her assistant, her hairdresser. Even in the palace, there were guards outside her door and servant girls in her room.

"I won't be gone long. You need clothes and there's not much food here. Keep the door locked. I'll be back before you know it."

His gaze raked over her one last time before he opened the door and left.

❧ 3 ❧

M ia paced the length of the living room chewing on a loose cuticle on her thumb. Rafe had been gone almost two hours. In that time, she snooped and found no personal mementos, no family photographs or other personal items. Who was this guy? An enigma, for sure. When she tired of looking through his things, she started obsessing about her own situation.

She left her phone in the car. She had no way to contact anyone, not that she would know who to contact. Who to trust. Her parents were halfway around the world. They would learn of the attack soon enough. Would they come after her or send more men to find her? She couldn't hide out in Rafe's apartment forever. Sooner or later she would have to come clean and tell him everything.

The one man she trusted was dead. Another wanted her dead.

She halted, staring out the window as she thought about Armond. He said he didn't want to hurt her. That he wanted her to come quietly. But why? What were his motives? Why would the Drakana want her?

The apartment door opened and Rafe returned carrying a large brown paper bag with grease stains along the bottom cradled in an arm. In his other hand he held two oversized shopping bags. He kicked the door closed and paused in the doorway.

Something about the way he assessed her sent chills through her. And she didn't get chills. He entered the room and dropped the two shopping bags on the floor.

"I guessed your size."

Mia moved to the bags and peered inside at a pile of denim and cotton. There were a couple of shoe boxes in the bottom, too. As she pulled the pieces out, he made his way to the kitchen and started unloading the bag of food. She noticed the logo on the food bag and pinpricks of cold danced along her spine. It had a flaming dragon's head and read Bar Inferno with the address and phone number printed on it.

The universe had given her a gift. Bar Inferno was the place she needed to find—the place owned by Mario Anderson. Now she had the address. Now she could find him and get back the Blood Stone.

But first, she had to stay on task. She held up a pair of distressed jeans. Below that in the bag was another pair of faded jeans. There were no heels or hose in sight. She flushed as she looked over at him, wondering how he knew that's what she wanted.

Her breath caught as she watched him portion out food onto plates. She couldn't get her eyes off his muscular hands or the way a vein flexed in his biceps when he moved his arms just so. It mesmerized her and was oh-so-sexy.

"I hope you like greasy bar food." He said it without looking up.

Something about the act of him bringing her food and buying her clothes made things feel ridiculously domestic. And normal. There were no commitments, no appointments, no appearances, no airs. He was just a guy and she was just a girl.

Mia hiccupped to keep from laughing or crying—she couldn't decide which—and scooped up the bags of clothes. "I'll change and be right back."

His gaze followed her as she hurried through the apartment to the bedroom. She straightened her back a little more as she hurried by and the realized what she'd done and immediately slumped again. She didn't need to be sexy for this guy. He may have been her savior but she wasn't going to let herself get attached to him.

No, she had a mission she had to complete. A mission that

wouldn't happen by her sitting around in this posh apartment eating bar food with a sexy guy.

In the bedroom, she closed the door. She dumped the entire contents of the bags onto the bed and went through everything. He had even thought to buy her underwear.

Heat flooded her, making her body temperature rise by several degrees. He had to put a lot of thought into the things he bought for her—which meant he must have been thinking about all her female parts and probably why he sized her up before walking out the door. The bras and panties were of the softest cotton in feminine colors of pink, purple, blue, cream. She couldn't fathom his thought process when he picked them out. Had he envisioned her in them? Her lower belly quivered with the idea.

She shoved away her silly notions and focused on what really mattered. She could not allow his kindness to dissuade her from getting to Bar Inferno. She still had to find Mario and the Blood Stone.

She stripped and dressed in the faded jeans and an oversized shirt. He bought her sneakers and she stepped into those. Mia gave herself a once over in the mirror, smoothing her hair into place. Her cuts and scrapes healed with the help of her shifting. She was glad. Mascara smudged under her eyes. She headed to the bathroom and did a quick rinse of her face. Only then was she ready to open the door and step out.

He stood in the kitchen, holding a plate eating. He had no idea her true identity. It had been a mistake to stick around and wait for him to return. She should have bolted from the apartment while he was gone. A risk, she knew. Though her face wasn't as well-known in the States as back in Andonia, there were some who would still recognize her.

"There's your food." He gave a nod toward a take-out box left on the counter.

Something about the way he said it, the way he gestured toward the container and the way he now refused to look at her angered her. She stole a glance at the front door, trying to decide if she could get out before he caught her.

She decided it was worth the chance. She took off at a run. His plate clattered to the counter before she had taken a second step and the next thing she knew, he clamped strong arms around her.

"Where do you think you're going?" His heated breath tickled the top of her ear.

Without thinking, she elbowed him in the gut and stomped on the top of his foot. His arms loosened as he grunted. She wiggled free and headed for the door again. She skittered to a halt at the door, pulling it open. Rafe reached over her shoulder and slammed it closed. How did he move so fast?

"I asked you a question, Freya." She could see sparks flickering through his steel gaze. "Or maybe I should call you *Mia*."

Her eyes widened. "You know who I am? How?"

"The news about the missing Princess Mia from Andonia is on every station everywhere. Authorities are combing the city for you."

"You saw it while you were out," she said on a breath.

"I would have figured it out eventually."

"Would you?" He sounded so confident she almost laughed. Who was this arrogant guy who thought he knew so much? She folded her arms over her chest and cocked her head to the side.

He scowled. "Your personal bodyguard was killed," Rafe said, ignoring her question.

She couldn't stop the stab of hot tears that pricked her eyes. She hadn't been prepared for that. She refused to allow herself to think about everything that happened. "Helmut. Yes. He was shot."

His gaze softened, his voice dropping low. "I'm sorry for your loss, princess."

Her throat threatened to close as tears burned her eyes. "Helmut was with me from the day I was born. He was the only one I trusted with my life."

It was hard to get the words out around the lump in her throat but she swallowed back the tears. She didn't want to fall apart in front of this man, this stranger. She would fall apart later. A flicker of guilt crossed his face so brief she might have missed it if she hadn't been standing so close to him.

"The rest of your people were killed?"

"Not all."

Not Armond. She had no doubt he hunted her. All the more reason to get the Blood Stone back as quickly as possible and get to the embassy. But poor Freya and Louisa were dead in the most horrific way. And she did nothing but flee.

"Why did you lie to me?" he asked.

"Because I didn't know if I could trust you. I still don't."

"I said you could." He didn't bother to hide his annoyance.

"Saying it and proving it are two different things."

"I brought you food and clothes. I think that's a start. Tell me what happened." It was more of a demand rather than a request. Like perhaps he already knew some of the details, but he wanted her to confirm them.

She huffed out an annoyed breath. "The Drakana attacked my motorcade. The man who was to replace Helmut when he retired tried to kidnap me."

"It was an inside job. You froze them, didn't you?"

She stared at him, silent. It hadn't occurred to her Armond could have planned it all from the beginning but likely Rafe was right in that it was an inside job. She tried to decide how to answer his question. He had been aware of some of the details. It would have made the news about the unusual circumstances surrounding the attack. Frozen men, dead men and a tipped over box truck would be odd clues humans wouldn't be able to figure out. Using her dragon's breath on the men was her only option.

"You're a cold-drake."

He sounded triumphant when he guessed what she was. She scowled. "Aren't you Mr. Know-It-All? You've figured everything out, haven't you?"

"Not everything. I don't know why the Drakana are after you."

"Nor do I."

"Then I guess we better figure it out."

"We?" She shook her head. "Not we. I can take care of myself."

He regarded her coolly as he looked her over, his gaze searching her face in a sensual way that made her insides jingle. "You think you can take on the Drakana alone?"

"I plan to go to the embassy after I find—never mind. I'm going to the embassy."

"Find what?" he demanded.

"Nothing. It doesn't matter. I command you to let me go."

"You can command me to do nothing." Fire flashed in his eyes. "I am not under your rule, princess."

"Then I demand it."

He laughed. "I take orders from one person—me."

"Do you intend to imprison me here?"

"No, I intend to help you whether you like it or not. I've been in this city a long time. I have connections you don't have. If the Drakana are hunting you, it's not safe for you out there."

"You misunderstand. I don't want your help anymore."

Annoyance flickered over his face before he got it under control. "Fine." He twisted the knob and swung open the door, letting it bang against the opposite wall. "Go."

She blinked. "Go?"

"The embassy is the safest place for you. Better than staying here. They'll think I kidnapped you if they find you here and I don't need that kind of trouble. I release you, princess."

She couldn't believe it. Her freedom was only a few steps away. All she had to do was take it. Fear and anticipation swept through her as she took a deep breath and stepped into the hall. He wasted no time before he slammed the door and she heard the distinct click of the lock. She was completely and totally on her own.

Against his better judgment Rafe let her go. He watched her walk out the door and waited until he could no longer hear her footsteps in the hallway before he slammed the door with enough force to shake the building. He wasn't used to a woman refusing his offer of help.

Fuck all. He shouldn't have let her go. He should have insisted she stay with him until he could find out why the Drakana wanted her, even though he suspected he knew why they wanted her. Whoever was giving the Drakana orders must also know Mia was somehow important. Drakana had hunted Logan before. That was to destroy the clan so Lord Archer could take over. Why, then, would they go after the princess? For a similar reason? Or something else?

When he was out getting food and clothes for her, he saw the news. He even went by the scene of the crime to see if he could pick up any more clues as to why the Drakana would want her. If what Logan told him was true, she was one of the missing links for the enchantment he wanted to cast to save the Hidden Lands. Perhaps they wanted her as much as Logan did and if that was the case, she was in more danger than he first suspected.

Rafe stalked to the wet bar and poured a drink, gripping the glass in his fist as he moved to the windows and stared out at the late afternoon. Sleet still fell but was now mixed with snow. He couldn't help but think how much the weather reminded him of Mia.

It had been a mistake to touch her, to put his hands on her, but he couldn't resist. He couldn't stop himself from touching her. Her skin was so cold to the touch it sent a chill right to his bones. The second he did, something inside him changed. He felt it. He wondered if she felt it.

He shoved those primal instincts down deep hoping to never resurrect them. Until Mia. Until now. Even his ancient dragon noticed her.

The fury surged through him with such great speed, he clutched the glass hard enough to shatter. A crack and then whiskey sluiced over his fingers. He cursed and took the shattered remnants to the kitchen, dropping them in the trash. He washed his hands, trying to get her out of his mind.

What kind of dragon knight was he to let the girl go into the city alone, unprotected?

He glanced at his smartphone and grabbed it off the counter, trying to resist the urge to check on her. He swiped at it until he found the app he wanted and opened it. Rafe thought Mia might take an opportunity to bolt. He hadn't expected it to be so soon. He hoped he could gain her trust and find out the real reason she was in New York. But she hadn't been so willing to talk.

That's why he had put a tracking device in the shoes he bought her. When he called up her location, he saw she headed straight for Hell's Kitchen. Bar Inferno was in Hell's Kitchen.

He suspected she was here looking for the Blood Stone, why she went to Bar Inferno. Somehow, she had managed to track it there and knew it landed with Mario and then Bree. How was he going to tell her she would never get it back? Logan was determined to keep it. He also didn't know how he would extract a tooth from her in dragon form.

She said she was going to the embassy. It was Midtown East in the opposite direction. With a curse under his breath, he headed out his apartment to follow her.

⸜ 4 ⸝

Armond leaned against the brick building deep into the shadows on West 48th Street, hands shoved into his pockets, as he waited for Bar Inferno to open. It'd been sleeting for the last hour as he waited. Despite the cold, he had nowhere else to go. He'd searched the city for Mia before trudging to Hell's Kitchen to meet his contact that afternoon. He was supposed to deliver the princess as promised but that was clearly not going to happen.

He'd lost her.

More specifically, she'd flown away.

When Mia shifted into dragon form, all Armond could do was watch. He couldn't stop her. As she flew from the tunnel, her massive tail swiped the box truck, knocking it over as though it was nothing more than a toy.

He could have followed her, sure. But two dragons flying over New York City would have aroused way too much suspicion and the last thing he needed was more unwanted attention. He was going to get enough as it was.

After the bar opened, he remained outside to watch and wait. There had been one attempt on his life. He wouldn't put it past Herrick to try again. The bastard had betrayed him, made him promises and then broke them, and for that he would have to get even.

It was a good thing he planned ahead and had a contingency plan in place. It was supposed to be a simple job. Get the princess away from Helmut and the others and bring her to the rendezvous point in Hell's Kitchen. With King Alfred and Queen Karina away, too, it made the kingdom easy to conquer, easy to claim for himself. Or so Herrick promised.

Something, though, had changed. Something that made Herrick renege his agreement with Armond.

As the afternoon turned into early evening, people and supernaturals trickled into the bar to warm up with a few drinks. He waited outside for as long as he could. When a line started to form at the door, he decided to enter to try to find his contact. He would have to be on guard every second he was in the bar to avoid a repeat of earlier that day. He would not be taken for a fool twice.

Inside, it was warm and cozy with only a few patrons at the bar and few more scattered throughout the rest of the place. Glancing around, he took a spot at the bar. The mirrors behind it would give him a complete view behind him.

The girl behind the bar greeted him with a smile. "What can I get you?"

"Gin and tonic."

As she made the drink, he saw the movement in the bar's mirrored wall. Armond put his hand on the concealed handgun under his coat, ready to shoot first and ask questions later. The man slid onto the stool next to him with a fluid motion, his otherworldly scent a dead giveaway that he was a dragon-shifter. But this was not Lord Herrick.

"Good evening, Armond."

"And who the hell are you? You aren't Herrick."

"His servant, sir. I am Lucas." He bowed his head in a brief nod. He glanced around the crowd before turning his attention back to him. "I understand there was some difficulty with the girl."

The bartender arrived with his drink. "Anything for you, sir?"

Lucas waved her away with a shake of his elegant head.

"Difficulty?" He gripped the glass tight in his fist. "Is that what you want to call it?"

"Lord Herrick regrets the actions of his men earlier today. It appears there was a miscommunication." The corners of Lucas's mouth lifted in a wan smile.

Miscommunication his ass. Those men acted on orders from Lord Herrick and knew exactly what they were doing. There was no doubt in Armond's mind. They wanted him dead and out of the way, so they could capture the princess themselves and use her for whatever nefarious deeds they wanted. Something about wanting one of her dragon's teeth for some reason in which Armond wasn't particularly interested.

Herrick had altered the plan but didn't account for Mia being such a wildcard.

And now Armond was going to alter the plan again.

"Where is the girl now?" Lucas asked.

He almost snorted. As if he didn't know. "She got away."

"Did she now? Would she happen to be the very dragon that flew over the city earlier today? You should have gone after her."

Armond's hand tightened on the glass until his fingers ached. The man knew the answer to the question, so why ask it? A television over the bar showed the scrolling newsfeed about the missing princess and all in her entourage dead. The explosion had rocked the tunnel and it wasn't long before first responders arrived. He had been lucky to escape unscathed. He wasn't sure where Mia would go. He'd checked the embassy and she wasn't there. At any rate, it wouldn't be long before the king and queen were alerted to their daughter's disappearance and that would ruin all his plans. The local news was whipped into a frenzy. He had to act before things got too out of hand.

"I couldn't shift into dragon form, too, now could I? I'll find her. But I want what was originally promised to me."

Lucas inhaled a deep breath through his nose, then exhaled. "Lord Herrick thought you might say that. He's willing to offer you something else in addition to rule of the kingdom."

"And what is that?"

"To rule a kingdom requires an heir, I believe. An heir with royal blood. Once Lord Herrick is finished with princess, she will be handed over to you."

The princess. He thought back to the ride in the car from the airport. How she crossed her long legs, how smooth they looked. How iridescent her skin was, the way she felt when he touched her, took her by the elbow. He'd found numerous ways to brush a hand here or there. She had either recoiled or moved away.

Having her was all well and good but she wouldn't cooperate much with him. He knew that. He would need something more to force her to comply with him. Good thing he left a few of his most trusted men behind in Andonia. Armond suppressed the smile that wanted to erupt.

There was one obstacle, though, he had to eliminate.

"What will the king and queen say?"

"Likely not much since they'll be dead," Lucas said. "Lord Herrick has a plan for them the moment they land in Australia."

Armond stiffened. He hadn't intended for that to happen. Yes, the monarchs were the obstacle he wanted removed, but he hadn't intended to kill them. Letting them live out the rest of their days in exile was more his style. The skin at the nape of his neck tingled.

"Why?" Armond asked.

Lucas looked bored and annoyed as he glanced over his perfectly manicured nails. "Not that it's any of your concern, but there are obsidian glass forges in Andonia he wants to control. And if you wish to rule Andonia…well, then they need to be out of the way, don't they?"

Why the hell would Herrick want control of the obsidian glass forges? Those weapons were poisonous to dragon-shifters and Drakana.

"Just find the girl, will you? Before the Chief Magistrate discovers she is one of the missing pieces to his puzzle."

If he hadn't already, Armond thought.

"I'll get her back."

"Good. We're counting on you. When you do, we'll be in touch."

"You'll know when I find her?"

The man gave him a chilling smile. "We know everything."

He left Armond with the creepy feeling his every move was

being watched. He ran his finger around the rim of his glass before downing the remaining gin and tonic. The alcohol left a delightful buzz through him as he reached for his smartphone.

Armond dialed the one person he could trust back in Andonia.

"Karl, it's me. We have a situation and we have to act fast."

Mia scarcely noticed the sleet pelting her as she hurried through the streets of Manhattan clutching the stolen walking map of the city. Rafe's apartment building was near Times Square which wasn't that far from Hell's Kitchen. Armed with the address of the bar she memorized from the paper bag, she charged down the street to find it. Determination coursed through her and all she could think about was the Blood Stone.

As she made it to West 48th Street, she was aware of the sidelong glances she got from passersby as they hurried down the street bundled in their oversized coats, hats and scarves. Whereas she didn't have a light jacket. They didn't understand her. They wouldn't understand her. She was accustomed to much colder climates than this. This was nothing compared to Andonia's frigid temperatures. Even on the coldest days of winter she only needed a light sweater.

She ignored them all as she hurried down the street and then halted. In the gray afternoon light, through the haze of sleet and snow, there was the neon sign proclaiming Bar Inferno. The relief that sputtered through her was enough to warm her.

Mia hurried toward the entrance and pushed through the door. A giant of a man stood on the other side with the biggest forearms she'd ever seen folded over a massive chest. She faltered, taking a tentative step backward as he looked her over with a congenial smile.

"You look lost, missy."

"Is this the bar owned by Mario Anderson?" She got right to the point.

A shadow fell across his face as his brows pinched together. "Who's asking?"

"I need to speak with him. It's important."

"'Fraid that's not possible, missy."

She glanced around the bar. It was far from packed for a late afternoon. Only a few patrons filled the seats at the bar and even fewer at the tables and chairs. She turned her gaze back to the bear of a man.

"Why not?"

"Mr. Mario passed away a few months ago."

All hope died within her when she heard that. Her shoulders slumped. "He's dead?"

"Did you know him?"

"No." But he had been her only hope in recovering the Blood Stone. He was her only lead and now that was gone.

"You do business with him?"

She shook her head. "No, I...he had something of mine I'm trying to recover."

The man snorted. "Yeah. That's what they all say. Man had more shady business dealings than a vampire."

She cut him a glance, unsure what that meant. She knew vampires existed, but she had never come across one. "Who owns the place now?"

"His daughter."

Hope returned as she glanced around again. She spied a young woman tending bar. "Is that her?"

"No, missy. That's Miss Meg. You sure ask a lot of questions." He peered at her intently. "You look familiar. Have you been here before?"

Her palms broke into a cold sweat. "I think I'll get a drink."

She had to get away from him before he figured out who she was. Maybe she could question the bartender and get some answers since the big guy at the door was less than willing to share. She needed to find the Blood Stone and get the hell out of there. The longer she stayed out in public, the more likely she'd be spotted by

Armond or one of the Drakana.

Mia perched on the edge of a stool. She hadn't any money, so she wasn't sure how she was going to buy a drink. The woman greeted her with a smile and she noticed her nametag read Meg.

"What can I get you?"

"Water with ice, please."

She frowned only for a moment before she filled a glass and pushed it toward. "Ice water on such a cold day?"

"It's my way." Mia took a healthy gulp. "That man at the door told me this place once belonged to Mario Anderson."

Meg halted wiping down the counter as she met her level gaze. "What of it?"

"Do you mind if I ask what happened to him?"

"I do mind. It's not something I discuss."

Her tone held a finality that told Mia she wasn't interested in talking about it further. But Mia was persistent. She had to find out what happened to him and the Blood Stone.

"I understand his daughter owns the place now."

Meg leaned across the bar and got right in her face. Her eyes narrowed to suspicious slits. "Who are you? What do you want?"

"I-I just want to know what happened to him. Could I talk to his daughter?"

"Bree's not here. You can talk to me. I'm the manager."

Mia started to ask another question when she sensed someone staring at her. She turned to see Armond leaning on the end of the bar eyeing her with quizzical speculation and a smirk lifting one corner of his mouth. A hunter finally finding his prey. She sucked in a sharp breath and tumbled off the bar stool, ready to bolt. He shook his head slowly from side to side as if to say not to run because he'd catch her.

What was he doing here? She had been so stupid. She should have listened to Rafe and now she was handing herself over practically on a silver platter to the one man she was trying to escape.

"Hey! Quit staring, you Neanderthal," Meg shouted.

Armond scowled as he turned back to his drink. But he kept a watchful eye on her in the mirror behind the bar.

"Thanks, but I should be going."

Mia started to leave but Meg clamped a hand around her wrist. She sucked in a sharp breath when Mia's cold hit her and pulled her hand away. Meg clutched her hand to her chest, wiggling her fingers, but said nothing as she eyed her.

"Do you know that guy?" she asked, her voice low.

"Yes. But he's not a friend, if that's what you want to know."

She lifted one thin brow and glanced down the bar at him. "I can have Bear remove him if he's bothering you."

"No, that's not necessary."

She shook her head. "I this it is necessary."

"What do you mean?"

Meg leaned forward, dropping her voice to a conspiratorial level. "I've been in this business a long time. I know people. He looked at you as though you were a side of beef ready to be served. If you walk out of here now, I have no doubt he'll follow you." She cut Armond a glance. "And I don't like the looks of him."

She swallowed hard and nodded because she couldn't deny it. It was the same feeling she got when Armond looked at her. Meg was right. If she bolted now, he'd definitely follow her. She could run but the embassy was still a few blocks away according to the map. She wouldn't make it before he caught up to her again. And since he was working for the Drakana, he probably had some of them waiting outside for her.

Yes, she had been monumentally stupid.

"I should have listened to Rafe," she muttered.

"Rafe?" Meg straightened. "You know him?"

"I met him today."

"He's a regular. He was in here earlier picking up food." Her gaze narrowed as she looked her over. "Wait a second."

She glanced up at the television that played over the bar. There was no sound, but the breaking news headline was clear. *Princess Mia of Andonia Missing.* Meg looked back at her with recognition

45

written all over her face.

"That's why that guy was looking at you like that. He's here to find you. You're the missing princess. He doesn't look like he wants to do you any favors."

Curses. She should have known she wouldn't be able to walk through the city without being recognized. "Of course, I'm not."

But Meg was nodding before she finished her sentence. "Yes, you are. You arrived today and——"

"Please." Mia implored her with her eyes.

She lowered her voice. "You're afraid of him, aren't you? I'll get rid of him."

Meg glanced toward the front door and conveyed some silent communication to the burly bear of a man at the door. He sauntered over, a crooked smile on his face as he reached Armond.

"You got it, Miss Meg."

Before Armond realized what was happening, Bear collared him and hauled him off the stool. He objected and tried to swing around but the big man held him at arm's length and carried him to the door. He tossed him out like yesterday's garbage.

Meg gave her a wide smile. "Bear won't let him back inside. You're safe here. How about a drink on the house?"

Safe here, but for how long? As soon as she stepped outside, Armond would be waiting for her, waiting to capture her. She had no idea what his end game was. She glanced around the near-empty bar, looking at all the patrons and wondering why she had thought it was a good idea to come here. Mario was dead, his daughter wasn't here, and she'd basically hit a dead end in her search for the Blood Stone. Even worse, she was trapped here with a henchman lurking outside the bar.

She should have stayed with Rafe.

Mia shook her head as she stumbled off the stool. "No, thank you. I should go."

The door burst open. They both watched an irate Rafe charge inside. He halted when he saw her sitting at the bar. Mia sat a little straighter, her heart hammering in her chest at the sight of him and fury etched all over his face and emanating off him in waves.

Meg's head swiveled between the two of them as they stared each other down. "Boy, does he look pissed."

Mia ignored her and was thankful when she scurried down to the other end of the bar as Rafe stomped toward her. Ice crystals dotted his hair and shoulders. If she didn't know any better, she was certain she saw steam coming out of his nose and ears. His face was flushed. He stopped next to her, his gaze roving over her.

"What are you doing here?" His voice was low as he spoke through clenched teeth.

She turned back to the bar, grabbed her ice water and downed it. "None of your business."

"Oh, it is very much my business. You made it my business."

"*You* made it your business. Now I'm unmaking it."

He snorted and then wrapped his hand around her elbow, the warmth of him pressing into her, through her, chasing away frozen shadows. "Listen carefully, princess. There are a half a dozen Drakana outside waiting for you to step out of here. I'm not sure what you did to piss them all off. Either you're going to let me help you, or you're going to die when you step foot out that door."

Cold dread punched through her. A half dozen Drakana? How? She'd seen none when she walked through the city and landed here.

"They won't kill me." The words shuddered out of her.

"Are you sure about that?"

"They want me alive. Armond wants me alive."

"I wouldn't count on that. Not with so many stalking up and down the sidewalk salivating at the thought of getting their hands on you." He released her elbow and then placed his hand at the small of her back. Heat licked up her spine with the simple touch. "You're going to come with me *now*."

She had no choice and he was right. She had to go with him. She couldn't risk falling into the hands of the Drakana or Armond.

"How are we going to get out of here?" she whispered.

"You have to trust me."

She turned her head and met his liquid silver gaze. Something she saw in his eyes made her understand he meant everything he'd said. She could trust him. He would protect her.

"All right," she said at last.

Rafe looked down the bar at Meg who trotted back toward them. Gone was the cheerful bar maid. Her expression was all serious.

"You need a way out of here," she said.

"Can you help us?" he asked.

She clucked her tongue at him. "Is that even a question? Come with me."

She called to the other bartender she was going on break as she headed from behind the bar. Mia hopped off her stool and followed Meg, acutely aware of Rafe's warm form close behind her. It gave her comfort to know he was there, and he was willing to keep her safe. Meg led them down a shadowed hallway past an office to a door. She halted and turned to them.

"This will lead you to the back alley."

"Thanks, Meg. I owe you."

She gave him a grin then glanced at her. "Good luck."

Meg pushed open the door to the cold dark. With his hand still on the small of her back, Rafe propelled her into the night.

❦ 5 ❧

"Why did you leave?" Rafe demanded as soon as the door slammed. They were alone in the alley.

She shivered, not from cold but from the shear heat in his words. She clutched her elbows. She wasn't ready to tell him about her attempt to get back the Blood Stone. It had been in her family for generations and it was once again lost to her, lost to her family.

"I'm...I had to."

"Why?"

She looked up at his towering figure bathed in the light from the street lamp. He stood in the circle of light, sleet and snow dotting his hair, his shoulders, his heavy coat. There was no mistaking the rage in his features as he gazed down at her. He must have realized she stood in the cold with nothing more than the thin T-shirt because he unzipped his coat, throwing it over her shoulders. She wanted to tell him the cold didn't bother her, but the warmth from his body heat still lingered on the material and swept through her, giving her a sensual shudder. She could smell his scent on it, too, something dark and mysterious and delicious.

"We'll discuss it when we get back to the apartment." He took her hand and led her up the alley.

Silence stretched between them. Even though she knew she wasn't off the hook, she was glad at least they didn't have to talk about it right now. She knew she was going to have to tell him the truth sooner rather than later, but she wished it was so much later. She chewed on her lower lip as they exited the alley and he looked left, then right. Even at this hour, in this weather, the traffic zipped along the street.

He turned left, his hand still clutching hers as they walked along. He picked up the pace and she sensed something wasn't right.

"We're being followed," he said.

She didn't dare turn around or question how he knew. "What are we going to do?"

"Keep walking and do exactly what I tell you."

She didn't argue. They headed toward 9th Avenue, the hairs on the back of her neck sticking straight up. She squeezed his hand, knowing he was the only defense between her, Armond, and the Drakana.

"We're going to have to lose them before we get back to the apartment." He never turned to look at her as he spoke. "We don't want them to follow us there."

She nodded, not saying a word. She didn't want to let on terror swept through her. She had placed her life in his hands without knowing it when she accepted that blanket from him on the roof.

Even though it was only a ten-minute walk back to his place, it seemed like an eternity as they navigated their way down the street. Sleet mixed with snow pelted them. She glanced at him and saw enough to know he was probably cold but making a valiant effort not to show it. His upper arm muscles strained against his shirt, gooseflesh on every inch of exposed skin.

She should have refused his offer of the coat but she feared he would be offended.

Mia lifted her gaze and watched his keen eyes take in everything around them. Eyes like a hawk that missed nothing.

"There are two one the other side of the street ahead of us," he said. "Two more behind us. I don't know where the other two are yet."

She tore her gaze from his chiseled features and glanced around the street but saw nothing and no one out of place. How did he know them? Did they have some tell-tale sign that revealed they were Drakana? Or was he simply that good?

"We're going to stop at the corner. An associate of mine will be waiting there. You're going with him and you're not going to question me about it. Do you understand?"

"An associate?" Her voice quivered.

"Yes, an associate. I called him on my way to the bar to find you. He's someone I trust with my own life."

He came to a halt where a tall, broad-shouldered man stood on the corner of Broadway and West 48th, his hands shoved deep into the pockets of his coat. He wore a black knit North Face cap that covered his ears. It was clear he was not fond of the frigid weather.

"Jaxson," Rafe said with a nod of greeting. The man glanced her way, then back at Rafe and returned the nod. "This is Mia."

He took his gloved hand out of his pocket and extended it to her. Rafe placed her hand in his.

"He'll take good care of you," Rafe said to her.

"What about you?" she asked, her breath quivering out in a plume of frost.

"I'm going to handle our little problem."

She shook her head. "No, it's my problem. I can't let you—"

"You *can* and you *will*. Besides, you don't have a say in the matter." He met Jaxson's gaze. "I'll meet you at the rendezvous point. Go and hurry."

Jaxson nodded and they headed up Broadway toward West 50th, but Mia couldn't help but glance back one more time as Rafe planted his feet shoulder width apart and prepared to take on the Drakana.

Rafe gave her a little nudge and watched them hurry down the sidewalk. His heart was in his throat. He was glad he had the forethought to call Jaxson when he left his place on the off chance something like this would happen.

He had to find out why the Drakana wanted her so bad.

He faced the two men charging him. Likely the remaining two

would follow the princess, but Jax could handle them with ease. He was no stranger to the Drakana or what they could do. It had been a long time since Rafe had to fight, but he still remembered how.

He didn't want to fight them in the middle of the street in case things got ugly, so he took off at a dead run and hung a left at the next corner. On his way, he picked up the other two Drakana, so now he had four on his tail.

At the first sighting of an alleyway, he dove into it making sure the four henchmen followed him. In the shadows, he turned and faced them, ready to fight. The four of them paused, side by side, at the mouth of the alley, nothing but a shadowy blockade shoulder to shoulder in the darkness. Rafe grinned and cracked his knuckles. It had been too long since he'd had a fight like this and he was looking forward to expending some of his pent-up energy on their faces. Inside, his dragon came alive, also spoiling for a fight.

"You can hide the girl from us," one of them said, "but we'll still find her."

"Oh, yeah?"

Rafe stood his ground as they advanced. None appeared to be carrying a weapon. If he had to, he'd use his dragon magic but only if his fists didn't finish the job. As if sensing his thoughts, his inner beast unfurled, stretched and yawned, ready to do damage.

"We know where she is," he said.

"That's great, but my associate won't give up so easily."

One Drakana stepped into a circle of light from a dim street lamp overhead. His smile was feral. "Oh, I hope not."

The man charged.

Jaxson practically dragged Mia down Broadway to the subway stop. He shoved her down the steps, their feet pounding them as they hurried to the platform. The overwhelming smell of piss and unwashed bodies accosted her sensitive dragon senses. She gagged, trying not to breathe it all in.

"Where are we going?" She eyed the turnstiles.

He took her by the hand again. "Stay close."

He pushed her in front of him and, reaching around her, swiped his metro card. Crowding her, he shoved her through the turnstile. He swiped his card again and stepped through after her.

They walked fast down the platform dodging people. Her legs ached and her lungs burned. Two men moved in front of them. One of them pulled out a blade, the garish lights of the subway tunnel winking off the obsidian.

"End of the line," he said. "Hand over the girl and we'll let you live."

She glanced at Jaxson. He gave them a faint smile. "I made a promise to someone. She stays with me."

"A promise, eh?" He laughed. "I guess we'll have to make you cooperate."

Jaxson laughed but lunged at the one with the blade. He wasn't ready for his attack and they stumbled backward. Jaxson landed a punch before the guy regained his footing and angled the blade at him. Jaxson held his wrist in his iron grip, holding him in place. Mia took a step backward, trying to decide if she should run or cower against the dirty tile wall.

She didn't have a chance to make up her mind when the second guy skirted around the two struggling with the blade between them and grabbed her. Startled, she yelped as the adrenaline kicked in. She kicked the guy in the shin, then spun toward him and used the heel of her hand to smack him in an upward motion in the nose. Frost burst from her fingers, covering his face. She heard a crack as he stumbled backward, blood spurting out his nostrils, coating the sheen of ice.

"You bitch!"

Jaxson was at her side, his assailant writhing on the ground. He'd managed to get the knife away from the man and gripped it in his hand. "Come on."

With his free hand, he took her by the elbow and they headed back down the platform. As they passed a trashcan, he stashed the blade inside.

"Nice moves," he panted. "Where'd you learn that?"

"Self-defense training," she said.

It was Helmut who had taught her how to do that, in truth, and she was grateful for it. Helmut, whom she still had not mourned for properly. Behind them, the men recovered enough to follow. The train arrived, the doors hissing open. Jaxson grabbed her hand and dragged her onto it. As the men caught up, the doors slid shut and the train launched away.

At the next stop, they exited. With his hand still firmly planted on hers, he led her down the platform to another exit. They took the steps two at a time and exited the subway and were back in the cold night as more sleet and rain came down.

"Where are we going now?" Her lungs burned.

"Somewhere safe," he said.

"Where is that?"

"You sure ask a lot of questions," he said.

"I have a right to know—"

"You have a right to keep your mouth shut while I take you where Rafe wants me to take you," he snapped.

Anger surged through her as she pressed her lips together, annoyed at the way he'd talked to her. No one had talked to her like that before. No one would have dared. And certainly no one would have gotten away with it if Helmut had been there.

She was a princess, not some commoner.

He herded her down the street, past a church toward the corner where he headed into a smoke-filled vape bar with loud music. The place was small, dimly lit with a few tables scattered about. He pointed to one of the tables at the back away from the live band.

"Sit."

"You can't just order me around—"

"I can." He leaned toward her, his voice low. "Now go sit at that table and wait for me like a good girl, *princess*."

She swallowed the biting retort as she stalked off to the table he'd indicated and plopped down in one of the chairs. He waited until she was situated before he turned to the bar to order drinks.

"Pig," she muttered under her breath. And only when she was sitting alone, did she think about Rafe facing four Drakana alone. She worried about where he was and if he was okay.

She chewed on the inside of her lip, keeping her eye on Jaxson as he ordered, then grabbed two glasses each with an amber liquid and headed back to the table. He placed one in front of her as he took the seat across from her, his dark eyes darting across the crowd, taking in everything.

"Who are you?" she asked.

"I'm a friend," was all he said as he continued to survey the place.

"Rafe said he trusted you with his life."

"And I trust him with mine." He never looked at her as she spoke.

She knew he must be a dragon-shifter, too, but she didn't know much more than that and he didn't appear to be in a sharing mood. Still, though, she worried what had become of her errant savior and if he would make it back to her.

"Is Rafe going to be all right?"

"He can take care of himself," he said, gruffly.

That wasn't the answer she wanted. "How long are we supposed to wait here?"

His nostrils flared as he sucked in a breath and downed his drink. He met her gaze. She could clearly see annoyance etched on every line of his face.

"You really do ask a lot of questions. Too many."

"I need an answer." She folded her arms over her chest, defiant.

He squeezed the glass in his grip until his nailbeds turned white. "We're to wait one hour. If he doesn't show up in one hour, I have specific orders to make sure you're taken care of."

Her brows knit. What did that mean? Make sure she was taken care of? She sniffed derision and turned her head to look at something, anything, else.

"I only go with Rafe."

"Then you better pray he makes it to us, princess."

It didn't take long to have two men on the ground, groaning. The other two were on their feet still and making a valiant effort to put Rafe on his back. His knuckles were red and raw, his fists throbbing from the beating he gave two of the Drakana.

Now he was faced with two more. Two more who held obsidian blades, each. He eyed them and knew the damage those blades could do. Logan had been stabbed with one when he made his entrance from the Hidden Lands into this realm and nearly died from the poison.

He knew he couldn't fight them both. Not when they were armed with those deadly daggers.

His dragon was awake and restless. Like a giant cat ready to pounce, it wanted out and it wanted blood. But now was not the time for that. Perhaps he could appease his dragon beast inside him and take care of the men another way.

As an elemental, he could harness the power of fire with nothing but a thought. He lifted his arms, palms upward and formed a ball of blue-white flame in each one. He threw it at them as though he were tossing a ball. They both ducked, crashing to the ground with a thud.

Rafe let the magic surge through him again. He palmed the flames as the men got to their feet. He tossed another flame at them. This time, they didn't stand a chance. The blue-white flare hit them, surged through the two standing and the two of the ground, burning hot. Incinerating them in a flash so fast, they didn't have time to scream.

Rafe, being fireproof, walked right through ash and flames. He had to get back to Mia.

❧ 6 ❧

As Mia sat at the table, she clutched her elbows. The loud music from the rock cover band pounded through her, making her jangled nerves vibrate. She continued to ignore the drink in front of her. The only thing she could think about was Rafe. She had no idea how much time had passed since they split off from him, but the longer he was absent, the tighter the knot in the pit of her stomach.

"He'll be here," Jaxson said loud enough for her to hear. He downed his second drink and eyed hers.

She shoved it toward him, her stomach too tied in knots to want it, and clasped her hands in her lap. He downed hers in two gulps. She didn't know what it was, and she didn't care. All she cared about now was getting back to Rafe.

At last he arrived, looking cold and tired. Relief sputtered through her, the knot in the pit of her stomach started to unravel. He took the seat next to her, his big hands on the table. His knuckles were split and bleeding, his skin red from being exposed to the cold but other than that, he looked unscathed. She wanted to fling herself at him, tell him she was glad he was still alive, but she remained rooted to her chair, refusing to move. She kept her hands clasped in her lap and her mouth shut.

"Any trouble?" His voice was muffled against the noise from the crowd and the band.

"Only two. One had an obsidian blade. The other she handled."

He thumbed her direction. As though she wasn't a princess but a fellow henchman instead. It irked her.

"Thanks. I owe you."

"Just pay the bar tab." He flashed a grin and got to his feet.

"And try to stay out of trouble."

That was that as Jaxson strode away and exited the bar. That left her and Rafe alone. He leaned back his chair, dropping his hands into his lap.

"Are you all right?"

"Fine," she said, sounding stiffer than she had intended.

"What did he mean by you taking care of one of them?"

"I know self-defense," was all she said, her throat tight.

"Good." He stood. "Let's go."

"Where?" she asked, clipped.

"Back," he replied, also clipped.

She got to her feet and slipped off his coat, extending it to him. Question flickered in his steely eyes.

"I don't really need it. You do."

He took the coat from her. "Thanks. Let's go."

She followed him out the door.

Her teeth were chattering by the time they returned to the apartment. Not from the cold but from the adrenaline and the fear rushing through her. The tight knot was back in the pit of her stomach from worrying about how things were going to go down once they were inside his place. Her nerves were shot, ready to fray any second now. She was tired and hungry, lost and alone.

They entered the darkened apartment, Rafe closing and locking the door behind them. The only light was that of the city lights twinkling outside the windows.

"We're safe here. They won't be able to get in," he said. "This place is like a fortress."

She only nodded. He shucked the coat and dropped it on one of the sofas. They'd taken a taxi back so they wouldn't have to walk in the damp weather.

"You should let me look at those knuckles," she said.

"They're fine. You want to tell me why you went to Bar

Inferno?" he asked, dismissing his injury.

"No," she said simply. "I don't want to talk about it. I'm tired and I want to go to bed."

His nostrils flared. She could see that even in the half-light.

She started to head to the bedroom when he snatched her arm, holding her there. She turned back, ready to question him when she halted her acidic retort. There was something dark and sexy in his face. Something that made all the fight go out of her. Not that she wanted to fight him. She wanted him to keep looking at her like that.

A curious swooping went through her lower belly. She focused solely on his hand. The way his fingers wrapped around her upper arm in a tender but firm grip, warming her cool skin. The way his body tensed next to hers. The way his heat radiated over her and through her.

"Is your skin always so cold?" His voice was low and sultry.

"Yes." The word hissed out of her in a roughened whisper. "You said it yourself. I'm a cold-drake." She tipped her head to the side. "But what are you?"

"An elemental."

She had heard of them. The elemental dragons could harbor the magic of the elements—earth, wind, fire, water. She had never encountered one. Her life had been rather isolated in Andonia and it had taken a lot to convince her parents to allow her to come to the U.S. alone. Her parents. Where were they? Were they safe? Did they know she was missing yet?

She shoved aside those thoughts, not ready to deal with those yet. She was still trying to get past the whole Drakana and Armond trying to kill her thing.

"What kind of elemental?"

"What do you think?" It was a challenge.

Rafe was somewhat of an enigma to her. He seemed to have figured her out and yet she knew virtually nothing about him. She studied him. The hard lines of his face, the stubble of beard on his cheeks and chin that looked as though he hadn't shaved in days, the liquid silver eyes that reminded her of the color of mercury. His tawny hair was cropped short and her fingers itched to run through the short strands.

But studying him did not yield the answer to her question.

As she scrutinized him, he looked her over. His features softened as his gaze went from her eyes to lips and back again. If she had to guess what elemental he was, she would guess fire. He was always warm to the touch.

"I have never seen eyes that color before," he said.

The comment caught her off guard making her forget everything. She was momentarily taken aback. She had never thought much about the color of her eyes—they were a deep violet and were like her paternal grandmother's—nor had anyone commented about them. To her, there was nothing spectacular about them. To those around her, it was nothing out of the ordinary.

She had always been surrounded by people who'd known her since the day she was born, who had known her family. She had been treated well and pampered and spoken to with respect. But this man talked to her as though she was nothing special.

And maybe she wasn't. Crown princess, yes, but of such a small country it didn't matter in world affairs.

His hand slid up her arm to her shoulder and paused on the curve of her neck. Mia shivered from the sensual touch. He leaned closer to her. His lips parted as though he was ready to kiss her.

To her surprise and delight she wanted him to kiss her. It seemed like something so natural and so normal she couldn't stop the desperate need flowing through her. As a princess, she had always done what was expected of her. Saw who she was expected to see. Did what she was supposed to do. There was never anything reckless about her behavior. Her suitors were approved by her parents before they could court her.

And there was no kissing. Ever.

Rafe was different and when she was with him, she was no longer a princess. She was a girl who wanted to be kissed by her dragon protector.

He released her and stepped away, taking with him his heat. It left her wanting more. More of his touch. She sucked in a breath, disappointment slicing through her as he moved away from her. It was as though a rug had been ripped out from under her.

"Why did you stop?" she demanded.

"Because you're a princess. It's not my place to be kissing you."

"I'll be the one to decide that," she snapped.

He faced her, not bothering to hide his smirk. "Is that so?"

"It is."

"Then what is your bidding, *your highness?*"

Now he was mocking her and she knew it. She returned his smirk. "I demand you finish what you started."

He lifted an eyebrow as he looked her over before closing the gap between them. She could once again feel the heat radiating from his body as he stood close, so close. Her heart fluttered and her stomach twisted into a knot. A warm sensation pulsed between her legs. She wanted nothing more than to feel his touch.

"You're quite demanding, aren't you? You can't order me around."

"Why are you standing so close to me?" she challenged.

He clutched her by her arms, looking down into her eyes. "I'm far past playing courtship games, princess. I've long since passed *ka kladou.*"

Ka kladou, when dragon males sought their mate. Typically, they mated for life. If he had surpassed that phase of his life, he was much older than she suspected or he already had a female bonded to him.

"Are you saying you have a mate?"

"No, I'm saying I don't need a mate. Whatever you do, whatever you try, you will not bond me to you."

She stared at him in shock. He thought she was after a bonding? It hadn't crossed her mind but she was relieved to know he hadn't found a mate, though that wasn't an option for her. He was an elemental. She was a cold-drake. Her parents would force her to marry one of her kind even if she did not love him.

"I don't wish to bond, if that's what you're worried about."

"Then what do you wish to do, princess?"

That was the burning question. She wanted something she couldn't have—him. If she gave herself over to him, then what would become of her? Would she forsake all that she was for a commoner? Her parents would never allow her to marry someone who wasn't nobility. She would never abdicate her royal title, either.

Mia looked into those steely silver eyes as her body warmed with need and desire. She wouldn't lose her kingdom or her crown or her head with one kiss. That's all she wanted. Just one kiss.

"Just what I said. Finish what you started."

"You don't know what I intended to start, if anything."

"You said you shouldn't be kissing me."

"I did but that doesn't mean it's all I shouldn't be doing or thinking about doing with you."

Her breath caught and she wasn't quite sure what to say to that. "I…"

"Do not presume I find you irresistible."

Ire flashed through her, hot and wild. "Why do you look at me like that?"

"Like what?"

"Like you *want* to kiss me."

"Because, dammit, I do."

He didn't wait for a reply as he pulled her to him and his lips captured hers in a searing kiss. The moment his mouth landed on hers, it warmed her all over. His arms tightened around her as he held her against him, his body pressing into hers in such a way she could feel every hard-muscled plane, every inch of him. His mouth did a sinful dance over hers as his tongue delved deep into the recesses of her mouth, tasting her.

Mia sighed against him with the sweet pleasure of his mouth against hers. She never wanted it to end. She never wanted him to stop. She wanted to stand there until eternity with his arms around her as his mouth made love to hers.

Everything changed in that moment when he kissed her. It rocked her world on its axis. It was enough to make her forget she was crown princess, heir to the throne of Andonia. Enough to make her forget the real reason she was in New York City. Enough to make her forget about the Blood Stone and the Drakana and everything.

Everything except Rafe.

He kissed her with all the reckless abandon she had always craved. It made her knees threaten to buckle. It was everything she ever thought a kiss could be and more.

When he broke from her, he still held her in his arms. Her head fell back, her eyes closed, and she was certain she could still feel his lips on hers.

"Happy now?" he asked.

Was she happy? Had she ever known true happiness? If she compared every moment of her life to this one moment, then yes, she could say she was happy. She straightened and pulled herself together, moving away from him. The heat radiating off him was heady, making her light-headed. Making her want more. She smoothed her hand over her shirt and moved toward the windows to calm her erratic breathing.

"I got what I wanted."

Rafe stared at her rigid back. She actually had the nerve to tell him she got what she wanted. He could have kicked himself for giving it to her. But she had fluttered her eyelashes and gave him swoony looks since he returned with food and clothes and, after that, when he saved her life from the Drakana. She looked at him with those big violet eyes and lured him.

He walked right into that, didn't he?

What a fool.

He should have resisted her. In the past, he'd resisted more alluring women than her. But something about her pulled him in, made him want to kiss her and more. As he held her, the chill to her skin thawed and warmed to his touch. Something inside him shifted, changed. He felt it and knew she felt it too because she kissed him back, matching his fervent need.

"Well, then. I'm glad you got what you wanted. As did I."

He said it to hurt her, to anger her, to keep her at arm's length. Because an angry princess was a princess he didn't want to kiss.

She didn't move as he stalked to the wet bar and poured a whiskey. He gripped the glass as he watched her, his eyes narrowed. She clutched her elbows as she continued to stare out the window. He could see her reflection in the pane of glass. Her face was impassive with the hint of a frown as she watched the traffic below.

"I'm glad I could satisfy your urges," she said at last, her voice strained.

The fury surged through him as he clasped the glass tight, his hand aching. He immediately reigned it in. He'd shattered one glass he didn't need to shatter another. He stalked to the kitchen, downed the drink and stood in the dark, trying to decide what to do with her.

If he turned her over to the embassy, he could be done with her. He'd be free of her. But he would never forgive himself if something horrible happened to her. He was certain the Drakana would continue to hunt her until they got her.

"Why do the Drakana want you?"

"I told you. I don't know." She continued to face the window, her body stiff.

He tried another question. "Why are you in the U.S.?"

"I'm here on an official diplomatic visit." Her flat tone indicated it was a practiced, canned response.

"While that sounds great for the press, princess, I don't believe it." He moved to stand behind her. "Why don't you tell me the *real* reason you're here?"

She stiffened. The movement was so imperceptible he might have missed it if he hadn't been standing so close to her. She was hiding something but she was too afraid to tell him what it was. He suspected it had to do with the Blood Stone.

"A friend of mine had a visit from an investigator who was looking for a velvet pouch of precious gemstones," Rafe said, testing the waters.

Mia went motionless. She was so still he wasn't sure she continued to breathe. The temperature around them suddenly dropped. A chill tickled his arms.

"Oh?" The word shuddered out of her on a breath. A breath that crystallized the air around them. She turned her head enough to look at him over her shoulder. Ice crystals formed on her eyelashes.

Clearly, he'd struck a nerve.

"Is that why you're here? You're looking for the gemstones?"

She looked away, her body shivering as she stared out at the night. The temperature continued to drop in the apartment. He had never seen a dragon-shifter with so much power.

"Do you want to know where they are?" he taunted.

She turned back to the window and shivered. "Not particularly."

He knew she lied. Whatever he'd said about the gemstones was definitely getting to her. But she was too afraid or too stubborn to share the information with him.

He took her by the shoulders and spun her to face him. She dropped her arms, surprise evident on her pretty features. The temperature dropped another few degrees. Ice formed on the inside of the windows. Her eyes had clouded over as she used her magic. He realized she didn't know what she was doing.

"Whatever you're doing, Mia, stop it." He gave her a little shake.

She blinked, her eyes clearing, and shook her head. Slowly, the room thawed back to its normal temperature.

"Cut the crap, Mia, and tell me the truth. Are you here looking for the stones?"

She swallowed hard, her throat working. "And if I am?"

"Were they stolen from your kingdom?" He knew they were. Logan told him.

Again, she swallowed. "We had royal gemstones stolen, yes."

"Did one of them include the Blood Stone?"

❦ 7 ❧

Her heart rammed hard in her chest as soon as she heard the words Blood Stone. How did he know about that? She stared at him. Her mouth had gone desert dry. She wasn't ready to tell him the truth. She wanted to keep that to herself for as long as possible but he had already figured it out.

Was she that transparent?

"Well?" he prompted.

She shrugged, forcing her body to relax and act as natural as possible. "I have no idea. It's been a long day and I'm tired."

She shoved by him, hoping she could scurry away and get to the safety and security of the bedroom. Thankfully, he didn't stop her. She closed the door with a snap. Then she fell onto the bed and stared at up at the ceiling wondering what she was going to do. If he knew about the Blood Stone, couldn't he help her?

The door flew open with such violence, it smacked the wall next to it. Rafe stood in the doorway, his outline a silhouette. She bolted upright, her hand fluttering to her chest, her eyes wide, her heart pounding a wicked tattoo.

"Don't walk away from me." Anger and annoyance lined his face. "You're going to tell me the truth. Everything from start to finish. Or I'm carting your ass to the embassy and leaving you there for the Drakana to find."

She wanted to retort he wouldn't dare but something stopped her. He *might* dare and he *might* actually do it. He was pissed off at her and with good reason. She had been less than upfront with information. Mostly because she had been so lost and so alone, she didn't know what to do or who to turn to. And when she'd landed on that rooftop, naked and terrified of what she would do next...there he was. Standing there with that blanket in his hands looking for all the world like a hero.

Her hero.

She couldn't stop the tears welling in her eyes. She couldn't stop them from burning through her defenses, those defenses she had so meticulously built to keep her nerves in check. But her nerves were raw, frayed beyond any recognition, and all she wanted to do was fall apart into a thousand tiny pieces.

And she hated herself for that. Hated she could no longer hold it together. Hated she wasn't as strong as she wanted to be.

Helmut was dead. Freya and Louisa *were dead.* Her remaining guards were dead. Armond had betrayed her. Her parents were on the other side of the world, probably worried sick about her not knowing if she was dead or alive.

She pressed a fist against her trembling lips and let the tears fall. They burned a hot track down both cheeks. The next thing she knew, he was sitting on the bed beside her, pulling her into his strong arms and holding her so tight she didn't think he'd ever let her go. She buried her face into the side of his neck, letting the warmth of him sink into her, letting him comfort her and hold her while wracking sobs shuddered through her as he gently stroked her hair.

Mia cried until she couldn't cry anymore, until she was doing nothing more than sniffling, trying to regain some semblance of control.

She was a princess after all. She was not a sniveling wreck of a woman.

When she was silent, all she could hear was the steady rhythm of his breathing and feel the calming beat of his pulse. His scent wrapped around her, consoling and soothing her. She still pressed her face into him, his skin damp and his shirt soaked with her tears.

Embarrassment burned into her quick and hot and she pulled away, slid off the bed and stood with her back to him. She ran the back of her hand across her nose and sniffed again. Gods, she was a mess.

"Better now?" he asked, his voice tender in the quiet of the room.

She took a deep breath and cleared her throat and when she spoke, her voice was stronger than she thought it would be. "I'm sorry about that."

"I'm not. You needed it."

Damn his empathy. It made tears spring back to her eyes. She blinked them away, took another deep breath.

"Do you want to tell me what happened to you? Why you shifted?" His tone was gentle and encouraging, as though he really did want to help her.

She pushed her fingers through her hair. No, she didn't want to tell him anything, but if she didn't, she may break down again.

"When we arrived at the airport, everything seemed normal. I only traveled with a few people because my parents are on their own diplomatic trip to Australia. Helmut was…my bodyguard. He was preparing to retire and was training a replacement, Armond. I never liked him." She scoffed. "I guess I know why now."

"Why?"

"Because he betrayed me. There were two cars taking us to the hotel. Helmut, Armond and me in the first car. Freya, my personal assistant, and Louisa, my stylist, and the others in the second. Armond wouldn't let Freya join me." She paused, turned to look at him. Maybe if he had, she'd still be alive.

"I'm sorry," he said.

She clutched her elbows and looked away. "We left the airport and headed to the hotel. We got stuck in traffic in the tunnel. That's when all hell broke loose."

The memory of what happened next burst through her mind, making her shudder. He waited while she collected her thoughts and steeled herself to continue.

"There was a box truck ahead of us. I knew something was odd about it. Several men with guns came out and started shooting.

Helmut was…"

"You don't need to explain," he interrupted. He understood.

"Armond tried to get me out of there, or so I thought. There were men dressed as police. Men who demanded Armond turn me over to them because he failed, they said. They argued. I tried to get to the others but the car blew up." She clenched her jaw.

"And you used your dragon magic on the men who attacked you?"

She nodded. "It was the only thing I could think to do. I missed Armond, though. I shifted and flew out of there. I knew I had to land quickly. It just happened I landed on your roof."

"I'm glad you did," he said, not moving from his perch on the side of the bed. "What are you doing in New York?"

She didn't want to tell him but he'd already mentioned the Blood Stone and the missing gems. "Just a diplomatic visit."

He shook his head. "No, there's more to it."

Huffing, she ran her hands through her hair again. "I'm trying to recover the missing royal gemstones. They were stolen several months ago. Do you know where they are?"

His face hardened as he considered his answer. Finally, he said, "Yes." He didn't offer any more information, maddening her.

"Then you can help me get them back and I can go home."

He didn't respond but she could see his mind working behind those steely eyes.

"With you and your parents away, is there any reason why anyone would want to overthrow the kingdom?"

She stared at him, her heart doing a wild beat. It had never crossed her mind that was why they wanted her out of the way. What, then, had become of her parents? Did they make it to Australia? Were they all right?

"I don't think so."

"But you're not sure?"

"Andonia is a small country, Rafe, there isn't much to rule. We are peaceful and have no weapons of mass destruction."

"No, but one of your primary exports is Andonia glass, isn't it?"

She nodded. "It is."

"And isn't Andonia glass one of the materials needed for obsidian blades?"

Her heart rammed hard as she stared at him. "I suppose."

"Obsidian blades that can kill a dragon-shifter because they're poisonous due to the way they're forged," he added.

"The dagger the Drakana pulled on me was an obsidian blade. Jaxson managed to get it from the guy. He tossed it in a trashcan in the subway."

He nodded agreement. "The Drakana I faced also had the blades."

She tapped her finger against her chin and paced. "That doesn't explain why Armond wanted to kidnap me. Why would he do that when he could just kill me and get it over with?"

"Perhaps to use you as a bargaining chip to get something he wants."

"Like what?"

He shrugged. "Money. Power. Your parents' cooperation. Access to the Andonia glass forges."

All she heard was *her parents* and panic lifted into her throat. "I need to know if my parents are okay. I can't call them. I lost my phone."

"Let me handle that."

She halted and stared at him. "They're *my* parents."

"And I need to make sure you're safe." He gave her a pointed look. "You're the crown princess."

"I know what I am." Her acid retort hung between them.

Fire flashed in his eyes, but he only said, "You should rest."

"I don't—"

"You do need to," he cut her off and rose. "I'll find out what's happening with your parents. I've been in this realm a long time. I know people who can get me the information without drawing a lot of attention."

Her shoulders slumped. He was right. She was exhausted and he knew it. He waved her toward the bed. Defeated, she moved to it and slumped onto it. He draped a blanket over her before heading out of the room.

"Rafe?" she called. He poked his head in. "Thank you."

He gave her a nod and closed the door.

❧ 8 ❧

When he realized Mia had given him the slip, Armond sent his Drakana henchmen after her. It didn't take long for them to be disposed of. Two returned, limping into the hotel room he'd secured in Times Square.

"What happened?" he demanded.

"She had help," his man said. "Two dragons. One of them was an elemental."

Armond stared at their bloodied faces. "Where are the others?"

The man gave him a grim look. "We found them dead in an alley. Burned alive. We could smell their remains in the ashes."

Armond's stomach cramped. The elemental must have had something to do with that. He dismissed them with a wave of his hand. "Go find something to do."

They scuttled to one side of the small hotel room, as if standing guard with their backs against the windows. Armond got up from the chair and paced the suite, the outside neon lights flashing across the floor in muted colors. Even as far up as they were from the street, he could still hear traffic and human noise. He didn't care for this realm at all.

How was he going to explain to Herrick he'd lost her a second time? The longer it took to recover her, the worse it looked for him.

All his perfect plans had gone to shit when she'd used her dragon magic in that tunnel and shifted. He hadn't expected her to do that. He'd expected her to cooperate.

It should have been simple. Hand her over to Lord Herrick and the Drakana and then he'd get his cash. Herrick thought to sweeten the deal by offering him the princess. But he knew Mia. The only way she would agree would be if he had some way to sway her, to force her hand.

Armond called Karl and together they hatched a plan to intercept the royals' plane at their planned stop in Singapore. If he could foil Herrick's plan by keeping them alive, he'd be a hero for Mia and she couldn't possibly refuse him.

A knock on the door halted his pacing. He stared at the door as another knock sounded. Opening it, he saw a man he didn't know and Lucas standing on the other side. The man gave him a thin-lipped smiled as he pushed his way into the hotel suite. Lucas followed. Armond closed the door.

This man could only be Lord Herrick. He was tall, thin with a long face, high forehead, black hair slicked back from it. His hawk nose and pointed chin accentuated his face and not in a kind way.

He hadn't been prepared to see him so soon.

"Armond, it's a pleasure to see you in person at last."

"Lord Herrick." He gave him a nod of greeting. "To what do I owe the pleasure of your visit?"

"My men tell me you lost the princess once again." He clucked his tongue. "A pity."

He fisted his hands, his pulse racing through him at breakneck speed. He resisted cutting a glance at the two who returned unscathed. One shifted nervously on his feet. He'd been betrayed by one or both of them. Before he could reply, Herrick continued.

"You continue to fail. I cannot, in good faith, make good on my offer to you if you cannot perform one simple task," he said.

"I need more time."

"You've had time. And now I understand that damned exiled dragon knight, Rafe, is helping her. How he managed to find her before you is beyond my comprehension," Herrick said. "You've managed to give him the upper hand, you imbecile."

Exiled knight? Armond needed more information about him but if he were to guess, Rafe was the one who helped Mia at Bar

Inferno. The elemental who killed his men. He needed to find him. Find Rafe, find the princess.

"I'll find her." He sounded sure of himself.

He scoffed. "You don't even know who Rafe is, do you?"

Armond stared at him, keeping his expression blank. No, he didn't know who this Rafe person was and he didn't particularly care. All he cared about was getting Mia back and handing her over to the Drakana so they could do whatever they wanted with her. He'd only taken the damn security detail job to ultimately get what he wanted. Now his plans were unraveling at a rapid pace. He needed to get them back on track and quickly.

"Should I?" he answered at last.

"The man was exiled from the Hidden Lands eons ago. He was captain of the guard for the royal families long before the council took over. Now he's a wealthy investment banker who knows his way around the city better than anyone because he's lived here so long. And the princess is in his possession." Herrick sighed as though he were annoyed with an errant child.

Perhaps Armond *should* care who Rafe was after all.

"Your six Drakana did nothing to help," Herrick continued. "He used his dragon magic on them as soon as he saw the obsidian blades. Your incompetence is ruining all my plans."

Armond clenched his jaw, the muscles aching so much it made his head throb.

"And what, exactly, are those plans?"

Herrick looked him over with a critical eye full of disdain. "Not that it's your concern, but I'll tell you. That meddlesome Chief Magistrate is trying his best to break the curse on the Hidden Lands. I intend to beat him to it and fight him for rule of the realm. There are certain things I need in order to do that. I need a tooth from the princess in her dragon form."

Armond stared at him for a heartbeat before he said, "You intend to steal one of her teeth? Why?"

"Logan isn't the only one who understands the Ancients texts. If the legends are correct, a tooth from the ancient bloodline of the

Gildhara will infuse power into objects. With her tooth, I can infuse power into the obsidian blades and overthrow the Council of Five and the Chief Magistrate. The Hidden Lands would belong to those of us who would see it go back to the great monarchy it once was when High Kings still ruled. Then the human realm will be ours for the taking."

Herrick paused as he let that sink in. He intended to proclaim himself High King of the Hidden Lands? He was insane.

"You and your Drakana will help us fight for and conquer both," Herrick said. "We will use the kingdom of Andonia as our home base and banners."

He was more insane than Armond thought. "Using my Drakana as your army was not part of the plan."

Herrick smiled. "It was always part of the plan. I never bothered to share it with you until now."

Armond swallowed the lump of anger burning in his throat. "What would you have me do?"

"I'd rather not have to do your job for you, but since you can't seem to find her on your own." He paused and motioned to Lucas who placed a slip of paper in his palm. "This is the address of the man's apartment. He lives in a high rise right here in Times Square. How fortunate for you."

Armond snatched the paper and stared down at the address. In truth, it was only a few blocks away. All this time, Rafe harbored the princess right under his nose.

"What you choose to do with that information is entirely up to you." He gave him another thin-lipped smile before he sauntered toward the door. He paused, turned back and said, "Good luck. Your future depends on it."

He was gone before Armond could even form a reply.

When the door closed, he turned to the two men who stood at the windows. He advanced on them.

"Which one of you betrayed me?"

They were both stony faced, refusing to answer. Armond said to the one on the left, "Give me your weapon."

76

He handed over his gun. Armond shot him in the head, then turned to the other one.

"Betray me again and you die. Clean that up and call the others. We have a princess to retrieve."

✎ 9 ❧

A t the closed door, Rafe listened as the mattress sighed with her weight. She sniffled a few more times before he finally walked away. He stalked to one of the sofas and sank into the soft cushions, staring out at the night.

He knew she wasn't telling him quite everything. If she was here, she was after the Blood Stone. He knew for a fact it had been in the velvet pouch with the other gemstones. The same gemstones Bree had recovered and subsequently handed over to Shi'Ann Jones, the investigator. He also knew that's where the gemstones were.

He doubted she knew anything about the Hidden Lands. He was going to have to educate her eventually, but for now he needed to make good on his promise to find out about her parents.

He made phone call after phone call trying to track them down. They had left Andonia a day before Mia had on their private charter, stopping in Singapore for a brief layover and diplomatic visit before resuming their flight to Australia.

They still had not landed. Which was worrisome.

He made more calls to friends in Singapore and Sydney. The private jet had left the airport in Singapore, but there was no one to confirm the king and queen of Andonia were actually on the plane.

Again, worrisome.

How was he going to break this news to Mia?

He wasn't. He didn't need to burden her with more trouble. What he needed to do was figure out why the Drakana and Armond were so hell bent on getting her in their clutches. He intended to find out before sunrise.

His cell phone rang. It was Logan. He answered with a clipped hello.

"I translated more of my father's journal," Logan said without preamble and paused, waiting for a response.

"And?" Rafe prompted.

"In the Whispering Mountains, there is a cave where this blood ritual is supposed to take place."

"And this blood ritual will break the curse on the Hidden Lands?" Rafe asked.

"From what I understand, yes." Logan said.

"There's something else I found," Logan continued. "I did some research on Mia."

He made it sound so ominous. "What did you find?"

"Her royal bloodline can be traced back to that of the ancient Gildhara."

That was a name Rafe had not heard in a long time. Gooseflesh erupted all over his skin. The Gildhara emerged as a powerful leader when the clan system took over the Hidden Lands. They were the strongest of the cold-drakes and ruled most of the realm. Fire-drakes and elementals claimed their own clans and mostly they all kept to themselves. Until the realm changed with the air slowing turning toxic as the curse began to take hold. War broke out between the clans. Those who did not want to fight—the Gildhara included—migrated to the human realm to find a new life and peace.

"Do you know what this means?" Logan asked.

"No," Rafe replied, his tone clipped.

"Legend states the Gildhara could infuse power into objects."

He paused again and Rafe let that soak in. If the legend were true, Mia's dragon tooth would be an integral part in this blood ritual necessary to break the curse. The real question was how did they expect to get it from her? Rafe couldn't force her to shift and let him extract the tooth. He would have to explain everything to her. He would have to make her understand how important it was for her to cooperate.

How could he do that when she'd never seen the Hidden Lands? How could he do that when he, himself, hadn't stepped foot in the Hidden Lands in more decades than he could count?

"I heard the news about the princess."

Rafe stiffened. With everything that had happened that day, it hadn't crossed his mind to contact Logan and tell him. And now, he wasn't sure he wanted to tell him. She'd landed in his lap.

"Yeah," was all he said.

"The state dinner was canceled for obvious reasons," Logan said. "I assume you knew that."

"I did." Though he hadn't given that much thought either because he'd been preoccupied with keeping Mia safe.

"Do you know where she is?"

Hearing the question made his skin tingle. He glanced toward the closed bedroom door where the princess slept. "Not exactly."

Lied. He'd just lied to his friend and immediately felt like a total and complete ass. But, he reasoned, it was for her protection.

"Keep me posted." Logan hung up.

Rafe tossed the phone to the cocktail table and leaned back once more into the sofa cushions. He blew out a breath. He shouldn't have lied to Logan about the princess. But if he'd told him the truth, that she was there with him, he'd begin to ask him questions about her shifting into dragon form and getting that dragon tooth.

Again, he glanced at the closed door. He couldn't stifle the overprotective feeling that swarmed through him. He didn't want anyone touching her. He didn't want anyone wanting to harvest one of her dragon teeth. Even if it was Logan and for a good reason. Even if it meant he'd be released from exile and could return to the Hidden Lands.

He heard the bedroom door open and Mia appeared in the living room wearing nothing but the oversized T-shirt. Her long legs were bare. He could feel a definite chill in the air as he looked at her and tried hard not to admire her pale iridescent skin that reminded him so much of her dragon self. Nor did he want to admire the lithe, toned body underneath that oversized shirt where he was sure she wore nothing.

Slowly, he came to his feet, worried at the frightful expression on her face. And what a pretty face it was. She had high sculpted cheekbones, full pink lips and those eyes…those big violet eyes fringed in dark lashes under perfect arched pale brows. Her silver hair was swept over one shoulder, so long it nearly reached her waist.

"Are you—" he started.

But she launched herself at him, threw her body against his and wrapped her arms around him. Her cold body hit him, sending a frosty punch through him. He was so shocked by the suddenness of it, it took him a moment before he wrapped her in his arms.

"What's wrong?" he asked.

"Something terrible has happened to my parents."

He stiffened. "What makes you think that?"

"I had a dream. A horrible dream. I think it was a message from my father."

Rafe swallowed hard. Families shared a bond where they could mindspeak to each other. He wouldn't doubt her if she said she'd received a message from her father. Still holding her, he sank to the cushions of the sofa. She curled against him, her icy skin thawing a bit.

"Tell me."

Her delicate palm flattened on his chest. He glanced down, admiring the long slender fingers, the perfectly manicured nails.

"He said the plane was highjacked in Singapore."

Rafe clenched his jaw until his back teeth ached. He had suspected as much. "By Drakana?"

"I don't know. That's all he said."

It was as he feared. When he couldn't track them down with all his phone calls, with all his connections, he knew something was terribly wrong. Now that she suspected, there really wasn't any reason to keep it from her.

"Did you find them?" Her voice was timid.

"No," he admitted.

Her hand clenched as she stiffened in his arms. He expected tears again, but to her credit she kept it together.

"Then you were right. Someone wants us all out of the way. Someone connected to the Drakana."

"Armond?" he queried.

"Possibly."

"I need you to tell me everything you can about this man," he said. "Every detail you know about him."

She stilled, barely breathing. "Why?"

"Because if he's the reason all of this is happening, I need to know how to defeat him."

"I don't know much about him. He's only been at the palace six months," she said.

"As your bodyguard's replacement?"

She nodded. "Helmut said he was highly recommended. They trained together weeks before he was assigned as a personal guard in the palace."

"Anything else you can think of?"

"When we were in the car before everything happened, he looked at my legs." She shuddered at the memory.

"You want me to kill the bastard?"

She knew he meant it in jest and giggled. "I think that's definitely a punishable offense at least with a fist to the face."

"I'll see what I can do." There was a smile in his voice.

"I don't want to talk about Armond anymore."

"What do you want to talk about?"

Her hand moved from his chest to his shoulder, her palm flattening there. She shifted in his arms, moving so that she straddled his lap. His brain stopped thinking but his body was on high alert. The chill she constantly harbored had thawed considerably as she looked down at him, those violet eyes flickering over his face.

"Why did you kiss me?"

"Because you wanted me to."

"Because you wanted to."

"Because we both wanted me to," he corrected.

He tried hard not to notice the curve of her breasts under the shirt or the way her nipples had peaked and pressed against the soft material. He tried, but failed. All he wanted to do was put his hands, his mouth on them.

"You said you'd been in this realm a long time," she said. "How long?"

"Too long."

"How long is that?"

"You ask a lot of questions."

A grin quirked the corner of her mouth. "That's what Jaxson said."

"He's right."

Her hands flattened on his shoulders as she shifted her hips and pressed her heated core against the bulge in his pants he'd suddenly developed. And then she rocked once against him. His hands landed on her small waist, his fingers digging into her hips. A breath shuddered out of her and her eyes sparked with some deep-seated desire he hadn't expected to see.

She had awoken his dragon from a long slumber with her sweet body and her sensual lips. It uncurled in a languorous stretch, happy to see the female who was ready and willing. His dragon purred, the hum strumming through his veins, heating his blood.

Pretty girl. Want.

"Mia..." It took all his self-control to keep his demanding dragon at bay.

His voice was hoarse, raspy. She was close to shattering his self-control, to making him do something he might regret.

Hell, he already regretted kissing her. He liked it. A lot. But he knew his place. He wasn't a man who should be kissing a princess or wanting a princess. He was a man who was sworn to protect, to honor.

But deep within, his dragon begged for her touch and

threatened to shred its way out of his human body if it didn't get what it wanted, if Rafe did not sate its desires.

"You're so warm," she whispered.

She pressed her hands against his stubbled cheeks. He knew what she was about to do and gripped her wrists, pushing her back a little.

"No, Mia."

The hurt flashed over her face before she controlled it. "No what?"

"We can't do this."

"You did before."

"That was before."

"Before what?" she demanded, her voice heated. "Before you decided I wasn't good enough for you?"

She released him in a huff and moved off him. A second later she was on her feet, padding toward the bedroom.

"You're too good for me," he countered.

That stopped her cold. She spun around, her hair flying and her eyes wild with fire. "You don't get to decide that."

"Yes, I do." He couldn't get up for fear the tell-tale sign still lingered in his pants. He didn't want her to know how she affected him. "I want to help you, but—"

"But you don't want be with me that way. I get it." She stomped toward the bedroom again.

He shot to his feet and stomped after her, grabbing her arm and spinning her around to face him. "Not like this, Mia."

"Like what?" she spat. Her eyes were like violet daggers ready to pierce his heart.

"You only want me because you're scared and alone. You think by having some sort of physical contact with me it will make you feel better. But it won't. All it will do is make you feel empty and more alone."

She snorted in a most un-princess-like fashion. "Do not presume to know what I think and how I feel. You don't know anything about me."

"I know enough to know that you're a princess and I'm a—"
He snapped his mouth shut. He didn't want to reveal his exiled
status.

Her eyes narrowed. "You're a what?"

He took a deep breath. "I'm a man you can trust. A man who
will protect you with his life if I have to."

They stared each other down for a long silent moment. Then
she said, "Find my parents."

She turned on her heel and headed back to the bedroom,
closing the door with a snap.

He watched her leave, remaining rooted in place as he balled his
fists. She'd sounded much like a demanding princess when she told
him to find her parents. Even though he knew he would, he still
didn't like being told what to do.

He almost charged after her when there was faint knock on the
door. He stared at it, wondering who could be at his place this time
of night. His senses on high alert, he padded over to it and listened.
He could hear nothing on the other side. Not even a breath. Odd.

He peered through the peephole and saw a petite woman
standing on the other side with Jaxson. She kept looking left and
right as though she were frightened. He opened the door.

"Jax?" Rafe glanced at the girl.

She had dirt smudged on her face. Her clothes were torn and
dirty. Her brown eyes were wide and red-rimmed as she looked up
at him. Jaxson practically shoved the girl at him.

"You'll be safe with him."

The girl stumbled toward him. Rafe caught her as Jaxson
charged back down the hall to the elevators.

"He said you'd help me." Her voice shook.

"Who are you?"

"My name is Freya. I'm looking for the princess."

❧ 10 ❧

Mia leaned against the closed door, her hands shaking. That old familiar frostiness returned to her bones, her skin, her entire body.

What had she been thinking? She was an idiot to fling herself at him like that. But the way he'd looked at her, the way his body went rigid when she straddled him left her breathless.

She shoved away the thoughts and raked her fingers down her face. Maybe he was right. They couldn't do what she so desperately wanted to do. She wanted to feel like she wasn't so lost, so alone, so isolated from everything and everyone she knew and loved.

But it didn't stop the hollow feeling from pressing through her. She was still alone and isolated. That dream of her father had been far more vivid than she made it out to be.

Her father had been speaking to her as though he'd been standing next to her. And while he looked normal, she knew it was only because of her dream state. He had managed to mindspeak to her when she was sleeping. When she startled awake, she'd lost the connection. Maybe because she had been sleeping was how he was able to make the link so easily. It didn't matter, really. All that mattered was her parents were in jeopardy.

And there was not a damn thing she could do about it. She was stuck here in this place with nothing but her wits. She had nothing. Not even her own clothes.

It was enough to make her want to break down again. To crumble and have another crying jag.

She shook it off, taking a deep breath. She was going to be

strong. If something truly had happened to her parents, then she, as crown princess, would inherit the kingdom. She had to remain strong for herself and her people. She could not let them down.

Mia padded to the unmade bed and climbed in, drawing her knees up to her chin and wrapping her arms around her legs. She had to believe everything was going to be all right.

Her stupid mind drifted back to Rafe. Looking down into those silvery eyes jangled her nerves. She could see his dragon-self warring within, wanting to claw his way out. She could see the feral look in those eyes that hungered for her. It made her weak in the knees, weak in the heart, weak in the head. There was something alluring about it, something that made her want him so bad she could not stop herself from climbing into his lap.

She was all too aware of how much he wanted her, too.

There was a soft knock on the door before it pushed open. Rafe stood in the doorway, nothing more than a shadow as light spilled in behind him.

"Mia, there's someone here to see you."

She blinked as she looked at him, confusion then terror slicing through her. She tamped down the terror. Rafe wouldn't tell her there was someone to see her if it was Armond or one of the Drakana. No, he sounded far too calm for that. She slid off the bed.

"Who is it?"

"Just come see. Oh, and you might want to put on pants."

He shut the door. She tugged on her jeans and hurried out of the bedroom. As she rounded the corner, she came to a jarring halt when she saw Freya standing in the middle of the living room looking like a terrified child. Her face was bone white, her eyes wide and round.

"Freya?"

Relief flooded the young girl's face and tears immediately welled in her eyes. They fell together, hugging each other as though they hadn't seen each other in years. Mia couldn't believe she was here. She thought she was dead, but she wasn't. She was here. In this apartment. Alive.

"Oh, gods, Freya. I thought you were dead!"

The girl hugged her back, hard. Mia put an arm around her shoulders and led her to one of the sofas. She noticed the wrinkled dirty clothes, the dried blood on her chin, the ripped hose and the scuffed shoes. The girl looked like she'd been through hell.

Rafe stood like a sentry between them and the front door, looking over them both.

"What happened?" the princess asked.

"It's a long story."

Rafe said, "I'm going to check the building to make sure she wasn't followed."

He left, locking the door behind him. Mia knew he did it to give them privacy so they could talk.

"Are you all right? Are you hurt? The car exploded—"

"Yes, Louisa and I got out before that happened."

"Louisa? Where is…" Mia's words died when she saw the sadness crease Freya's face. "She didn't make it."

She shook her head.

"What happened?"

"When we heard the gunshots, Louisa and I got out of the other car. We tried to get to you, but the other guards wouldn't let us. We saw something happening with you and Armond and the police who weren't police. And you…you froze them. Louisa grabbed my hand and we started to run." Her breath hitched. "One of the men…he…he shot her in the back."

"Oh, gods," Mia whispered. She hugged her tight. "But you got away."

"I just kept running." Thick tears ran down her cheeks. "I was such a coward. I should have stayed with her."

"No," Mia said, her voice hard. "You did the right thing. You lived."

She hiccupped. "The car blew up after that. And then you shifted." The girl cut her a glance. "You tipped over the box truck."

She nodded and had no remorse for that whatsoever. "Tell me how you got here."

"I went to the embassy first. The place was crawling with Drakana. They're desperate to find you, Mia."

"I know." But she didn't want to dwell on that. She'd think about that later. "Go on."

"I thought I'd be safe there. They let me inside, but something wasn't right. Something was off. I couldn't figure it out at first. I overheard one of them talking about the king and queen. Mia..." She paused, her eyes still wide and round and damp with tears. She grasped her hands, squeezed them. "Their plane was highjacked."

It was her worst fears coming to light and as her father said in his mindspeak dream to her. For a moment, the world tipped on its axis. The blood whooshed to her head, making her see pinpricks of light dancing in her vision. She rose from the sofa and paced.

"I knew it."

"How? How did you know?" Freya asked.

"My father mindspoke to tell me but that's all I know." She stopped, looked at the girl. "Did you overhear anything else?"

"Yes. They want you and them. They are planning a coup back home."

Gods. Terror exploded through her as she stared at the girl and her world tipped once again on its axis. Her stomach clenched with the terrible fear clutching her. How could this be happening?

"Who?" Mia demanded.

"I don't know. I never found out. When I realized you weren't there, I knew I had to get out of there, to find you. They tried to stop me. I fought back. I got out." Freya raked shaking hands through her hair.

"Where did you go?"

"I ran until I couldn't run anymore. Until I ran right into a man. Another dragon-shifter." Her lip quivered.

Mia's brows knit. "What did he look like?"

"Tall. Broad-shouldered. He wore a black knit cap," she said.

"Was his name Jaxson?"

"Yes." Her eyes widened again. "How did you know?"

"He's a friend of Rafe's. What happened?"

Freya worried her bottom lip. "He helped me. Drakana followed me and he got me out of there. He asked me who I was. I told him I was looking for you. He said he knew where to find you so he brought me here."

Mia stared at her. Rafe had said nothing about Jaxson bringing her here. Maybe that was why he left so quickly. She took a deep breath and sat next to her again.

"I'm glad you're safe, Freya."

She sniffed. "Me, too. But, your parents…"

"They'll be all right. I have to believe that."

Before the girl could reply again, Rafe returned, closing and locking the door behind him. He turned to look at both women, a feral look on his face. She didn't miss blood splattered on his shirt.

"What happened?"

"Drakana," was all he said. "We took care of them."

She didn't need to confirm Jaxson was part of that "we."

"They'll never stop hunting me, will they?" Mia clutched her elbows.

"Not likely. Now that they followed her, it's only a matter of time before they realize you're hiding out here." He swiped a hand over his face, his skin bristling against the stubble. "We have to relocate."

The blood drained from her head in a whoosh. Freya sucked in a sharp breath.

"You two should get some rest. I'm going to gather supplies. We'll leave at dawn."

"Where are we supposed to go?" Mia wanted to know.

"If my beach house in the Hamptons wasn't trashed, we'd go there. Since it's still being rebuilt, I have another remote location in mind." He gave her a conspiratorial smile.

"And where is that?" Demand edged her tone.

"A little cabin in the woods."

Something on her face must have expressed concern because he added, "Trust me on this Mia. It'll be safer if we leave."

"And then what?" She hadn't meant to sound so demanding.

"I find your parents and figure out why the Drakana want you so badly."

"Because someone wants to overthrow the king and queen," Freya said. "They're planning a coup."

Rafe cut her a glance, surprise creasing his face. "Who is?"

"She doesn't know," Mia said. "She told me before you came back. But if I had to guess, I'd say Armond was behind it somehow."

He gave Mia a nod. "Most likely."

"That makes it imperative I find my parents and get back to Andonia as soon as possible. I have to stop this rebellion."

There was an urgency to her tone she hadn't expected. But suddenly, getting home with her parents was the most important thing in the world. Forget the jewels and the Blood Stone. She had to find them, had to get home, had to stop this horrible thing from happening. Her kingdom and her people's lives were at stake.

"One thing at a time. Go rest, now. We only have a few hours before I want to leave this place."

"But—"

"I'm going to make sure you, your parents and your kingdom are safe, Mia. You have my word on that. But you have to trust me. Do you?"

She met his gaze and saw the truth there in his eyes and knew he would do whatever it took to keep her safe.

"I trust you."

With her arm around Freya, Mia walked back to the bedroom. As soon as they were inside the dark room, the girl kicked off her shoes. Mia went to the bags of clothes Rafe brought her earlier and rummaged through them. She brought out a shirt and a pair of jeans.

"Who is that guy, Mia?"

Mia turned to her, holding the clothes. "A friend."

"Are you sure you can trust him?"

"Yes," she said with a confirming nod. She handed the girl the clothes. "We'll talk more after you change. I think I have another pair of shoes but they may be too big for you."

"Thank you, your highness." For a brief second, her chin quivered.

She watched the girl enter the bathroom and close the door. Mia sank to the edge of the bed and tried not to let the worry and despair overcome her. A second later, Freya was out of the bathroom wearing the too-big shirt. She'd rolled up the cuffs on the jeans since they were too long. She'd washed the blood and dirt from her face. Freya dumped her dress clothes on the floor by the bed, then sat next to the princess.

"How did you end up here?" she asked.

"After I shifted, I knew I couldn't stay in the air long. I picked the first building I could find to land on. It just happened that it was Rafe's."

"He owns the building?"

"So he says," she said with a nod. "He saved me from the Drakana."

The girl glanced toward the closed door, as though envisioning him. "He's handsome."

"Don't," Mia warned with a playful smile. "He's not interested in me."

"I wouldn't be too sure about that," she said.

"Why not?"

"Because of the way he looks at you. I think he'd murder anyone who got between you and him."

The girl said it with a tone that indicated she was joking but Mia knew different. He'd made sure she was safe from those Drakana which meant he would murder anyone who tried to do her harm. How had he come to have a fierce protection of her in so short a period of time? They hardly knew each other and yet...she didn't think she would feel safe with anyone else.

"Perhaps," Mia said at last.

She put her head on Mia's shoulder. "I'm so tired."

"Me, too. We should try to sleep like he suggested."

She had no doubt the next few days would be long and difficult.

✥ 11 ❧

As soon as Rafe caught up with Jaxson, he knew the Drakana had followed him to the building. They'd fought the four of them, killing one and injuring the others. He wasn't happy about his friend leading them right to his doorstep but there wasn't much he could do about it now. The damage was done.

"You led them right to me," he'd said, his tone laced with accusation.

"I had no choice. They were going to use her to get to the princess," Jaxson said. "I'm sorry but I had to."

He knew he was right and he'd done the right thing, but it didn't wipe out the annoyance that swept through him.

"You realize we have to leave now," Rafe had said.

Jaxson gave him another heartfelt apology. And though Rafe was aggravated he'd managed to compromise their location he knew he had done the right thing. The girl was safer with him than out on her own. The princess seemed to genuinely care for the girl, so he couldn't very well turn her away. After all, Mia had used the name Freya when they first met, a sure sign she was fond of her.

His suspicion someone was trying to get their hands on Andonia had been spot on. Why was the real question, though. He didn't know who this Armond person was or why he wanted to turn Mia over to the Drakana or why he wanted to overthrow the king and queen.

He headed to the spare bedroom where he kept weapons in a safe. It was time to arm himself from head to toe. His next order of business was to get out of here and to the mountains before the

Drakana came back. He had to figure out where her parents were and get them back. He wasn't equipped for this much trouble. He was going to need help.

He cringed at the very thought of calling Logan and telling him he'd had the princess in his possession the entire time. He didn't have time to find out the information he needed about Armond. He needed his focus to be on Mia and finding her parents. He had no idea how he was going to do the latter, but he was going to do whatever it took to locate them.

He grabbed his cell phone and called him. Logan answered on the first ring.

"I have information," Rafe said.

"Did you find her? They're still combing the city looking for her."

"Who?" Rafe asked.

"The Drakana, the FBI, the police. You name it."

Getting out of the city with the princess may prove more difficult than he thought. Rafe paused. He had to tell him. "She's here with me."

There was a pause before Logan responded. "With you?"

"Long story," Rafe said, his voice gruff. "She's under my protection."

"You convinced her to stay with you?" Surprise was evident in Logan's voice.

"More or less," Rafe said. "Logan, there's another problem. I need you to find out everything you can about a man named Armond. He was Mia's security detail. He was supposed to take over for the man retiring who was killed in the tunnel ambush. Mia thinks he's trying to overthrow the king and queen and take over."

"I'll see what I can dig up."

"Good. Also, my place has been compromised. They know she's here. I'm going to have to move her."

"Where are you going?"

He hesitated. He didn't want to say in case somehow the Drakana had managed to clone his phone. It wasn't likely, but he'd rather be on the safe side.

"I can't tell you. At least not yet. I need to get her out of the city first."

"What about the dragon tooth?" There was hope in Logan's tone.

Rafe's hand tightened on the phone. He didn't want to tell Logan there was no way in hell he was going to rip out a tooth from the princess in her dragon from. "I'm working on it."

Another lie. He wasn't ready to tell Logan to stuff it and that he wasn't getting the tooth from Mia. He'd have to find another way, another cold-drake. But he didn't have the nerve to tell him that, not yet. At least not until he knew more about Armond and why he wanted to take over the kingdom of Andonia.

"Well, work on it faster."

Impatience bubbled through him at the demand. "It's going to take some time. She doesn't know about the Hidden Lands. The only home she knows is Andonia."

"Then explain it to her. Do whatever you have to do. We're running out of time, Rafe."

He knew Logan wanted more than anything to save his dying lands. That was his number one priority as Chief Magistrate of the Council of Five.

"How bad is it?" Rafe asked.

"More clans have left but there are a few who are determined to stick it out. Those are the ones that concern me. The ones that are determined to gain control of the Hidden Lands and the council. I can't allow that to happen. If I do, everything my father worked for will be for nothing."

Rafe gripped the phone harder, his hand cramping. "I know."

"I'll see what I can dig up on this Armond person. Just get me that tooth."

The line went dead. Rafe stuck the phone in his pocket, the anger surging through him to the point he wanted to punch a wall. He knew Logan meant well, deep down, and he knew he was only doing what he thought was best. But he didn't understand what a difficult position he'd put Rafe in by asking him to get a tooth from her.

Nor did he understand how the girl made him feel. Feelings that he thought were long dead had resurfaced. Feelings he refused to let get in the way of what he was supposed to do and yet…they were. He'd known the princess for less than twenty-four hours and suddenly he was fiercely protective of her.

He shoved away the thoughts and started arming himself. He put daggers in his boots, strapped one to his thigh and another to his belt. He tucked a handgun in the back of his pants and found a holster for another.

Months ago, when his apartment had been invaded by Drakana and Lord Archer, he and Logan had barricaded themselves inside and fought back. He could fight back, alone, if necessary.

He left the spare bedroom and padded across the apartment to the master where he paused at the door. Silence was on the other side of the door and he was satisfied to know the women were resting. At least, he hoped they were. He pushed open the door, a slash of light from the hallway beaming across the carpet and illuminating the two forms huddled on the mattress.

Rafe used his stealth to walk inside and find the keys to the cabin he'd purchased long ago. Two hours west of the city, it was his refuge when he needed to get away from the noise, the pollution, the people. He hadn't been there in a long while. He'd spent most of his time in the city trying to forget he was nothing more than an exiled knight who had failed and landed in the human realm eons ago.

As soon as he got the women there and settled, he'd make a run for supplies. They'd need food, water, firewood.

As he grabbed the keys, he turned back toward the door. Behind him, Mia rolled on the bed, sighing in her sleep. He glanced back at her, saw her face relaxed as she slept and was momentarily caught off guard by her stunning beauty.

She really was a gorgeous woman, if not petulant at times. Even if he didn't know she was a princess, he could tell she had a regal beauty that was inherent in her features. She carried herself with poise and a controlled calm that, he knew, came from years of royal training. The fact she let her emotions break through that unflappable exterior was a testament to her fragility. And she'd let him see every tear and hear every wracking sob.

It had nearly killed him to see her like that.

She pulled herself back together, regaining her composure in record time and pretending it had never happened.

Standing here in the darkness watching her sleep was doing nothing good for him. He turned away and crept toward the door, pulling it closed behind him.

And that's when his dragon senses picked up a slight noise outside his front door. He stiffened, strained his ears to listen and knew something or someone was out there.

He pulled one of the handguns, cocked it.

The door behind him came open in a flash. He sensed her behind him without turning around.

"What was that?" she whispered, her rough voice trembling.

"Stay in the bedroom," he ordered, keeping his voice low.

He took a step toward the front door, but she was at his side in an instant. "Where are you going?"

"Mia…"

He paused, turned to her, and saw the worry and fear etched on her features. Only moments ago, she'd been sleeping. He wasn't sure what had awoken her. Maybe she heard the same noise he had or maybe she'd heard the click of his gun.

"Go back in there. Stay with Freya. I'll handle it."

She visibly swallowed, glanced at the door and then stepped back toward the bedroom. She gave him a little nod as she closed the door. But he knew she stood on the other side, straining her ears to listen, to hear what would happen next.

He turned toward the front door as it blew open in a puff of smoke.

❧ 12 ❧

Rafe heard her yelp from the other side of the door. He put her out of his mind as he focused and headed toward the apartment door, his gun at the ready.

When Logan and Bree had stayed in his apartment while Logan was on the run from Lord Archer, his apartment had been broken into much the same way. Now, for a second time, it was being invaded. It sent ire and rage spinning through him.

His home had been his sanctuary for years. The idea Drakana could come into it and take what was his made him shake with violence.

Only smoke lingered in the open doorway, nothing more. No one had made an appearance.

"Show yourself." He aimed the gun at the doorway, waiting.

"I have a hundred men surrounding this building and twenty more in the hall with me." A voice emerged from the shadows beyond the threshold. "Put down your weapon. I'm unarmed."

Rafe's eyes narrowed as he stared down the barrel of his gun. "But your men are."

A laugh. "And you're one man. If I unleash them, you can't possibly defeat the all."

Bastard. Rafe lowered his gun but kept it in his hand loose at his side. He clicked on the safety. A man stepped into the threshold, his hands up to show he was unarmed. He was tall, broad-shouldered with black hair and bright blue eyes. In the second he moved into the doorway, they sized each other up. Rafe didn't like the guy.

"I find it interesting this apartment building is practically empty for a city this size." He looked him over. "You don't appear to need tenants."

It was true. Tenants started moving out after he and Logan fought off the last Drakana attack. He couldn't blame him. Ninety-percent of the apartments on this floor were vacant. It didn't matter to Rafe. He didn't need the income from the building since he already owned it.

"What do you want?" Rafe got right to the point.

"I'd think that was obvious. You have something of mine. I want it back."

This had to be Armond, the man Mia told him about. The one who tried to kidnap her and hand her over to the Drakana. His caged inner beast made another appearance and slammed against his skull. This time, it wanted blood. Desperate to rip this man into shreds, this man who dared to demand he hand over the princess.

"She doesn't belong to you," he said.

"She doesn't belong to you, either," Armond pointed out. "And yet you're keeping her hidden here. All I want is the girl and then I'll leave. I'll tell my men to stand down and not blow up the building as I've instructed them."

Rafe snarled. The beast banged against his head again. He hadn't been in his dragon form in so long, he wasn't even sure he remembered what it felt like. But the feral animal inside him demanded to be released, to sink his claws into this man's face and rip his skin to shreds.

"There are innocent people who live here. Their lives are not expendable."

"I suggest you give me what I want." Armond's tone was even and matter-of-fact. "And everyone will be fine."

There was no way in hell Rafe was handing Mia over to this man. To buy some time, he said, "What do you want with her?"

"That's none of your business," Armond said.

"But it's my business." Mia's voice lilted from behind Rafe.

He stiffened, refusing to turn around to look at her. But

Armond's gaze flickered behind him and he knew she stood there. A faint smile flickered over his lips.

"Mia, I'm glad to see you're unharmed "

"Oh, screw you, Armond," she snapped with such vehemence Rafe almost laughed.

"That's no way to talk to me after I saved your life."

"You saved my life?" She huffed out a humorless laugh. "Only to hand me over to the Drakana." She moved to stand next to Rafe, still wearing the jeans and T-shirt he'd given her earlier that day. She folded her arms, and shook her head. "I'm not going with you."

His eyes turned dark and dangerous. "Then your kingdom will suffer."

Rafe felt the temperature drop around them instantly, as though a cold north wind burst through the apartment. He cut her a glance. Complete and utter calm was on her face as she stood rock still staring at Armond. His own dragon inside calmed, stilled, as though having her near him was enough to tame him. Interesting. He would have to think about that more later. Right now, he had to find a way to soothe her.

"You dare threaten me, my kingdom. Andonia is everything to me. My home. My people. Not yours."

The air surrounding them smelled like pine and snow and he knew it was coming from her.

"But it will be." Armond's cocky smile showed off perfect white teeth.

An icy breeze ruffled Rafe's hair. He looked at her again, really looked this time, and saw ice crystals forming on her eyelashes.

"Where are my parents?" Her tone was as chilly as the room.

"Oh, you know about that?" He looked well-pleased she'd somehow gotten the information. "I'm impressed. How did you find out?"

"Where are my parents?"

The temperature dropped again. When Rafe exhaled, his breath crystalized in front of him. He knew Mia was using her dragon magic. Consciously or unconsciously. Either way, he had to stop her. He reached for her, but she shrugged him away and took a step closer to Armond. With her movement, Armond snapped his fingers. Men swarmed inside the door.

Armond hadn't been lying when he said he had twenty men in the hall with him. Most of them crowded into the apartment, all of them armed. All of them ready to do whatever it took to walk out of there with the princess.

Not on his watch. He clicked the safety off the gun and raised it, pointing it at Armond's head. The man cut him a glance that said he wasn't impressed but Rafe held steady.

"The royal charter was hijacked in Singapore. They are currently on their way here."

She stared at him, a flicker of icy light in her violet eyes. Frost formed around her feet and spread across the floor to Armond.

"Why here?"

"Because it was the only way to get you to do what I needed you to do."

"By handing me over to the Drakana?" she demanded.

"You don't yet understand how important you are. But you will. Even if I have to use your parents to do that."

"What are you going to do to them?" Her hands clenched and unclenched.

She dropped her arms by her side. Her fingertips were blue. The frost continued to move toward Armond and his men. They were trying to sidestep out of the way but the ice followed them, pushing them back into the doorway. Rafe glanced around, saw a thin coating of ice moving across the floor, covering the furniture and making its way up the walls and windows.

"I'm going to make them understand why you are so important," he said.

Hoarfrost coated everything now. It was so cold, Rafe shivered. Armond puffed out a breath as he took a step back to the open door.

"If you want your parents to live, Mia, you'll come with me.

102

Willingly."

"You bastard." Her breath plumed in front of her. "I will kill you for that."

She didn't waste a moment as she lifted her arms, her palms outward. She exhaled a sharp breath and, combined with the magic coming from her hands, she froze everything standing in front of her. Armond saw what she was about to do and tried to duck out of the way. Her icy breath hit him square in the chest, freezing him.

"Mia…"

Rafe's warning trailed off as he looked at the men frozen in front of him. This is what she'd done in the tunnel to save herself, to get away. He put the gun away and called to her again but she ignored him. He stepped in front of her, mindful of the slippery floor at her feet and grasped her arms.

Her skin had leached of all color and was bitterly cold. So cold, he sucked in a sharp breath and released her the second he touched her. Her lips were blue. Her skin shimmered with an otherworldly glow as her dragon magic surged through her veins. Her body quaked, though he suspected it was from rage rather than cold. From fear, from anger, from uncontrollable emotions beating through her. Emotions she had no idea how to handle. He wondered if she fought back the urge to shift.

"Mia, we have to leave," Rafe said.

With the men frozen, it was the best time to get the hell out of there. He'd figure out the rest of the details later. For now, he had to get them down to the parking garage, in the car and out of the city.

He used his own dragon magic to warm his fingers until a pale blue flame danced along his skin. He controlled it to keep it from burning her as he reached for her, placing his warmed hand once again on her arm. She blinked, then, as though seeing him for the first time as she met his gaze.

"Wh-what did I do?"

"It doesn't matter. We have to leave."

She looked from him back to the frozen men. "I didn't mean

to."

"I know." He gave her a gentle shake. She met his gaze again. "Listen to me. It's going to be all right. But we have to leave now. Get Freya. Can you do that?" he asked, his voice gentle, soft, urging.

She nodded. Color returned to her face, making the shimmer that had been there dissipate and disappear. She hurried toward the bedroom and returned a moment later with a sleepy-eyed Freya. It was amazing the girl had slept through all that. When she saw what had happened to the apartment, her eyes went wide.

"Your highness…what did you do?"

"We'll explain later," Rafe said. "Watch your step."

He took a tentative step on the icy floor and made slow progress across it to the door. Once they were there, he helped the women outside the apartment. In the hallway, the scene was much the same. But there was an inch of snowfall on the floor and ice covered the walls and ceiling. All the way to the elevator.

How had she managed that?

Every single last Drakana was frozen in a sheen of her ice, including Armond. He didn't particularly care if they lived or died, but he also didn't like leaving his apartment open as they left it behind. He'd have to call Logan and ask him to secure the place as soon as they got out of there.

Their feet crunched on the new-fallen snow as they headed to the elevator. Mia's color had fully returned. He could see the shame flooding her features as she looked down the hall at what she'd done. She gave Rafe a sheepish look.

"I'm sorry," she whispered, her breath still pluming in front of her.

"Don't be." He got them to the elevator and punched the button. "We have to hurry before the ones outside realize what's happened."

The elevator dinged and they got on. Freya huddled in the corner with her arms wrapped around her as they rode down in silence. In the garage, he shuttled them to the car and got them inside. Tires squealed as he drove out.

Armond wasn't lying when he said he had the building surrounded. He could see his men stationed up and down the street as they drove away.

"How long will they be like that?" Rafe asked, keeping one eye on the rearview window. "Will they live?"

"Yes." The word was icy on her lips. "I didn't hit them with the full force of my magic. Not this time. They'll come out of it soon."

"Good," Rafe said. "I don't plan to be anywhere near here when they do."

They were out of the city heading west toward the mountains in record time. Rafe had called Logan and told him what happened. He said he'd take care of the apartment and make sure it was closed up. Mia sat in the passenger seat with her arms wrapped around her middle as she stared out of vacant eyes out the window. She hadn't said a word since they got in the car. Freya huddled in the backseat, her eyes darting from the scenery flashing by to his in the rear view. Rafe did his best to ignore her and focus instead on the drive ahead and Mia's well-being.

"Mia, are you all right?"

She didn't respond. She continued to stare out the window. There was a stretch of silence, then Freya spoke.

"She can't control it," she said.

Rafe met her gaze in the mirror. "What do you mean?"

"Her dragon magic. Whenever she gets scared, her dragon magic takes over."

He cut a glance at Mia who was still catatonic. "What's wrong with her?"

"It drains her, when she doesn't shift," she said. "She needs time to recharge."

That explained why she seemed fine on the rooftop. She'd used her magic and shifted and flown over the city. He wondered, though, if the iridescent look to her skin when she was so cold indicated she was close to shifting. He thought he'd seen ripples of scales along her skin.

"I'm fine." Mia's voice snapped in the silence, her breath still crystallizing the air inside the enclosed car.

In an effort to calm her, he said, "We'll find them. I promise."

"Armond wants my kingdom, Rafe."

It wasn't the first time she'd uttered his name, but the way it rolled off her tongue sent a tingling sensation through him just the same. His inner beast purred. But now was not the time to get excited about that. He shoved those thoughts deep down.

"He won't get his hands on it," he said, sounding sure of himself.

"You don't know that. You don't know anything. You've probably never even heard of Andonia before you met me." A wave of bitterness emanated off her.

Her callous tone pissed him off. "I know plenty of things. I know enough to keep your ass out of Drakana hands which is what I intend to do. It's the only way Armond won't win."

She bristled at his arrogant tone and scowled at him. Freya leaned back into the cushion of the backseat. Her eyes were as wide as saucers. Rafe kept his eyes forward, ignoring her.

"You dare speak to me like that."

"I'll speak to you however I see fit." Still, he refused to look at her.

"I am a princess—"

"But you're not my princess." This time he turned his head and met her glare.

Fury sparked in her violet eyes. He thought he could see her dragon raging behind her dagger glare. A cold breath shuddered out of her right toward him, chilling him to the marrow of his bones. He knew she did it on purpose.

"Look out!"

Freya's shout from the backseat made his head snap around. The traffic ahead had come to a halt and was nothing more than a sea of red brake lights. He slammed on the brakes, making the tires squeal. Their seatbelts snapped, keeping them into position as they came to a jarring stop. Up ahead, white smoke curled upward in the night sky.

Next to him, he could hear Mia's breath shuddering in and out of her. "I don't like this."

She must have sensed something. He did, too, and he didn't like this situation, either. Not one bit. Like a fool, he'd gotten them on the highway and made them sitting ducks.

"Get us out of here," she said.

When she spoke, the temperature in the car dropped. He glanced at her. Frost had already started to spread on the leather seat around her.

"Mia, stop. You have to control it," he said.

She shuddered, clutching her elbows. "I don't...I can't..."

"She doesn't know how." Freya leaned forward and placed a hand on Mia's shoulder. "It's going to be all right, your highness. We'll be all right."

There was a commotion ahead in traffic. Lights from emergency vehicles flashed. Mia was right. He had to get them out of there, somehow, someway and before she decided to freeze the interior of the car. He glanced in the rearview mirror but saw nothing but headlights.

Rafe's cell phone rang. It was Logan. He answered with, "This isn't a good time—"

"Yeah, well, guess who just shifted and took off over the city? And destroyed your building in the process, by the way."

Shit.

The explosion only a few feet behind them rocked the entire freeway. They all turned to see a ball of fire light up the night sky. Cars went flying. There was sudden chaos on the highway as people fled their cars and ran.

"Get us out of here!" Mia shrieked.

He stomped on the clutch and threw it into first gear, jerking the wheel to the side to get onto the left shoulder. He sped as fast as he dared down the narrow lane looking for a way into traffic. But up ahead the shoulder was about to be no more.

"Rafe—"

"I see it," he growled.

There. He spotted an opening in the left lane as it started to move and floored it, diving into it. The car behind him honked and waved his hand out the window, middle finger extended. Another opening in the next lane and he took it, weaving in and out of traffic as they approached the wreck and the emergency vehicles that had stopped traffic. The right lane was closed off and there were no openings in traffic to let him in. He had to stop.

Rafe glanced behind them, saw the dissipating flames of the explosion.

"What was that?" Freya asked.

"That was Armond," Mia replied.

"Are you sure?" he asked.

She bent toward the door and looked up through the window, pointing. "Pretty sure."

A shadow moved through the night sky. A shadow that blotted out the stars, the falling sleet, the street lamps. It seemed to be nothing more than a black hole but Rafe knew better. He could see the faint outline of wings flapping in the night air, the black leathery skin gliding overhead.

This was not good.

"Fuck all. He's a shadow dragon."

"Yes." Mia nodded. When she looked at him, there was a sort of calm in her purple eyes. "He tracked us."

"How the hell did he do that?"

"I don't know."

But Mia touched the pale blue stone of the necklace she'd worn from the time he found her naked and shivering on that rooftop. She gripped the chain in her fist and yanked hard until it snapped.

"What are you doing?"

"I think this is a tracking device." She rolled down the window and threw it as hard as she could. Somewhere in the distance, the stone landed with a tink on the pavement. She turned back to Rafe. "Drive."

Rafe looked through the windshield at the stopped cars and the dark shadow banking and turning back around to face them. The opening of the maw and the bubbling of fire deep inside the beast.

"Rafe, drive!"

He punched it in gear and floored it, sideswiping two cars as he went by. The shadow dragon moved over them. He emitted a high-pitched squeal that indicated he was not happy about them getting away.

"I thought you said he didn't want you dead," Rafe said as he weaved through traffic, finally finding a clearing. He kicked the car down a gear, pressed the accelerator to the floor. The car took off, shooting down the highway at breakneck speed.

In the backseat, Freya cowered down, trying to make herself as small as possible. Mia held onto to the door handle as she peered in the side mirror no doubt watching for Armond's return.

"And I thought you said no one was getting in your apartment building unless you were dead. You said it was a fortress."

He didn't like she threw his words back at him and scowled. But she was right. He thought he'd secured the place but hadn't. The Drakana had gotten through anyway. All because he'd let his guard down. Because he'd let Jaxson deliver the girl to him. He took a curve too hard. Freya emitted a squeak of terror while Mia merely sucked in a sharp breath.

"I guess I was wrong, princess." Rafe steered the car around another bend and never took his eyes off the road.

"And maybe I was, too," she admitted. "But I doubt it. Likely he's trying to kill you to get to me."

"By blowing us up?" This time he stole a glance at her.

The door handle had frosted over. Snowflakes danced around her head. In any other situation, he would find that completely fascinating, but right now it was not amusing whatsoever.

"Armond knows me." Her eyes were pinned on the windshield ahead. "He knows what sort of defense I have."

"And what is that?"

"I'll show you."

She pressed the window button. As it rolled down, she unclipped her seatbelt and stood up, pushing her upper body out of the car.

"Mia, what the—"

But that was as far as he got when suddenly a burst of cold wind went through the car. He glanced into the mirror to see the entire freeway iced over behind them. He slowed the car down so she wouldn't fall out the open window.

There was a sudden ear-splitting shriek from above and then the shadow dragon fell from the sky. He landed with a resounding boom on the iced over pavement and skidded. He tried hard to get his footing on the slick ice, but it was useless.

Mia dropped back down into the seat. Her face was drained of color. Her skin had that iridescent shimmer to it as it had before when she used her dragon magic in the apartment and snowflakes still danced around her face. Ice crystals had formed in her hair, on her eyelashes. Her nose and lips were blue and her eyes—those amazing purple eyes—were wild with her fury.

"Now get us out of here."

Rafe floored it.

❧ 13 ❧

Mia sagged against the seat as Rafe sped out of town. Snow fell from the night sky, dotting the windshield as they put more distance between them and the city. The necklace wasn't an heirloom, but it had been the last thing Helmut had given her before they left Andonia. She could recall his words as though he'd said them to her moments ago.

This will ensure your safety if there's any trouble on this fool's errand of yours in Hell's Kitchen. I'll be able to find you.

Only now did she understand what he'd meant.

She hadn't really thought about it when she put it around her neck, but the pale blue teardrop stone must have been some way for him to track her. Armond had figured out how to track her, too. She knew she had to get rid of it by tossing it out the window without hesitation. She hated she had to let it go.

A soft snore came from the backseat. Freya had curled in an awkward position and slept soundly.

"Are you all right?" Rafe's voice was soft in the darkness.

"Fine." It came out a lot more curt than she intended but he didn't understand how deep that wound went where Helmut was concerned.

"I'm sorry about the necklace."

"It's not about the necklace." She gripped the door handle, her nails scraping along it. She took a deep breath, closing her eyes and exhaling. "I didn't mean to snap at you. That was my last link to Helmut. He gave it to me before we left Andonia."

"He meant a lot to you, didn't he?"

111

Streetlights flashed by in a rush as she stared out at the night, tears burning the backs of her eyes. "More than you know."

It was nearing dawn by the time they turned down the dirt road and headed through the mountains and the sunlight dappled trees. Mia leaned her head against the window and watched the scenery go by as he made turn after turn, winding his way through the woods and going deeper and deeper until at last he parked in front of a small cabin.

She stared at it through the windshield. "This is your place?"

"It is." He pushed open the car door.

Freya came awake, yawned and stretched. "Are we there yet?" she said through a yawn.

"Yes," Mia said.

Before she could open the door, Rafe opened it for her. She peered up at him in surprise. He held his hand down to her. Her stomach knotted as she reached for him, placing her fingers in his palm. His hand closed around hers, giving her a gentle tug as he helped her step out of the car.

His warmth spread through her, pulsing under her skin and chasing away the chill. No one else had made her feel that way and she couldn't help but marvel at the way his touch affected her. He clasped her hand and led her from the car to the small cabin, unlocked the door and led them inside.

The living room furniture was covered. Rafe released her, the warmth from him sucking away from her. He uncovered the furniture and snapped on the lamps on either side of the sofa. He tossed the covers aside.

The living room had a three-seat sofa, two chairs and a cocktail table facing a wood-burning fireplace. A richly colored area rug covered the bamboo flooring. Behind the living room was a small dining area with a table for four right next to the kitchen that had only the bare essentials.

"There are only two bedrooms." He met her gaze.

A wild, hot flush went through her. "Freya and I can share."

But he was shaking his head before she even finished. "No, princess. You're staying with me."

"I most certainly am not."

"You are and you're not going to refuse." His voice was hard, determined. She saw a hint of desire in those silvery eyes. "I can protect you better that way."

"Oh, don't worry about me then. I can take care of myself," Freya snipped.

Mia's head snapped at her but the girl was giving her a hint of a smile. A smile. One that Mia had never seen on her assistant before.

"Freya, don't you think it's inappropriate I spend the night in the same room with him?" She thumbed in Rafe's direction.

"Desperate times, princess," she said. "I think you should listen to the man."

Mia flushed again, so hot she was certain her cheeks burned bright red.

"Yeah. Listen to the man," Rafe repeated. "Freya, I'll show you to your room."

He waved her after him and Freya happily followed leaving Mia alone in the middle of the living room. Frustrated, she huffed out a breath. How dare he demand she sleep in the same room with him? He was far too bold.

Or was he?

Maybe he was merely doing his job to keep her safe. A job, she reminded herself, he had volunteered for. He wasn't her security detail.

She clutched her elbows and glanced around the room. It was devoid of any personal items, much like his apartment in the city. He returned a moment later, car keys still in hand.

"I'm sorry it's cold in here, but I haven't been up since last summer," he said. "I turned on the heat. It should be warm in no time."

"I hadn't noticed." And she hadn't. Her skin had returned to its normal iciness.

"Is your skin always like that?"

"So pale and cold? Yes. Always." Except when he touched her. She experienced a warmth she had never experienced before. A warmth that made her feel as though she were finally normal.

He moved closer to her, his gaze never leaving her face. "I was going to say is it always so iridescent?"

She blinked surprise. "What do you mean?"

He reached for her. His fingers trailed down her arm, leaving a burning sensation in his wake. Did he know he did that to her?

"Iridescent. When the light hits it just right, I can see all the colors of the rainbow."

Her mouth went dry. "You can?"

"I can. In the sunlight, it shimmers. It's lovely."

No one had ever told her that her skin was lovely or even described it in such a manner. There was a curious swooping in her lower abdomen. He dropped his hand and reached for the gun at the small of his back and clicked off the safety, then held it out to her.

"What's that for?"

"We need supplies. Take it." He indicated the gun.

She stared at him. "I've never used a gun before."

He clicked the safety back on. "I'll show you how." He waved her toward him.

Mia moved closer. He wrapped an arm around her, holding the gun in front of them.

"This is the safety. You click it off like this." He switched it off. "Keep it on unless you think you need to use the gun." He clicked it back on. "Do you know what kind of gun this is?" She shook her head. "It's a revolver. It's already loaded. All you have to do is point and shoot." He held it up to demonstrate. "Now you try."

She took the gun from him, but it felt awkward in her hand.

"Like this?" she asked.

He repositioned her hands, so she was holding it properly.

"There. Like that. Good."

"And then what?"

"Point and pull the trigger. But make it count. You only have six rounds." His breath tickled her ear as he spoke. "Can you handle that, princess?"

Her heart kicked into a quick beat with his nearness, the way he held her, touched her. Her body reacted to his warmth in the way it had with all his other little touches.

"I think I got it."

"Good." He dropped his arms and moved away from her, leaving her devoid of all that delicious heat.

"Do you think something is going to happen?" she asked.

"No, but you should be prepared. Don't shoot me when I come back." He flashed her a smile and was gone.

She watched him walk out the door. As soon as he was gone, she dropped the gun on the cocktail table. She didn't want anything to do with the gun.

"He's so dreamy."

Freya's voice from behind her made her jump. She pressed a hand against her fluttering heart. "You scared me."

"Don't you think so, your highness?"

Your highness. She bristled at the title and almost snapped at her not to call her that. But isn't that what Mia was? She was a princess, though Rafe didn't treat her like anyone else.

"I hadn't noticed." Mia moved the furniture covers and plopped down on the sofa.

"Are you certain about that? You blushed at him when he told you he wanted you with him."

"I did not."

"Oh, you did. I saw your cheeks turn pink." Freya was smiling again.

"Don't you have something to do?" Mia snapped.

"I lost my iPad and I napped in the car, so no." She moved around to the other side of the sofa and sat next to her. "I think it's sweet he wants to protect you."

115

"I think he's being a pain in the ass." Mia folded her arms over her chest and stared at the offensive weapon on the table.

"He's not. He's trying to keep you safe. That's more than Armond did."

Armond. That bastard.

"I don't understand him," Freya said.

"Nor do I, but it doesn't matter why he's doing it, only that he's doing it."

"I'm sorry about the necklace. I know it was special to you."

"It was nothing." Mia tried to shrug it off. She didn't want to think about it too much because it upset her.

Silence lapsed between them, then Freya said, "What do we do now?"

"I guess now we lay low and wait to see what Armond's next move is," she said. "And in the meantime, let's see what's in the kitchen."

As soon as she said it, Freya's stomach rumbled. "That sounds good to me."

Freya and Mia found a bottle of merlot and a couple of wine glasses in one of the cabinets.

"Isn't it a little early in the day to drink?" Freya looked at her watch.

Mia shrugged. "It's five o'clock somewhere."

"Good enough."

She had to go through every drawer until she finally found a corkscrew and could get it open. The refrigerator was devoid of all food. There were only a few ice cubes in the freezer. The cabinets had one box of stale crackers and a can of expired tuna, which Mia tossed in the trash.

So, they opened the wine and had half the bottle gone by the time Rafe returned. He carried in two grocery bags full and placed them on the counter.

"There's more in the car." He headed back out.

Mia unpacked the groceries. He'd bought enough food to last them a couple of months in the woods. She wondered if he was expecting them to be there that long. He returned with two more bags and left again. These were full of frozen goods and dairy products as well as toiletries. When he returned again, he had an armload of bags that were full of cold-weather clothes. Hats, coats, gloves, thermals. She gave him a questioning look.

"There's only clothes here for me and it's about to get cold. You'll both need that."

He nodded to the clothes and left again. When he returned, he had an armload of firewood. He quickly set about making a fire while Mia finished putting away the groceries and Freya drank more wine.

Something about the way he built a fire as she put away the food felt so domestic. Like it was perfectly natural for the crown princess of Andonia to play house with her dragon protector.

"Well, this is cozy," Freya said from her place at the dining table. There was a smile in her voice.

Rafe had the fire going, warming the small interior with a golden glow. He entered the kitchen, saw her holding the wine glass and spied the half-empty bottle.

"I hope you two are enjoying that," he said. "It's a two-hundred-dollar bottle of merlot."

She grinned. "No wonder it's so good."

He nudged her aside to rummage through the cabinet for another wine glass. He poured one for himself and took a sip, nodding approval. "I forgot I had it."

"How does one forget they have a two-hundred-dollar bottle of wine in the cabinet?"

"Like I said, I haven't been here in a while. I see you made yourself useful by putting away the groceries."

"I'm very useful," she said. "I can do all sorts of things."

"Like what?" His eyes narrowed as he looked at her over the rim of his glass.

She flushed as her mind raced to try and come up with something but she was at a loss. She was a princess. She had been pampered her entire life from the moment she was born until the moment she stepped foot on that plane to come to the United States.

"Mia can spin pillows on one finger," Freya announced.

"Freya!"

She giggled and downed her wine, then rose and reached for the bottle. Mia snatched it away before she could grab it.

"I think that's enough wine for you," she said.

"You can spin pillows?" Rafe raised an eyebrow. "I'm intrigued. Show me."

"No." Mia stuck out her bottom lip in a pout.

"Pouting isn't going to make me change my mind," Rafe said. "Though I can tell that is one of your most spectacular talents."

She wanted to punch him.

"Show him, your highness." Freya walked over to the sofa and picked up one of the side pillows, tossing it to her.

Mia caught it and held it a moment, staring down at the red and gold pattern and feeling ridiculous.

"Yes, show me." A hint of a grin tugged the corners of Rafe's mouth.

She huffed and held the pillow, balancing it on one of her forefingers. She kept it balanced as she pushed one corner, then the next and the next until it started spinning like a top on the tip of her finger. Freya clapped her delight.

"Impressive," Rafe said. "How did you learn that?"

"When I was ten, I broke my ankle in three places ice skating. I'd tried to do a triple salchow and didn't stick the landing. I had to have surgery." She lifted the edge of her jeans to show him a faint scar around her left ankle. "I spent a lot of time being babied and stuck in bed, so I learned to spin pillows to pass the time."

She stopped the pillow and tossed it back to Freya.

"That's really not all that useful," Mia added.

Rafe grinned. "I suppose it is when you're bored. Do you still ice skate?"

"No, my mother made me give that up. My ankles were too weak after the accident."

"She decided to race cars instead," Freya piped up.

Mia glared at her. "You really need to learn to keep your mouth shut, Freya."

"Wait a second. You race cars?" Rafe's eyes were wide with surprise.

"Sure. But only at the track with no one else around and only in a car that won't go over a hundred and sixty kph," Mia said. "Though I confess I've driven faster than that before. I like the dirt tracks better than the asphalt tracks."

Again, that hint of a smile tugging at the corner of his lips. "Why is that?"

"Because the track changes and you can sling dirt everywhere when you turn just right."

He laughed out loud. "Princess, you surprise me."

"When my mother found out, she was furious." Mia couldn't help but smile.

"You mean, your mother the queen?" he asked.

"Yes."

A loud snore erupted from the sofa where Freya had passed out. Mia sighed.

"She doesn't hold her wine so well," she said.

"I'll take her to her room."

He put down his glass and went to the sofa where he hefted the girl into his arms. Watching his muscles flex and work sent a familiar heat sweeping through her. A heat that crept into her cheeks. She looked away and took a sip of her wine, trying hard not to watch. He returned to the kitchen and opened the fridge, pulling out vegetables.

"I tucked her in."

"Thank you for taking care of her," Mia said and meant it.

Rafe got out a green bell pepper, an onion, ham and cheese. He started to cut up the green peppers. "I'm glad Jaxson brought her to me and she found you."

"Me, too." She ran her finger around the rim of her glass, watching him chop the pepper with expert precision. She chewed her lower lip, wondering if she should come clean with the real reason why she'd come to the States—to find the Blood Stone. Oh, he probably suspected since he'd already mentioned the Blood Stone once. She'd managed to sidestep talking to him about it, but she wasn't sure how much longer she could keep it to herself.

Instead, she asked, "When are you going to tell where I can find my stolen gemstones?"

He didn't pause in his chopping when he spoke. "I told you the investigator had them."

"Yes, but not how to get them back."

"As soon as all of this is over, you and I will find out how to contact this Shi'Ann Jones and get your gemstones back."

He finished with the peppers and moved on to the onion, slicing it into bite-sized pieces.

"You don't know how to contact her?" She sipped her wine, letting the fruity flavor linger on her tongue.

"Not exactly, but I'm sure Logan or Bree does."

"And who are they?"

"Logan is a dragon-shifter and the new Chief Magistrate of the Council of Five in the Hidden Lands. Bree is his very pregnant wife."

"The Hidden Lands?"

He moved on to the ham, cutting it into small pieces. "It's the realm we all come from." He cut her a glance. "Even you, Mia."

She narrowed her eyes at him. "I come from Andonia, as does my whole family."

"Yes, but once, long ago, we all inhabited the Hidden Lands. Cold-drakes ruled their own kingdom there until they migrated out."

He scooped the pepper, onion and ham to the side, then turned to the fridge and got out the eggs. She watched him crack several into a bowl.

Her brow creased with confusion. She had never heard of such of thing. Cold-drakes in the Hidden Lands? Her parents had never told her about that place. As far as she knew, Andonia had been ruled by the Draynor family for the last four generations.

"Why would they do that?"

He whipped the eggs as he melted butter in a pan. Once it had melted, he poured the eggs into it and added the other ingredients making her stomach growl.

"Because the Hidden Lands is cursed. Only a few clans are brave enough to remain." He met her gaze.

"How did that happen?" She was truly interested in this place and why it was cursed.

"No one seems to know. Logan is searching for a clue in his father's old books but neither he nor Bree can stay there long."

She drained her glass and reached for the bottle, pouring more in hers and the remaining into his glass. He folded the eggs in half and slid it onto a plate. He handed it to her. She looked down at it and then back at up him.

"No one has ever made me an omelet before."

"You seem to have had a lot of firsts with me, princess."

She took the plate from him and grabbed a fork, digging in immediately. She couldn't remember the last time she ate and had a hard time controlling the urge to shovel the eggs into her mouth at a rapid pace. He reached for more eggs, this time scrambling them.

"I guess I do," she said around a mouthful. "So, what's your story?"

"My story?" He stirred the eggs, cooking them until they were no longer runny.

"You said the Hidden Lands is the realm you all belong to. How long have you been here?"

He froze for a long moment, a contemplative look on his face. He plated his eggs and found a fork. "I told you before. Too long."

"And that's still not an answer." She put down the empty plate. "That was delicious."

He smiled, well pleased. "I'm glad you liked it." He took a bite, then turned to the coffee pot.

"Are you going to answer my question?" she prodded.

"No."

Annoyance flashed through her. She folded her arms over her chest. "Why not?"

"Because it's none of your business."

She huffed. "Not fair. You get to know everything about me but I don't get to know anything about you? Obviously, you're rich because you own this cabin and that building in the middle of the biggest city in the U.S. You have pretty decent taste in cars if that Jaguar we drove up in is any indication. You like fine wine." She motioned to the now-empty bottle. "You know a thing or two about security. And you know how to cook a mean omelet."

"You know everything you need to know about me."

She huffed out another breath. "You're impossible."

He put down his fork, staring at his plate with only remnants of scrambled eggs remaining. "I was once a knight."

She had visions of him in a full plate armor carrying a sword and looking dashing and it sent her heart into a quick pitter-patter. If he was once a knight, he believed in chivalry and protecting a lady's honor. Suddenly all she wanted to do was fling herself into his arms and kiss him senseless. The very idea of him as a knight was incredibly hot and sexy.

"A knight?"

"Yes, and that's all you ever need know." He turned to her, his silver eyes dark and dangerous and his face indicating the subject was closed. "And now, princess, you have a date with a pillow."

⊰ 14 ⊱

Mia didn't protest much when he took her by the hand and
led her to the bedroom. In fact, she was downright pliable
in his hands. Her cheeks had turned pink from the several glasses
of wine she'd had and her body didn't feel as cold as it normally
did when he touched her. He guessed that had something to do
with the alcohol making its way through her veins.

She climbed into the bed without a word, pulling the blankets
to her chin. She was asleep within minutes.

Rafe crept from the room and closed the door behind him. He
paused in the hall and blew out a breath.

Questions. She was so full of questions and needing answers
about everything from the gemstones to who he was. How the hell
was he going to explain to her about the Blood Stone? She would
be furious when he told her she wouldn't be getting it back.

It had been a long time since he'd thought about his past. He
didn't want to start thinking about it now. He'd buried those
memories deep inside him, hoping they would never be
resurrected. And yet, the princess had somehow found a way to
dredge them all back, much to his dismay. He was not interested in
remembering anything about his past and he didn't want to talk
about it with her or anyone.

Logan mentioned he knew, but Rafe wasn't sure how much he
really knew or what was in those Ancient texts he'd mentioned.
Logan was giving him a chance to regain what he'd lost—returning
to the Hidden Lands. He wanted that. He wanted that since the day
he was exiled. He wanted to help Logan break the curse for the

realm.

But at what cost? He didn't want to do it at Mia's expense. The more time he spent with her, the more he realized he could not ask her to shift and hand over one of her teeth. It was an impossible thing to ask of her, especially because she had no idea what the Hidden Lands were or even what they meant to the dragon clans who left them so long ago.

She would never understand and he could never fully explain it to her.

He would have to tell Logan he couldn't give him what he wanted, knowing it would crush Logan's hope of breaking the curse. He wasn't sure what that would do to their relationship. He'd helped Logan when he needed it the most. Now it seemed as though he was abandoning him at his most desperate hour.

It made him feel like a total ass.

He signed and ran his hand through his hair. How the hell he was supposed to sleep next to the princess? When he told her he intended to share a room with her, he said it to see how she'd react. And she'd reacted exactly how he thought she would—annoyed and a little turned-on. He wasn't immune to the blush rising in her cheeks, giving her a pretty color to her pale skin.

Nor was he immune to how she felt when he touched her. How she warmed to him. How she wanted him to continue to touch her. It was why he skimmed his hand along her arm. Even his dragon wanted to continue to touch her.

It took all his strength not to cup her face and kiss her right there, right then.

But Freya had been there looking on with hope in those wide dark eyes. He didn't want an audience. Not when he wanted Mia all to himself. Having the girl here put a damper on any romantic involvement he and Mia might have, but he also couldn't turn her away. She was lost and needed someone to help her.

Rafe needed to find out where Armond was keeping Mia's parents and how to get them back unharmed. But, at the moment, he hadn't any idea how to do that. All he knew was they were in a safe place and he was bone-tired. He headed to the fireplace and added more kindling. Then he stretched out on the sofa, crossed his legs at the ankles, and promptly went to sleep.

He awoke to the chatter of two female voices and the smell of something cooking. When he pried his eyes open, he could see the fire had died to embers and the two women were in the kitchen cooking and chatting. He pulled himself to a sitting position and peered over the back of the sofa at them.

Mia caught a glimpse of him and gave him her best winning smile. She looked rested. The dark circles under her eyes were gone. Her pale hair was damp and hung over her shoulders. She'd put on clean clothes.

"Morning. Or maybe I should say evening. It's nearly dusk." She held up a mug. "Do you want some coffee?"

He ran his hand through his hair and over his scruffy face, his skin bristling against his stubble, and nodded. He needed to shave and couldn't remember the last time he'd showered. "That would be great."

He pried himself off the sofa and headed into the kitchen, the aroma of something baking hitting him full force and making his stomach growl with a ferocious roar. She poured him a cup of the dark brew and pretended not to notice.

"How do you take it?"

"Black," he said. She raised her eyebrows, looking impressed. "Does that surprise you, princess?"

"Not in the least." She refilled her cup. "It's a little strong. Maybe it'll put hair on your chest." She gave him a lopsided grin.

"I don't need more of that."

She giggled.

Standing so close to her, he could smell the clean scent of her soap and the faint aroma of her shampoo with the undertone of a crisp winter day—her natural scent. Desire tingled through him, a reaction he hadn't been prepared for. Freya, too, had on clean clothes and appeared to be rested and relaxed.

"I hope you don't mind but we raided your kitchen," Mia said. "I had no idea Freya could cook."

"My mother taught me," the girl said and beamed, looking well-pleased.

Rafe leaned down and peered through the oven window to see the whole chicken he bought roasting to perfection surrounded by potatoes, carrots, celery and onion. His mouth watered at the sight. His last meal had been a couple of scrambled eggs. He'd been lacking in taking care of himself since Mia landed on his rooftop.

"You made that?" He looked at the girl.

She nodded, proud of her efforts. "It was easy."

"Doesn't look easy," he muttered.

"Did you have other plans for the chicken?" Mia was unable to hide her smirk.

He took a sip of coffee. "Not at all. Cooking breakfast is what I'm best at, though I do have a few other culinary skills."

One pale brow lifted in surprise as she looked him over, impressed with him. At least they wouldn't starve to death.

"Good to know. We were hungry, so Freya whipped this up. She has a knack for having recipes floating around in her head. It should be ready soon."

Outside, they could hear the crunch of tires on the gravel drive as someone approached the cabin. Mia stiffened. Freya froze. Rafe put down his mug and headed for the gun still on the cocktail table.

"No one knows we're here." He snatched up the gun and clicked off the safety. "You two go barricade yourselves in one of the bedrooms while I handle whoever this is."

They didn't argue as they scurried away. He heard the click of the bedroom door.

Moving to the window, he peered through the blinds and watched as the car came to a halt, its headlights beaming right into the window, blinding him. A figure flung open the door and stumbled out. Whoever it was sagged against the open car door for a moment before slamming it and staggering toward the cabin.

It was Jaxson. He held an arm against his side where his shirt hosted a large blood stain. Rafe clicked on the safety and stuck the gun in the waistband of his pants at the small of his back. He flung open the door and caught Jaxson as he lurched across the threshold.

His friend's skin was pale and beaded with sweat. He clutched Rafe's arms. It was clear it was an effort to keep on his feet.

"What the hell happened to you?" Rafe kicked the door closed and helped him to the sofa.

"Drakana, that's what," he said. "This Armond person is desperate to find the princess." He took a deep breath as though speaking was a labor. "I came to warn you. He's brought the fight into the human realm, Rafe."

"What does that mean?"

"It means humans know about us. Armond and his Drakana tore through the city looking for her."

His gut twisted. He should have known something like that would happen when Armond shifted and tracked them down on the highway. He hadn't anticipated that, though.

"How did you find me?" he asked.

"Don't worry. I wasn't followed this time. And I've known where your hideout was for a long time." He winced with the pain and then grunted, rolling to get more comfortable.

"Why come here? You could have called," Rafe said.

"I came because…" A fine sheen of sweat glistened his face.

Suddenly, Rafe realized why he'd sought him, why he'd come to find him. "Let me see your side." He eyed the side Jaxson held when he tumbled out of the car.

Jaxson pulled up the edge of his blood-stained shirt to show him the wound. "I may be too far gone. It was an obsidian blade."

The female gasp alerted Rafe to Mia's presence. He looked up at her. Color had drained from her face as she pressed her fingers to her lips. Snow danced around her head. He needed to distract her, to keep her from freezing the inside of the cabin and get her dragon magic under control.

"Mia, now is not the time for that. Get the first aid kit. It's in the bathroom under the sink." He turned back to Jaxson and examined the stab wound. "Looks bad."

"You helped Logan once. I hoped you could help me."

"How long has the poison been in your system?" Rafe demanded.

"Too long." He leaned his head back, staring up at the ceiling, his breathing labored. "Like I said. I may be too far gone."

"So was Logan when he found me. I was able to help him. I can help you, too." Determination laced his words.

Mia returned with the first aid kit, Freya on her heels. She handed him the small red zippered bag. Rafe pushed up his shirt and saw where the blade had stabbed him, leaving a gaping wound. He'd already lost a lot of blood and would likely need stitches.

"You're not going to like it," Rafe said. "The wound needs to be cleaned and stitched. Plus, you'll need the antidote. Mia, I'll need your help stitching him up."

She pressed her lips together and he could tell she didn't like the idea of helping him stitch Jaxson back together. But she didn't complain as she came around the other end of the sofa. Rafe pulled out a syringe and a medicine bottle with an amber liquid.

"What is that?" she asked.

"Something to counteract the poison from the obsidian blade in his system." He poked the syringe in the bottle and filled it, then spoke to Jaxson. "When you're feeling better, you can tell me how you ended up with a stab wound from an obsidian blade."

"Sure. It's a great story." Sarcasm dripped on his words.

"I need a vein," Rafe said, giving Jaxson a pointed look.

He eyed the syringe with less than excitement. "I hate needles."

"I don't care. We can do this this hard way or the easy way. Personally, I prefer easy way."

"And what is that?"

"You roll up your sleeve and I give you the shot and we're done." Rafe reached for a tourniquet and waved it in front of him.

"If you don't want to cooperate, we do it the hard way by me knocking you out."

With a sigh, Jaxson pushed up his sleeve. Rafe handed Mia the band of rubber. "Put it on his upper arm. Make a knot." Then to Jaxson, "Make a fist and hold it."

As he did, Rafe felt the bend of his elbow for his vein. Satisfied he found a good vein, he didn't give any sort of notice before he plunged the needle into his arm and pumped in the medicine. Jaxson sucked in a sharp breath, his body going stiff.

"Oh, and it stings a little," Rafe said.

"You might have warned me," he said through clenched teeth.

"I didn't want you to give me any more shit." He removed the needle and set it aside. "You'll feel the medicine in a minute."

"What will it...do..." His words drifted off as he passed out seconds later.

"That." Rafe glanced up at Mia. "Help me get him into the bedroom. Freya, I hope you don't mind having a roommate."

Rafe hoisted Jaxson's dead weight up on one of his shoulders and put his arm around his waist. Mia took the other shoulder and did the same. Together, they dragged the poor guy into the other room. Freya scooped up the first aid kit and followed, hot on their heels.

He eased Jaxson down onto the bed and then lifted up the shirt to expose the hideous wound. Jaxson had managed to stop the bleeding, but it still oozed. A white foamy substance oozed around the opening. Rafe knew that was the poison at work. Freya gasped. Mia sucked in a sharp breath.

"It looks bad," Mia said.

"This is what an obsidian blade does," he said.

He thanked Freya for having the forethought to bring in the first aid kit. He got out gauze, a small needle and what looked like thread. He set it aside on the nightstand, then reached for hydrogen peroxide and antibiotic ointment. He doused a piece of gauze with the hydrogen peroxide and gently cleaned the white substance and blood from the wound until he could see the jagged opening.

Freya gagged and looked green about the whole affair. When the timer on the oven dinged, she happily ran out of the room to remove the chicken. She didn't return.

It was just as well. He didn't need her in here getting sick over a few little stitches. Mia seemed to handle it well enough as she handed him the needle. After Rafe made his final stitch, he covered it with a bandage.

"Will he be all right?" she asked.

"He'll live." He padded to the bathroom and washed the blood and poison off his hands. "As soon as that antidote makes its way through his system, he'll heal a lot quicker."

Mia perched on the edge of the bed, looking at Jaxson, her face contorted with worry. "I never knew what an obsidian blade could do."

"Logan was stabbed with one when he came through the portal to the human realm. I had to patch him up, too, so I'm familiar with those types of wounds." He dried his hands and halted in the doorway.

Her brows were knit with question. "Portal?"

"How we travel between this realm and the Hidden Lands." He tossed the towel back onto the bathroom counter, then held his hand out to her. "Let's go see how Freya is doing with that roasted chicken."

"You drop a bomb like that on me and expect me to ignore it? I need to know more about this portal. How does it work?"

He dropped his hand realizing his mistake in mentioning it too late. "Logan can answer that. He knows more about it than I do."

It was a small lie. He understood the concept and how portals could be opened and closed with Dragon's Breath, but he didn't want to get into that right now. It was too complicated.

"What did Jaxson mean when he said Armond had brought the fight into the human realm?" She stayed put. It was clear she wasn't moving until she had an answer.

He hadn't realized she'd overheard their conversation and wondered how long she'd been standing there before she made her presence known. He didn't want to answer her, but he knew she wasn't going to let it go. He sighed.

"It means, princess, Armond is determined to find you. He doesn't give a rat's ass if humans see him in his true form, nor does he give a shit who he hurts, destroys or kills in the process. It means he will do whatever it takes to get his hands on you no matter what."

She pressed her lips together so tightly, they leached of color. She glanced back at Jaxson, as if seeing the first victim of Armond's war and worried her bottom lip.

"Why? Why is he doing this?"

He didn't know the answer to that, but he was intelligent and had lived long enough to guess. He'd seen all manner of man—dragon-shifter and human alike—to know power and money could corrupt even the best person. Mia was crown princess of a small kingdom. She would be a valuable asset to him.

It was something he hadn't considered until now, something that had been gnawing at him about the whole situation from the beginning. Armond wanted—needed—Mia alive because she was crown princess. She would inherit the crown and rule of Andonia but if he staged a successful coup and took over, he would need a stronger claim to the throne. He'd need her.

"If you're wondering if it has to do with more than just your kingdom, I think you'd be right," he said. "You have something he wants and he's not going to stop until he gets it."

Slowly, she turned her head and met his gaze. Worry lines creased her forehead. "And what do you suppose that is?"

"If I had to guess, princess, I'd say he wants your hand in marriage."

She shuddered. "What makes you think that?"

"Because with the king and queen dead, he can move to take over the kingdom, but he'd need royal blood to produce an heir." He gave her a pointed a look.

Revulsion flickered over her features. "I would sooner die than let him get his meaty paws on me."

"We better make sure that never happens." He held his hand out to her again. "Come on. Let's go eat."

∽ 15 ☙

A wave of horror and disgust went through her at Rafe's suggestion Armond wanted her for nothing more than an heir. She could not deny the real threat Armond posed to her and her kingdom. She shoved away the horrible thought and focused on more pleasant things. Like the hot dragon-shifter in front of her.

"Something doesn't make sense. If he wants me for himself, why would he try to kidnap me and hand me over to the Drakana?" she wanted to know.

He continued to hold his hand out to her. "Only he can answer that. There could be numerous reasons. To break you. To take you prisoner until he's secured the kingdom with his men. To do other things."

Her stomach tightened into a knot. Those other things were not things she wanted to consider. She was glad he didn't voice them.

"I need answers." She stared at him, as if she could find them there in his face.

His expression was impassive as he continued to hold his hand down to her. "We'll find them. Come on. I know you're hungry."

Relenting, she reached for him. His warm fingers closed around her cold ones, sending that lovely heat up her arm and spreading through her body. He made no move to lead her from the room. She made no move to release his hand. They stood there for several heartbeats, looking at each other while he held her hand.

"All of this is happening because of me." Her voice was timid and quiet.

"No." He shook his head. "It's happening because Armond made it happen. You and your parents got caught in the middle."

She glanced back at Jaxson who slept peacefully in the middle of the bed. "I'm sorry about your friend."

"He'll be all right once he sleeps off the antidote. He'll be weak for a while, but he'll pull through."

"I never wanted anyone to get hurt."

"Mia, you can't do that."

"Do what?"

"Beat yourself up like this."

He tugged her hand, pulling her to him and wrapping an arm around her waist. She tipped her head back to look up at him. Her breath caught in her throat as she met his liquid silver gaze. Her heart picked up the pace and that curious swooping feeling was back in the pit of her stomach. His body heat washed over her, chasing away winter shadows making her feel normal again. He brushed back a lock of her still damp hair with the back of his hand.

She couldn't stop from running her hand over his chest, halting at his shoulder. She liked the way his muscled form felt under her hand. Liked even more the way he looked at her. They'd shared a kiss before and she'd been a bitch about it. She didn't want to admit how much that kiss affected her or how much she liked.

Her life had never been her own with her duties and responsibilities. She always had someone telling her what to wear, where to go, how to behave, when to smile, when to wave. Since she'd been with Rafe, she'd had a sense of self. He didn't treat her like a princess. He treated her like an ordinary woman. As though her status and title didn't particularly matter to him. Even though the situation was less than ideal, even though she felt as though she could not be ordinary, it was somehow different. She knew he kept her hidden to keep her safe, to keep her alive.

"Thank you for helping me and Freya," she said. "I don't think I could have survived without you."

He cupped her face. "You would have. You're a strong woman

and a survivor, Mia. You would have found a way."

A part of her melted. She had never thought of herself as strong or a survivor. She was nothing more than a pampered princess who had unlimited access to the best haute couture and designer labels. That didn't make her a survivor. That made her a spoiled brat. She didn't know what to say to that. Freya made a sudden appearance and they jumped apart as though they were two teenagers caught by their parents. It left her body devoid of his warmth once again.

"I—I'm sorry. I was just...the food is ready." She scurried out of the room.

Without another word, Rafe followed the girl, leaving Mia empty and alone and cold. With a backward glance once more at Jaxson, she left the room, closing the door softly behind her.

After dinner, Freya insisted on cleaning up the dishes. She shooed Mia out of the kitchen. Rafe put more kindling on the fire, making it an impressive blaze. With both of them busy, it left Mia with nothing to do.

"I need some air." She stepped to the front door.

"Don't go far," Rafe warned, sounding more like a concerned parent than anything.

She rolled her eyes behind his back as she opened the door. "I'll be fine."

It was early evening, but the sun had already set. A blanket of snow covered the ground and the two cars. And though her breath crystalized in front of her, she wasn't cold. She was in her element. This weather reminded her much of Andonia.

She couldn't stop the wave of homesickness passing through her. She clutched her elbows and looked up at the clear night sky. Out here, away from the city lights, she could see the stars blinking against the inky backdrop. The moon shown bright, making the new-fallen snow glisten with a blue-white light.

Despite being in this peaceful beauty, it was hard for her not to worry about her parents, her kingdom, her own well-being. She had so many questions and Rafe, by no fault of his own, had no answers to give her. She didn't know who she could turn to, who she could ask, who she could trust back in Andonia. Armond was nothing but a traitor to the crown. When she was back in Andonia, she would see to it he was punished. He would pay for everything he'd done to her and her family.

The door opened and Rafe stepped out onto the small porch. Golden light slashed from the interior of the warm, cozy cabin for a brief moment before he closed the door and stood next to her. He had a contemplative look on his face.

"Freya is watching over Jaxson," he announced.

"That's good. It will give her a task. She'll feel useful." She tipped her face up to the night and blew out a breath, watching it plume white in the air.

"Aren't you cold?" he asked.

"No. Are you?"

He blew out a breath. "A little."

"I'm a cold-drake," she said. "Andonia is in a deep freeze right now. This is balmy compared to that."

She wasn't sure what compelled her to do it, but she lifted one hand, palm upward. The dragon magic inside her surged, making her skin pale to that iridescent color he'd called it. She could see it, then, the way her skin shimmered in the moonlight, and marveled at it. Snowflakes appeared and danced in the palm of her hand.

"I thought you couldn't control it," he said.

"Freya wasn't quite right when she said that. Sometimes I can, when I'm calm and can think about how the dragon magic feels inside me. Like now."

"How does it feel?"

She considered his question. She had never really thought about it before and tried to put it into words. "Like frost is flowing through my veins. Like winter lives deep in my soul." She lifted her gaze to his. "And like my dragon wants to come out."

"Does it want to come out now?" His voice was thick with

desire.

It sent arousal spiraling through her. The snowflakes disappeared. Her shuddering breath left a plume between them. She could see something ancient and otherworldly behind those silvery eyes of his and wondered if his dragon eyes were the same color. If he had scales to match. If he truly was a fire elemental, would his flames be red and gold or burn hotter in blue and white?

Deep inside, her dragon was restless. The magic pounded against her skin, pulsing a wicked beat. She shoved it back down to keep it at bay. To keep it quiet. But she knew her history and she knew it would not remain quiet for long.

"It does," she said.

Rafe closed the gap between them, his heat radiating off him as though he were nothing more than a portable heater. Her portable heater. The overwhelming desire for him nearly made her come undone. Her powerful feelings for him scared her. Snowflakes danced around her head, unbidden by her.

"Are you doing that on purpose?" he asked.

"No," she breathed.

He lifted his hand, a blue-white flame dancing in his palm. It gobbled up the snowflakes around her head. She sucked in a breath, watching the flickering flame in his hand. She at last had her answer as to what his dragon fire looked like. It was the most beautiful thing she'd ever seen.

She fell into his arms. He snuffed out the light as he caught her, held her close. He warmed her from the outside in and all she wanted to do was kiss those sensual lips of his once again. Their mouths fused together in a mutual bonding. It burned through her at a rapid pace, chasing away the bone-chilling cold and lighting her up inside with a warm brightness.

A soft mewl bubbled up her throat. His hand tangled in her long hair, fisting at the nape of her neck. She leaned into him, kissing him with reckless abandon, with everything she had ever felt. Fire flashed through her veins and all her worries and fears melted into a puddle at her feet.

A literal puddle at her feet. The ground hissed, steam rising where there was once snow. They broke apart and both looked down to see they stood in a small circle of melted snow and ice.

"It appears," he said slowly, "our dragon forms like each other."

✣ 16 ✣

It had been many years since Rafe had shifted into his dragon form. He hadn't used his dragon magic until recently. Until Mia landed in his life. The first time in eons he'd used his dragon magic was in that dark alley in the city. He'd forgotten how it surged through him, made him want to shift, made his dragon form want to claw its way out. His skin itched at the thought of it. It took all his strength to suppress it and keep it at bay.

All because he'd kissed her. All because he'd warmed her. He knew his elemental heat chased away her cold-drake frost. He had never expected to want her the way he did.

She blinked her violet eyes, her cheeks pink with arousal. Her skin no longer held that luster it normally did, and he knew it was because she still stood in his arms.

"What do we do now?" she asked.

He knew what he wanted to do. He wanted to scoop her up and carry her inside and bed her. He wanted to see the color remain high in her pretty cheeks, her lips damp from his kissing, her skin rosy and dewy from lovemaking.

He also knew what he should do. He should release her, send her back inside the house, and sleep on the sofa.

"It stands to reason that if our dragon forms like each other," she continued, "we should do something about that." A breath shuddered out of her. "Shouldn't we?"

With her face still tipped up to his, he could see the flutter of her pulse in the long column of her throat. He wished he hadn't seen that because it did nothing to abate his own state. He couldn't take her back inside and ravish her, even if that was what he wanted. She was a princess. She deserved better than an exiled knight. She deserved better than him. She deserved royalty.

He took her by the hand.

"Walk with me."

Momentary confusion flickered over her face, but she fell in step beside him. They walked down the slope from the small cabin into the snow-dusted woods.

"Where are we going?"

"Just a short walk to get some fresh air." And clear his head and hopefully make this unshakable need for her go away. "You were right, you know. I had never heard of Andonia until we met. I don't know where it is."

It wasn't entirely true. Mostly, he wanted her to distract him from the arousal in his pants. He was familiar enough with the little kingdom to know what its top export was and where it was located on the map.

"It's in Western Europe. A tiny sliver of a country surrounded by Belgium, Germany, and France. It's been ruled by the Draynor family for generations."

He knew this, of course, because he knew the history of the Hidden Lands. The Draynors had migrated to the human realm and infiltrated the small country. They took it by force with an army that was largely dragon-shifters and usurped the throne.

"The alabaster palace is in the capital city and sits atop the stone cliffs overlooking the landscape. It's likely snowing there."

Her face took on a wistful expression as she glanced up at the tree-crowded night sky. He knew she worried about getting back home, about securing her kingdom and about her parents' safety. He squeezed her hand.

"By mid-winter, most of the roads in the higher elevations will be impassable. We'll be snowed in until the first Spring thaw," she said. "You'd think in a palace one wouldn't get cabin fever."

"But you do?" He grinned at her.

"Even life in a palace gets boring. I think I've read every book in the royal library. Twice. The horses like it, though. They get a lot of attention from people other than the groomers."

He snickered at her shy smirk as she looked up at him.

As they neared the small creek, he could hear the babbling of the water. At the edge of the tree line, they stopped to take in the view. The water danced over jagged rocks and broken logs. Moonlight glinted off the surface, giving it an ethereal glow that reminded him of a place he once loved in the Hidden Lands.

"It's lovely."

She breathed the words as she stepped to the water's edge, looking down the creek as far as she could see. The night was calm, cold and still, the only sound that of the trickling water.

"This is why I bought this place." He moved to stand next to her. "It gives me a sense of peace in a world of chaos."

"The world is chaos, isn't it?"

She crouched down and dragged her fingers through the water, watching the ripples sparkle and dance. He knew the water was likely ice cold just as he knew it wouldn't bother her one bit.

"A few yards that way, there's a small footbridge," he said. "But it's too cold and too dark to go exploring tonight."

"I'd like to see that sometime."

She picked up a smooth rock and stood. With a flick of the wrist, she tossed it down the creek, watching it skip and skip and skip until it smacked into a larger boulder and disappeared with a plop.

"I'd like to show it to you sometime," he said and meant it.

But he knew they would likely never get to do that because this was merely the quiet before the war. It wouldn't be too long until Armond discovered where they were hiding out. He only hoped it would be when Jaxson was healed and could help him fight back.

And there was the matter of her parents and where they were, if they were still alive. He pushed that thought aside, not wanting to think how it would change her, and gazed out over the water once again.

"It reminds me of the Hidden Lands. Of home." He hadn't

voiced that to anyone. Not even Logan.

A pang of longing went through him as he thought of the place he once lived, the life he once led. He was a different man. A knight in a world where chivalry and honor still mattered. A world where two lives were cut short and destroyed because if his own impudence.

She tipped her face toward the moonlight to look up at him. Her could see the pale light dancing in her dark eyes. Her skin had returned to its normal iridescence, making it shimmer under the pale blue beams, kissing her skin and making it glow.

Gods, she was beautiful. It took his breath away.

"You sound wistful," she said.

Maybe he was. Maybe he was more sentimental than he thought. He hadn't missed the Hidden Lands until of late when Logan dangled the promise of exoneration in front of him. He'd been thinking about it more than he had in the last few decades.

"It's been a long time since you've been there, hasn't it?"

He shook out of his reverie, coming back into the real world. "Too long." Far too long. He took her by the hand again. "Come on. We should get back before Freya starts to wonder where we've gone."

They headed back up the slope, through the snow-kissed trees. In the distance, he could make out the glow of lights in the cabin windows and see the smoke curling in lazy tendrils from the chimney. In any other time, any other place, they would go back into that cabin and be alone, together, and he would have his way with her.

"I miss home, too, you know," she said.

He hated she'd picked up on that but didn't respond. Instead, he buried those feelings of longing and belonging deep.

"When the snow melts in Spring, we have a flower festival. There are fresh cut flowers in every room of the palace. The gardens are so fragrant and green, I can't wait to get out and explore to see what the head gardener planted that year."

Something tugged at him, hearing her talk about her homeland

142

as though she were never returning. To distract her, he said, "What's your favorite flower?"

"I've always been fond of poppies."

She liked poppies. He filed that way for future reference. After all of this was over, though, she may never speak to him again when she discovered what he was after. In the meantime, he'd enjoy holding her hand and maybe kissing her every now and then.

"Pink ones," she added as an afterthought.

"Tell me about this flower festival." He tried to keep his mind occupied and distracted from how her skin glowed in the moonlight.

"We host the three-day event every year on the grounds with vendors who come to sell their wares. Everything from rose-scented soaps to candles to special bouquets. You can buy a crown of flowers to wear. It ends in a gala in the palace ballroom where anyone is invited. The ballroom is bursting at the seams and the crowd spills out onto the balcony and lawn. There's music and dancing and so much food."

They crested the slope and ended up back in front of the cabin, pausing at the foot of the porch steps. He was reluctant to let her go, though. She didn't seem in a hurry to release him either.

"Sounds fun," he said.

"It is."

They stood there, looking at each other in the cool moonlight. He should release her, make her go inside. But he couldn't.

"Rafe, I…" She tugged her lower lip through her teeth.

He liked when she said his name. His voice was gruff when he responded. "Yes?"

She leaned into him, her hands on his chest as she stood on tiptoe. "Thanks for the walk."

Her lips barely brushed his in a swift kiss. She bounded up the porch stairs in two steps and was inside the cabin before he could move. He shoved his hands deep into his pockets, wishing he had the nerve to go after her. Instead, he shivered alone in the moonlight.

Mia closed the door and sagged against it, her heart racing at such a rapid pace she pressed her hand against it, trying to make it slow to a normal speed. She had no idea what his intentions were when he followed her outside or when he walked her down to the creek. But she understood him a little more. He was like her. He was homesick.

He wanted nothing more than to return to his Hidden Lands. For some reason, he couldn't or wouldn't. He had said he was once a knight. She had hoped he would open up to her, tell her more about what had happened to him, why he was here in the human realm. That was why she had babbled on endlessly about the ridiculous flower festival.

There was no flower festival in Andonia. She'd made it up. The more she talked, the more nonsensical it sounded. She should have kept her mouth closed, but she couldn't stop herself. She didn't know why she'd made it up, exactly, only that she wanted to talk to him and she wanted to tell him something of Andonia. Telling him the kingdom did nothing but thaw in the Spring sounded boring. The only sliver of truth to her story was she loved strolling through the gardens when they were in full bloom and she was fond of pink poppies.

She pressed her fingertips against her lips still burning with the brush of the kiss. She had wanted more than that, but she wasn't nervy enough to go after what she wanted.

Freya made her way out of the bedroom carrying an empty coffee mug. She paused when she saw Mia standing at the door, question in her eyes. Mia righted herself, dropped her hand and smoothed it down the thigh of her jeans.

"I was outside getting some fresh air." It sounded like she was trying to cover up some wrong doing.

"Okay." Freya looked suspicious, as though Mia had been caught doing something she shouldn't have.

She cleared her throat and changed the subject. "How's

Jaxson?"

"Resting," Freya said. "I think I'll sit with him tonight while I check my email." She pulled her smartphone from her pocket.

"You have a phone?" Elation hit Mia with a burst of emotion. She hurried across the living room to Freya and snatched it from her hand.

"It was the only thing I managed to keep on me," she said. "I thought you had yours?"

"No. I left it in the car when…"

"Oh," Freya breathed. "I'm so sorry, your highness. I should have given it to you sooner."

She was already punching the number to her father's phone. "It's all right. I have it now. I can call my parents."

"There's only a little battery left—"

Mia held up her hand to silence her as the phone rang. Once. Twice. Then an answer.

"Hello, Freya."

She stiffened, her hand tightening on the phone and the blood draining from her head. It was Armond. She froze. Her eyes were wide and round as she looked at Freya, uncertain what to do next. Freya snatched the phone from her. She punched the speaker button.

"Who is this?"

"You know who it is." His silky voice drifted from the phone. "I'm glad to hear your voice. I worried when I didn't find your body in the wreckage."

Mia clenched her fists, anger surging through her. But Freya was the epitome of calm. "I'm sorry to disappoint you that I'm still alive."

He chuckled. "I assume you calling the king means you've found Mia and wish to give him a message."

They stared at each other. Mia shook her head in silent communication. Freya said, "I haven't found her."

"Then why are you calling?" he demanded.

"He is my king." She used her best snooty tone. "And my

employer. Am I not allowed to contact him to see about his well-being?"

"I think you're calling for another reason and I think it has to do with Mia. Where is she?"

Her heart rammed hard against her chest, the fear coursing through her. It was time to stop hiding. She snatched the phone from Freya who clearly wanted to protest.

"I'm here, Armond. Where are my parents?"

There was a long pause. "Hello, your highness."

Oh, how she hated him. "My parents, Armond."

"You do have a one-track mind. That's what I like best about you. They are fine. They landed several hours ago in New York City and are safe and sound with my men," he said.

"Where?"

"That's none of your concern, as yet. If you're willing to turn yourself over to me, I will make sure you are reunited with them."

Freya was shaking her head.

"What do you want?" Mia asked.

"I thought that was clear. I want your kingdom and I want you as my bride."

Bile surged to her throat. Freya looked like she was ready to vomit. "That will never happen," Mia said.

"Then I'm sorry for your loss."

Panic replaced disgust. "What does that mean?"

"You're a smart girl, I'm sure you can figure that out."

Freya reached for her free hand, squeezed it.

"You mean to kill them?" Mia did her best to hide the terror in her voice.

"I will if you refuse to marry me, yes. I'll give you time to think about it. Forty-eight hours. I want an answer. If the answer is yes, you and I will live happily ever after." He paused.

Her stomach turned. There would be no happily ever after with Armond. "And if the answer is no?"

"Then your parents will die. Forty-eight hours, your highness. Call me at this number with your decision."

The line went dead.

Mia held the phone in her shaking hand, staring dumbly down at it. Ice chilled her to the marrow of her bones as snowflakes appeared around her head. Frost spread beneath her feet.

Freya whimpered. "Your highness, what are you going to do?"

Just then, the door opened and Rafe stepped in. He saw them standing together, saw the look of shear fright on both their faces, saw the snowflakes and the frost and took two giant steps toward them both. Concern flickered over his features.

"What happened?" He reached for her, placing a hand on her arm. It instantly chased away the cold but the snowflakes remained.

"Armond has my parents."

❧ 17 ❧

Dark anger creased his face in a brief moment before he got it under control. He lifted a hand with the fire in his palm and gobbled up the snowflakes. "Calm, Mia, and tell me whose phone that is. Did he call you?"

She swallowed hard. "It's Freya's. I called my father. I-I had to know if they were all right."

He clenched his jaw, the muscles ticking along the edge. It was clear he kept his temper in check. "Where is he holding them?"

She shook her head. "He wouldn't say other than they'd landed in New York City. I don't know anything else. All I do know is he wants me to turn myself over to him. He..." She swallowed the bile that rose into her throat. "It's as you said. He wants me to agree to marry him or he'll kill my parents. He gave me forty-eight hours to make a decision."

She sensed the rage emanating off him in heat waves, but he didn't explode or let it overcome him. He swiped his hand through this short-cropped hair and took a deep breath.

"Where are you to meet him?"

"I'm to call him with my decision."

He grunted annoyance. "I don't like the way that sounds."

"Me, either. It sounds like he's stalling."

He paced the length of the small living room, clenching and unclenching his hands. She knew he was angry and he had every right to be. She was stupid to think she could call and get her father on the line. She knew Armond had highjacked the plane and yet a little glimmer of hope made her think he would be all right. That somehow her parents got away from Armond like she had.

"That doesn't give me much time to figure out a plan. There's nothing else we can do about it tonight" He looked at both of them. "Let's talk about it in the morning."

Mia handed the phone back to Freya who took it and bounded back to her room without a word. She stood a moment longer, watching him as he crouched in front of the fireplace and put on more kindling.

"Are you coming with me?" Her voice was timid, tentative.

"I don't think so."

Those four words sent a dagger to her heart. It felt as though a wedge had been driven between them.

"Rafe, I'm sorry. I had to."

"You did what you thought you had to do." He used a poker to arrange the firewood, making the flames go higher. "I can't fault you for that."

She remained rooted to her spot, watching the powerful muscles in his hands and arms.

"Go to bed, Mia. We'll figure out something in the morning." He never looked at her as he spoke.

Guilt flooded her as she turned on her heel and fled.

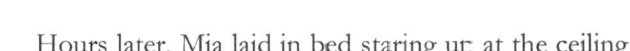

Hours later, Mia laid in bed staring up at the ceiling as guilt still pounded through her. Sleep eluded her. She could not forget the way Freya's face had paled when she heard Armond's demand on the other end of the phone. Nor could she forget the expression of disappointment and anger on Rafe's.

She sighed. She had been such an idiot. Why did she think calling her father was a good idea? At least she had some peace of mind knowing they were still alive, though she had no idea how Armond was treating them. How could he do this to his sovereigns, to her and to the kingdom?

She flipped over to her side and stared at the door. She knew

Rafe slept on the sofa. He hadn't wanted to share the bed with her and she wondered if it was because he was angry at her. She couldn't blame him.

And just when she thought they were connecting while they walked hand in hand through the trees down to the creek. It was so magical and peaceful. Now everything was ruined.

Or was it?

Perhaps there was a way she could make things right again. She didn't want him mad at her. She also could not fathom never kissing him again and feeling the warmth of him burning through her cold.

Mia flung off the blankets and got up. She stood beside the bed, staring at the door as her heart pounded so hard, she thought it might burst through her chest. He had refused her before because he thought she was using him to not feel scared or lonely. Maybe he had been right then but now things were different.

If things went horribly wrong with Armond, if her parents ended up dead and she was shackled to that miserable man for the rest of her life, didn't she deserve a little bit of happiness? She couldn't stop thinking about what Rafe had said, that their dragon forms liked each other. Hers had purred approval when they were close. She knew what that meant even if neither of them wanted to speak the words aloud. And though he said he didn't need a mate, she disagreed.

He needed her as much as she needed him. She saw the way he looked at her when they stood by the creek, the way he gazed at her as though she was the only one for him. It had made her heart trip in her chest, made her want to fling her arms around his neck and kiss him. Made her want to pull him down to the cold ground and let him take her right then and there.

But she hadn't. She'd stood there as he mentioned the Hidden Lands and heard the longing in his voice. She understood then he'd been separated from his kind and in the human realm for a long, long time. It pained her. She didn't know how she would survive in a world without other dragon-shifters, without her kind. How had he?

Mia shed her clothes and stood naked in the center of the room, a shudder pulsing through her. Not because she was cold, but because of the desire and need pounding every part of her. She moved to the full-length mirror in the corner and examined her form. She had to be satisfied with the smooth skin, the thatch of hair between her legs because she didn't want to waste time primping and grooming.

Glancing around the room, she snatched the quilt off the end of the bed and wrapped it around her shoulders, holding it closed in front of her. Her heart thumped a wicked tattoo as she reached for the door and pulled it open. Taking a deep breath, she walked from the bedroom into the small living room, the quilt dragging behind her like a dress train.

Rafe was stretched out on the sofa. He'd kicked off his shoes and crossed his legs at the ankles. His arms were folded over his chest. Firelight flickered in an orange and yellow glow over his features, softening the hard-chiseled lines of his stubbled face.

For a moment, it stole her breath and almost made her lose her nerve.

He turned his head to look at her, those molten silver eyes meeting hers. He didn't move. He kept his face impassive. If he was surprised to see her standing there wrapped in a quilt, he didn't show it.

She dropped the blanket, letting it tumble around her feet and stood there, waiting. She kept her gaze on his, watching and waiting to see his reaction. His face remained stubbornly impassive as his eyes locked on hers. But she could see the desire sparking there.

His gaze slipped down from hers, over her bare breasts with peaked nipples, down the smooth plane of her abdomen and down some more to her thighs, pausing briefly on the V between her legs and again on her breasts. His smoldering gaze landed back on hers.

Her breathing had become erratic, shuddering out of her. Her stomach tightened. Her core heated.

Oh, gods, what was she thinking? She clenched her fists,

resisting the urge to snatch up the quilt and scurry back to the bedroom. She almost did when he unfolded his tall, muscular form from the sofa and got to his feet. He stood there looking at her, never taking his gaze off hers. For the longest, most silent moment in the history of the world she thought she might break into a thousand pieces and die of embarrassment right there. The only sound in the room was that of the crackling fire.

His movements were slow, methodical as he pulled off his shirt and tossed it aside. She almost wept with joy. She could not stop her eyes from gliding over the hard lines of his chest sprinkled with dark hair, the washboard abs, the rounded curve of his biceps. He unbuttoned his jeans and shoved them down his thick thighs, stepping out of them and kicking them aside. He left the boxer briefs on, but she could clearly see he was not disappointed to see her naked.

"Is this what you want, princess?" His voice was deep and thick with arousal.

Oh, hell, yes, it was. Her mouth had gone dry and she couldn't form any coherent words. Her brain had stopped functioning. He took a step, two toward her and stopped with only a breath between them. His heat, his glorious, delicious heat, radiated over her chasing away the ever-present chill in her bones.

If he could do that standing so close to her, what, then, would he do to her when they... No, she couldn't think about it. Her mind shut off. She didn't want to allow the fantasy to take over the reality. This was real. He was real, and he was standing right in front of her.

"Is it?" he asked, his voice low and sultry.

"Yes." The word hissed out of her on a breath.

"Are you sure?"

She placed her hands on his chest, letting her fingers slide through the smattering of hair there. "Absolutely."

In the most brazen move she could muster, she palmed him. The heel of her hand ran down his hardened length. Desire flickered through those silvery eyes turning them into quicksilver.

His jaw clenched tight, the muscles working along the edge. She was certain she could see his dragon behind those eyes, wanting out, wanting her.

Without another word, he dropped to his knees, his hands on her buttocks as he pulled her to him and tasted her. His tongue slid into that wet heat. Her head fell back and suddenly it was hard to breathe. Her fingers tangled in his hair, gripping the short strands as she held on for dear life. When she was at the brink, he pulled away.

Her feet were rooted into place. Her mind was utterly devoid of all thought. She couldn't think and, thankfully, she didn't have to. He snatched the quilt from the floor. With one powerful shove, he pushed the cocktail table out of the way and spread the quilt on top of the area rug before the crackling fire.

Oh. Her heart skipped when he held a hand out to her in invitation.

Mia placed her cold fingers in his. His hand wrapped around her and he gave her a gentle tug. She moved to him and for a long moment, they stood together. He traced the lines of her body. His hands landed on her waist as he pulled her to him. Their bodies came together, skin brushing skin in an intimate touch that sent her senses reeling. Gods, he was warm. It was like a heady drug she couldn't get enough of. She wondered if he was always this warm, if fire flowed through his veins.

Taking her hand, he pulled her down to the quilt. She stretched out in front of the fire as he took her wrists, putting her arms above her head. He positioned his body next to hers, propping up on one elbow and looking down at her with a sort of reverence that made her heart twist. As though she were the most beautiful woman he'd ever seen.

He cupped first one breast, then the other, running his hand down the length of her. Appreciation flickered through his eyes as she focused solely on his face. There was a hungry promise of more in his eyes. The way he looked at her while touching her made her weak. So weak. And she was thankful she wasn't standing because she was certain her knees would buckle.

A delicious heat flooded though her from his fingertips. Everywhere he touched warmed her from the inside out.

How long had she waited for this? An hour? A lifetime? It seemed as though they belonged together, they were made for each other. He chased away the winter frost inside her with every masterful touch. He was fire to her ice. And for the first time in her life, she had at last thawed from a deep freeze.

She reached for his hand, then, pressed his palm against the flat plane of her belly and nudged it downward. His pulse in his throat jumped as his hand slid down and into the heat where his tongue had been only moments ago. She stretched her arms over her head again, arching her lower back, opening to him to touch her.

A groan rumbled through his chest.

"Do you like playing with fire, princess?"

Her skin tingled. For the first time in her life, gooseflesh erupted along every exposed inch of it. Oh, yes, she very much liked playing with fire. His fire.

"Are you fire, sir knight?"

He blinked surprise, momentarily taken aback by her calling him sir knight. A long, slow smile tugged at the corners of his mouth. "You're a smart girl. Don't you know the answer to that?"

She knew. She rocked her hips against his touch. "Show me your fire."

He removed his hand and lifted it above her, a blue-white flame dancing in his palm. Warm yet not hot enough to burn her which fascinated her. Did he control that? It lit up his face, casting long shadows around them and blotting out any other light. She wrapped her fingers around his wrist and pulled his hand toward her until it was close to her lips. She blew a gentle breath and snuffed out the flame.

The pulse in his neck beat hard. Smug satisfaction swept over her.

"Are you proud of yourself?" His voice was thick with desire.

"I am."

He cupped her breasts and then caught one dusty pink peak between his lips and sucked. A mewl escaped her at the shear sensation of his mouth on her. She reached for him, pulling him on top of her. He pushed her legs apart and nestled his big body between them. Her legs wrapped around his waist, her heated core landing on his hard length, pressing into her. She rested her hands on his shoulders and marveled at the corded muscles there. She rocked against him but she still felt the offending cotton between them and emitted a small whimper.

His hand fumbled between them, pulling his hardened length from his underwear. Without wasting another moment, he plunged deep inside her. Her breath caught on a gasp as he pumped into her. A spark, bright and white and brilliant, sang through her veins, searing her. He paused only a second before he plunged inside her again. Again, that brilliant light flared deep inside her, punching through that constant hoarfrost, thawing it completely.

Their mouths fused together in a searing kiss, each of them pouring all the pent-up sexual need and want and fervor into the other. She tightened around him, her core slick with heat. Her hips matched his rocking rhythm while he never stopped kissing her and their tongues did a sinful oral tango. She dug her nails into his back as the orgasm flashed though her and his followed seconds later. He swallowed her moan with another kiss and then it was all over.

Rafe rested his face against her neck, his heated breath tickling her damp skin. She slipped her hand up his back to the nape of his neck and tangled her fingers in his hair. The only sound was that of their labored breathing and the crackle of the fire.

They laid together, not moving, neither wanting to break the connection.

Finally, he said, "Now, princess." He kissed her cheek. "How about I carry you to the bedroom and bed you properly?"

❦ 18 ❧

The sight of Mia standing in the small living room with nothing but that quilt around her sent his senses reeling. When he met her gaze, he knew what she meant to do, instantly giving him a hard-on. He watched the material whisper from her skin, pooling at her feet, revealing that shimmering iridescent skin.

Gods.

Firelight flickered over her bare form. He'd imagined quite a lot about her, but his imagination did not compare to the real thing. She stood there, her hands clenched into fists, and waited with a shudder of desire. He could hear her labored breathing and smell her arousal as she waited, oh so patiently, for him to react.

It took all his self-control not to leap from the sofa.

He reminded himself she was a princess and she deserved better. So much better than an exiled knight. But the invitation was clear and he intended to worship every inch of her and accept her seduction.

Even as he tried, he could not stop ka kladou, the mating. It had surged through his veins, unbidden. At the sight of Mia standing naked and ready before him, his inner beast awoke and demanded he take her now and hard and fast. Make her his. Claim her for his very own. He couldn't resist, even if he wanted to.

He had never intended to mate with anyone and definitely not with a princess. The moment they came together, the moment he pushed inside her, it happened. For most dragon-shifters, it was a mere touch that could bond them together forever. He wasn't certain why it happened for him now so late in his dragon life.

Perhaps it was because he had put duty and honor before anything else when he still lived in the Hidden Lands. Perhaps it was because no human female could ever understand him. Or perhaps it was because he had never desired a woman as much as he desired Mia. But it had happened and there was no going back. They were mated. For life.

Did she know? Did she realize what she'd done when she gave herself to him? He scented her desire, her need, her longing before she dropped that quilt. She had planned it. The thought of her coming to him with the intent of letting him take her made him hard all over again.

He kissed her cheek before moving off her and standing. He held his hands down to her and helped her to her feet. Her expression was one of contentment and smug satisfaction as he swept her, weightless, into his arms and carried her out of the living room, the quilt forgotten. He was going to spend the rest of the night making love to her, slowly, methodically, and he was going to enjoy every minute of it. He may not have another chance to be with her. He hadn't told her everything about the Blood Stone and the Hidden Lands and her part in it. It was starting to weigh heavily on him. He had to come clean and soon.

But not tonight. Not now. Not when she was pliable in his hands. Not when she was wet and ready and wanting. Not when she wanted nothing more than him. Not when she was his mate.

It had been so long since a woman wanted him for him that he wasn't sure how to feel, what to think. So, he shut that part of his mind off as he kicked the bedroom door closed, walked to the bed and laid her gently on the mattress.

Her gaze raked over him in a sultry, sexy, brazen way. He shucked his underwear and slid into the bed next to her. She rolled toward him, half on and off her side and pulled him close, kissing him. A wanton kiss.

He nudged her to her back with a gentle push. His hand swept over her breasts, first one then the other, before continuing a downward jaunt and slipping between her legs into her slick heat to touch her there again. Her legs fell open as he caressed her, brought her to the brink and stopped. She whimpered, stiffening against him in her frustration. He nuzzled her neck, nibbling her earlobe.

"I'm not done with you," he breathed against her skin. "Not by far. I intend to savor you, princess. All night."

Her tense body relaxed. In that moment, he knew she gave herself to him. She was his and he was hers.

Mia nestled against him, unwilling to be parted from him. She'd lost track of time and didn't much care if she ever slept again. She fought against the drowsy warmth, desperate to stay awake. Afraid that if she fell asleep, she would miss precious moments with him. She was content to lie next to him, letting him be her portable heater and keep her warm from the inside out. She never wanted that feeling to go away.

She knew in less than forty-right hours she would have to face her fate. She didn't want to think about that right now. She wanted only to think about Rafe and how he made her feel.

He made her feel a lot of things. He'd done things to her she had only imagined and had never dared fantasize about. Right now, she wasn't a princess. She was his woman and nothing more. Her title didn't matter.

She laced their fingers, lifting their hands upward and flattened her palm against his. His hand was much bigger than hers, his fingers dwarfing her long, slender ones. Hands that had touched every inch of her.

"I never want this night to end." She hadn't intended to say it aloud but couldn't stop the words from spilling from her.

"I'm afraid it will at some point."

"Shh." She pressed two fingers against his lips. He kissed them.

Emboldened, she rolled on top of him, looking down into his amazing eyes. His hands were in her hair, sweeping it back from her face. The way he looked at her shredded her heart because she knew, no matter how they felt about each other, there was no future for them. For now, though, she would live in the moment and not worry about the future or what was to come.

"What is it?" he asked.

"I like the way you look at me."

"How do I look at you?" His hands danced in her hair, the strands falling through his fingers in a waterfall.

"Like I'm the only woman you've ever—" She paused, biting off the last words.

One brow lifted in amusement, a smile threatening the corners of his mouth. "I've ever?"

"Been with. I'm sure that's not true."

She swallowed hard, knowing it sounded lame. She intended to say had ever loved but thought that might be pushing it. He wasn't in love with her any more than she was in love with him. Was she? Her heart did a funny thing in her chest as the words floated through her mind.

"If you're asking me if I've had other women, princess, the answer is yes. I'm old not dead."

She giggled. But then she wondered. He appeared to be quite a bit older than her. She could sense—and sometimes see—his ancient dragon behind his eyes. He had more life experience and was filthy rich. He indicated he'd been in the human realm a long time, but had refused to tell her how long.

"How old are you?"

"Old enough to know I shouldn't be bedding you."

"But I'm irresistible." She cocked a grin.

He dragged his fingers through her hair again. "That you are."

Her heart turned over. How much more could it take? It pumped blood at a rapid-fire pace, burning desire through her. She rolled off him and nestled against him once again, her arm draped across his mid-section. She listened to his even breathing as he continued to run his fingers through her hair.

He came from the Hidden Lands, but she hadn't a clue where

159

that was or how to get there. She didn't know it existed until she met him. He told her he was once a knight. She assumed in the Hidden Lands, which made her wonder if he was no longer a knight. And if that were the case, why? Did he give it up?

"Tell me about the Hidden Lands," she said, hoping to get him talking. Maybe she could piece together why he was in the human realm.

His hand stilled. "You don't want to hear about that."

"Yes, I do," she urged. "Where is it? How does one get there? Is it through one of those mysterious portals?"

"So many questions." He pushed her to her back and moved on top of her, nudging her legs open. "Too many questions."

Her lips parted and she started to ask something else, when his mouth covered hers. He plunged inside her and all thoughts about the Hidden Lands left her brain. Their bodies rocked together in an even tempo, each one keeping pace with the other. She tightened around him, holding on as though for dear life as the orgasm rippled through her. One last sinful kiss and then he was done, moving off her and tugging her against him, holding her as though he would never let her go.

But she still had questions.

"I know you do."

She blinked surprise in the darkness, going still against him. "You know I do what?"

"Have questions."

"You do? How did you know?"

"Princess, do you know what the mating is?" He deftly changed the subject.

"Yes," she said.

Then you can hear my thoughts, too.

She sucked in a sharp breath and sat up. "I can. How did you do that?"

I didn't. We did.

"But how?" she demanded.

Speak to me with your mind.

She bit her lower lip as she stretched her mind to his. How?

He smiled. Good girl. When dragons mate, they are connected to each other.

Had she inadvertently mated with him? She hadn't thought about it, but she was of age. Her feelings for him had been overwhelming when she stood naked before him. Had she emitted some dragon pheromone without realizing it?

"I don't understand."

"Yes, you do. I have never mated. You have never mated. You chose me when you gave yourself to me."

She stared at him wide-eyed, her mind racing as she thought back to their tryst on the floor in front of the fire. It had been magical and romantic and something had changed. Yes, she'd felt something burning through her, something hot and wild. Something that thawed her from the inside out. Her breath hitched. Was that what the mating felt like?

"Yes," he answered. "That's what it felt like."

Her mouth had gone dry. Not that she didn't want to be mated with Rafe. He was hot and sexy and all. But they hardly knew each other. And what would her parents think? To her knowledge, he wasn't royalty. She wasn't sure they would approve or give their blessing. Nor did she particularly want to confess to them they'd mated. For life.

Without thinking, without knowing what she was doing, she had made things more complicated than ever.

He dragged her back down to him, tucking her into his side. "Don't think about it now."

He held her as the silence pressed around them. She rested a hand against his chest, feeling the steady beat of his heart.

"Do you still want to know about the Hidden Lands?" he asked.

"Yes, I do. Very much."

He took a deep breath, as though speaking of the place was something he hadn't done in a very long time.

"The sky has a pink and purple tinge to it. Not at all like the blue we see here in this world. The earth is lush and green. There are rivers and glistening lochs. Small, quaint villages that are homes to the clans and their leaders dot the rolling hills. The Whispering Mountains border our realm, dividing it from the others. Hiding it. The snow-capped mountains are always shrouded in what others think is mist but dragon-shifters know it as Dragon's Breath."

The sound of his dreamy voice made her eyelids heavy. He spoke about the place as though he had a great love for it. As though it had been burned into his memory, never to be forgotten. A place where he longed to return and couldn't.

"Dragon's Breath?" she asked.

"The Ancients used their dragon magic to weave a spell around the mountains. They called it Dragon's Breath. It was how the Hidden Lands were born," he said.

"Why is it hidden?" She stifled a yawn.

"When the Ancients ruled and there were no clans, there were those who wanted to invade and take their lands. They fought back. Ienir the Great led the dragon-shifters to victory and used his magic to raise the Whispering Mountains. That's when he and the Ancients banded together, weaving their Dragon's Breath together to form the ever-present mist."

He continued and told her of the first High King, Ienir the Great, ruling with a fair yet stern hand. Then he told her stories about the old world, the land, the people. A part of him sounded wistful, as though he would never see it again.

He went on to tell her about the civil war between dragon-shifters and how the clans were each born, how the Hidden Lands had been divided into territories with each one ruled by their own Council. Logan, he said, was Chief Magistrate of his own Council of Five.

She smiled in the darkness, loving the history. Her parents had never told her anything of the old ways, the Ancients, or the Hidden Lands. All she knew was Andonia was their kingdom, they had ruled it and no one else would rule it. She would inherit someday and sit on the throne. But hearing his stories stirred something deep inside her, made her long to see this mysterious place she couldn't imagine.

"I'd like to see the Hidden Lands someday," she said.

"I'd like to take you there." He sounded like he meant it. "But I can't."

"Why not?"

He stilled, his breath halting. For a moment she wasn't sure if he'd answer. "The air has turned toxic there."

"Why?"

"The land is cursed. That's why most have been migrating into the human realm."

"Is that why you're here?"

He stiffened and in a low voice said, "No."

She didn't know what to say but she felt as though she asked the wrong question. He didn't move, didn't say anything else or offer her any more stories of his homeland. Every fiber of her wanted to ask why he was here but she couldn't. She thought it best to leave it alone.

"There's something you should know. About me."

Something about the way he said it sounded dire. She lifted her head and looked up at him. His hands went through her hair again.

"You may not like what I'm about to tell you."

Her skin tingled. Her stomach cramped. But she nodded, swallowing hard. "Whatever it is, tell me."

"It may change the way you look at me."

"Never." She said it with conviction, certain that whatever he had to tell her would never change the way she looked at him or the way she felt about him. "You said yourself we're mated. Shouldn't I know everything there is to know about you?"

A lazy grin tugged at the corner of his mouth. "Just because we're mated doesn't mean you love me or even want me."

Oh, she wanted him. She wanted him more than she could ever say. And right now, at this moment, she had him right where she wanted him. Likely he had her right where he wanted her, too. That was fine by her. She reached up, placed her hand against his roughened cheek. Feeling the stubble scrape against her palm sent white-hot memories pouring through her. Memories of their torrid night together. She nearly blushed.

"Tell me."

"I told you I was a knight once. But what I didn't tell you was I'm in exile. Never to return to the Hidden Lands.".

❦ 19 ❧

Rafe had intended to tell her the truth. The whole truth. Everything about the Hidden Lands, the curse, the Blood Stone, the dragon's tooth needed to complete whatever blood ritual there was to save the Hidden Lands and break the curse.

But he couldn't.

Not when she looked up at him like that with such trust and understanding. It nearly killed him to see that in her violet eyes.

He hadn't lied. Not exactly. Telling her he was an exiled knight was definitely something he wanted her to know. He wasn't sure he was one-hundred-percent ready to tell her the whole truth about his ugly past. In the short amount of time he knew Mia, he knew she'd ask a million questions until he spilled his guts and told her why he was in exile.

He hadn't intended to start waxing poetic about the Hidden Lands. Maybe he was more homesick than he thought. He hadn't realized it until he spoke of the realm far out of grasp.

Everything he'd told her had been true. From the Ancients to the Dragon's Breath to the Whispering Mountains. They were all part of his history. Her history, too.

Ienir the Great had been from the ancient bloodline of the Gildhara, the same as Mia's bloodline Rafe would wager she was more powerful than she realized. Did she know that about her history? She seemed not to. What had her parents, the king and queen, told her of their ancestry? Were they not proud of their heritage? Did they not want her to understand where she came from and who she truly was, deep down? A cold-drake, yes, but so much more. Even she didn't realize how much dragon magic flowed through her veins. She was magnificent and she didn't know it.

"I'm sorry," was all she said.

She didn't try to ask her usual barrage of questions. He had to admit he was a little disappointed.

"Don't you want to know why?" he prodded.

"Of course, I want to know why. But I only want you to tell me if that's what you want."

Gods, she was more than magnificent. He brushed the back of his hand over her cheekbone. "You're beautiful."

She blushed to the roots of her hair, staining those high cheekbones in a pale pink. Normally, her skin tone held that opaline luminescence that shimmered in any kind of light. Her skin held a constant chill from head to toe. But not now. Not since he'd bedded her. Now, her skin had warmed and changed from milky white to an ivory that had been sun-kissed reminding him of one of the Fae or possibly an Elf. She could pass for one, with her silver hair. She only lacked the pointed ears.

"You're getting off topic," she said.

"You're right. I am. I told you before I was once a knight in the Hidden Lands before there were clans. When the land was ruled by one ruler. One High King."

She blinked large owlish eyes up at him. No doubt she was surprised by his age. Even he couldn't believe he'd lived for as long as he had. Most of his years had been spent in the human realm. Alone. Far too many long, lonely years.

"High King Narsin gave me his kingdom to protect as well as his queen and their daughter, the princess. I was his Captain of the Guard." He remembered that time so long ago. Pain speared him. "I failed him."

She didn't hide her surprise. Her eyes went wide and round. "How?"

He clenched his jaw so hard his teeth ached. He had not told anyone the story for years. He had kept it to himself, lived with his shame for centuries.

She sensed his hesitation. "You don't have to tell me."

"I've never told anyone." He brushed hair back from her face. Though Logan claimed he knew the truth, they hadn't discussed it.

"Are you sure you want to tell me?"

"Yes."

She chewed on her lower lip, then asked, "Why?"

"Because I want you to know." He chose his words carefully. "Invaders came from a neighboring kingdom and attacked the castle. They intended to sack it and take it for themselves. I led the fight to defend the king and his castle. I sent the princess and the queen through the tunnels. I thought it would be safer for them if they went to their mountain home until the skirmish was over. They were heavily guarded, or so I thought."

He swallowed hard, his mouth dry. "My men were killed. The women were captured, tortured and murdered. The king blamed me and he was right to. He never told me to get them out. I made the selfish decision. Because I wanted to protect the princess." His throat clotted with emotion. "Because I loved her."

She said nothing as his words sank in. But he could see the quickened pulse in the long column of her throat.

"I got them killed. As punishment, he banished me. Cursed me. Exiled me here for the rest of my days, however long they may be."

He had not uttered those words to anyone since that fateful day. He had never faced it. Never acknowledged he had been a failure to the king and his realm. Never once acknowledged it was his fault the queen and princess died because of him. Because he made the wrong decision. That king no longer ruled the Hidden Lands. No, he was long dead, and he had been the only one who could grant his return and remove the curse. The stain upon his character. Until Logan had offered it up to him on the promise he would deliver one of Mia's dragon's teeth. Something he knew he could not do under any circumstances.

And now here he was, trying to protect another princess and her kingdom. This time, though, he was going to make damn sure nothing happened to her. Perhaps the gods had deemed to give him another chance, a way to redeem himself and right that wrong so long ago.

"I'm so sorry." Her face was unreadable in the half-light, her eyes dark orbs in the shadows.

"You don't think less of me?"

"Why would I?"

"Because I failed."

"You did what you thought was right." She brushed a kiss over his lips, then nestled down against him once again. "I'm glad you told me."

She had shielded her mind from him, burying her thoughts in a place he couldn't reach. Knowing his past mistakes and failures, would she still trust him? He couldn't read that on her face or in her mind.

Though she didn't judge him, he felt compelled to continue to explain.

"I have no way to atone for what I did. No way to go back and change what happened."

"No," she agreed, her voice quiet. She reached for his hand and laced their fingers. That small gesture made him understand what it meant. She didn't hold his past against him.

"That was a long time ago, wasn't it?"

He smiled, though she couldn't see it. It was yet another attempt to find out his age. "It was four centuries ago."

She stilled in his arms and then her voice was quiet. "Wow. You *are* an old man."

He pinched her and she squealed and then giggled.

"I may be an old man," he said, "but now I'm *your* old man."

"You are," she said with a smile.

"We should get some sleep."

She stifled a yawn. "I don't want to."

"Yes, you do. You're tired. I'll be here when you wake. I promise."

Her eyes drooped as she dropped her head onto his chest. It

didn't take long for her to drift into a deep sleep. He listened to her even breathing a long time before he gently pushed her to the bed, tucked her in and padded to the living room.

He hadn't checked his cell phone in a while. When he looked, he had several missed calls and a voicemail from Logan. He dialed his number, not thinking about the time or anything else until his friend answered with a groggy voice.

"Do you have any idea what time it is?" Logan growled.

It was still dark outside. He cringed, knowing he called in the middle of the night. "Sorry. I saw you called."

"Yeah, hours ago. I have information about this Armond person you asked me about. By the way, your escape from the city caused a bit of hysteria. Luckily, we have enough shifters in enough high places in the realm to downplay it."

Rafe could hear the rustle of material in the background and took it to mean Logan climbed out of bed next to this pregnant wife so he wouldn't disturb her.

"It's not my fault Armond followed us out of the city in dragon form. What did you find out about him?"

"He's Drakana," Logan said.

"Drakana? But he didn't have the starburst on his wrist." At least, not that he saw.

"He's one of their higher-ranked leaders, so he has it, just not in the usual place. My guess is back of the shoulder and instead of a tattoo, it's a brand. Shows a higher loyalty to their kind. That's why he's working with Herrick, why Herrick hired him."

There was a glacial tone to Logan's voice and Rafe knew he wasn't happy about that. Herrick took over when Lord Archer died, who had tried to wipe out Logan's entire family. Now Herrick was vying for control of the Council of Five and maybe all the Hidden Lands.

Drakana were scum dragon-shifters turned dragon hunters, willing to wipe out their own race and for what? For their own political agendas? To make sure only their kind survived? It was a form of genocide Rafe never understood and never would.

"What does he want?" Rafe asked.

"I couldn't say but my best guess is Herrick wants control of Andonia. He must think the Blood Stone is still there and wants to get his hands on it," Logan said.

"Or he wants to get his hands on the obsidian glass forges." Rafe didn't know if that was true but he thought he'd throw that out there to gauge Logan's response.

He *hmmed*, then said, "I hadn't thought of that. It's possible, I suppose. Why would he want access to the obsidian glass forges?"

"Because it's a weapon."

"Sure, but a weapon toxic to him, too."

"And you and me. And any other dragon who opposes him and the Drakana. You said yourself war is coming. Maybe it's closer than you think."

There was silence on the other end as Logan considered. "But taking over a cursed Hidden Lands makes no sense to me."

"Maybe he knows something we don't. Maybe he's trying to get his hands on that Blood Stone to perform the ritual himself. Who the fuck really knows?" Rafe had enough time since their arrival at the cabin to think of all the possibilities. He didn't like any of the outcomes that came to mind. "All I do know is Armond kidnapped the king and queen and wants Mia to turn herself over to him. He intends to marry her and sire an heir."

Logan made a choking sound of disgust on the other end of the phone. "To what end?"

"To rule Andonia. Why else?"

"Perhaps Herrick lured Armond into helping him with the promise of the kingdom," Logan said. "It makes sense, doesn't it?"

"Yes."

A stifled female gasp behind him made him realize he stood in the middle of the living room naked. He glanced over his shoulder in time to see Freya skitter from the room. He snatched up his discarded jeans with a scowl. At least she'd only seen his backside.

"If Armond was her security detail, why bring her to the States to kidnap her?" Logan asked.

Rafe recalled Freya saying someone—possibly Armond—had organized a coup. "Maybe it was easier that way to take over the country. With the royals out of the way, there would be no one to challenge them."

"So, we think this Armond person wants to rule Andonia with Mia as his wife and that Herrick wants to control the obsidian glass forges for an unknown reason. Did I get all that right?" Logan said.

Rafe nodded, though Logan couldn't see. "The only thing we haven't answered is why or how Herrick is involved."

"Maybe they're planning something bigger than trying to take over the Hidden Lands," he suggested, as though the thought had just occurred to him.

A chill danced up his spine and gooseflesh erupted over his exposed skin. "It's possible. I'll try to find out."

"And while you're at it, figure out how to get me that dragon's tooth."

Even now, Logan didn't know what he was asking Rafe to do. He clenched his jaw until it ached. "Yeah, yeah, yeah. The dragon's tooth. Don't worry. I'll get it."

He ended the call.

"What dragon's tooth?"

Mia's voice behind him made him freeze. He looked at her over his shoulder. She'd found one of his shirts and donned it. In the shadowy light, he could see her skin had returned to her usual pale color.

"It's not important." He pulled his pants back on, buttoning them, and then set about rebuilding the fire.

"Who were you talking to?"

Fuck all. He should have known she would have more questions, that she wouldn't take his dismissal and leave it. He placed several large logs on the ashes of the previous fire, then reached for a handful of kindling.

"Rafe?"

"I was talking to Logan. I asked him to do some digging on Armond." He struck a match and lit the kindling.

"And?"

The fire flamed to life. He sat back on his heels. "He's Drakana."

A frosty silence settled on the room, making him shiver. He turned to look at her, meeting her violet eyes. Her face drained of color, leaving her paler than her normal pallor. She stood in a circle of rime.

"You know this for certain?" Her breath plumed when she spoke.

"There's no reason to disbelieve what Logan told me."

"And you can trust the information he gave you?"

"I can." He rose and walked to her. He placed his hands on her cold arms. "We can't worry about it now."

"Can't we? Shouldn't we? In only a few hours, I'm to turn myself over to him or he'll kill my parents." Snowflakes whispered off her skin and danced around her.

"It's going to be all right," he said, his voice soothing and calm. "I won't let you hand yourself over to the enemy."

Her lower lip quivered. "Can you promise me?"

She tipped her head back and looked up at him with such hope and desperation in her eyes that he could not deny her. Here he was faced with an impossible task of keeping her safe when he didn't know for sure if he could. He had failed once before. He could not fail again. He could not let his mate die.

"I promise."

He hoped to the gods he could keep that promise.

⤛ 20 ⤜

Armond had gone to great lengths to intercept the plane in Singapore. It hadn't been easy but he managed to call in favors and use just about every resource he could to redirect that plane to the United States. The last thing he wanted was for it to land in Australia where Herrick's armed men waited.

He'd found an abandoned warehouse in Brooklyn that had once belonged to a pack of wolf shifters. The place had looked as though a brawl had taken place judging by the furnishings ripped to shreds. But it was intact, and it was the perfect place to hide out with the kidnapped king and queen. They would be well out of the public eye and away from the bustle of Midtown.

There was a small three-bedroom apartment above the warehouse. The living room had a three-seat sofa with one cushion absolutely destroyed, a rug that looked as though claws had ripped it to shreds, and a chair that had seen better days. There was an eat-in kitchen. The dining table had been tipped over. The chairs were unbroken, though, so Armond dragged two of them into the living room for the king and queen. He bound them to the chairs, their hands tied behind their backs. The queen gave him glares full of daggers. The king called him a traitor and would see to it he paid for betraying crown and country. Armond had snarled at him.

He paced the length of the shattered living room, his hands clutched behind his back. It had been a ballsy move to kidnap the reigning monarchs of Andonia and bring them here, but Herrick had left him no other choice. He'd made sure they weren't followed from the time they left the airport to the time they set foot in the building.

He hadn't counted on Mia calling her father. Perhaps the gods had smiled down on him for once and something was finally going his way. It might have been a mistake to give the princess that much time to turn herself over to him, but he needed to make his final plans.

Herrick had been breathing down his neck to find the princess. When his last attempt failed miserably on the highway, he had almost given up. He knew it was a mistake to shift into his shadow dragon form in the city, but it was a risk he had to take. It had thrown the city into hysterics but local political leaders were downplaying it as much as they could.

Even the supernaturals who inhabited the city knew he was an idiot for showing his true form to the humans.

Mia was a wild card he never counted on. He hadn't anticipated her using her dragon magic on the highway to knock him from the sky or freezing over the roadway which caused a pile-up of epic proportions.

She won that round.

"Whatever game you're playing," the king said as Armond paced, "you'll never win."

"Shut up," Armond snapped.

He had more preparations to make, more plans to finalize. He knew from his second-in-command, Karl, the coup in Andonia had gone off without a hitch. They had stormed the palace and taken it over with swift ease. Karl closed the borders to the small country and waited for Armond to return with his prize—the princess.

"Our people will not sit idly by and allow you to take control," he continued.

"I said shut up."

"I will not. I—"

Armond reeled on him, the gun in his hand before he even realized he'd palmed it. The queen shot her husband a look full of warning.

"You will," Armond said. "The only reason you're still alive is

174

because of me. I suggest you do what I tell you from here on out."

"Where is my daughter?" the king demanded.

"Not your concern," Armond snarled.

"It is and I demand to know—"

Armond moved with lightning speed to the king, pressing the muzzle of the gun into the side of his cheek. "You're in a position to demand nothing, your majesty. But since you're my king, I'll tell you that your daughter is shacking up with that dragon-shifter we tried to take out. Unsuccessfully, I might add." He straightened, lowering the gun to his side. "As for you two, you'd be nothing but cold skin and bones by now it if hadn't been for me. Herrick was planning to ambush and kill you in Sydney. You're welcome."

The queen stifled a gasp.

"I'm supposed to thank you for kidnapping us?" The king scoffed.

"And keeping you alive. Yes, you are. A little appreciation goes a long way, your majesty."

"How do I know you're telling me the truth? I don't even know who this Herrick person is."

Armond's nostrils flared. "You're going to have to take my word for it."

"Prove it," he challenged, lifting his chin a little higher.

Armond snarled again. Fine. He'd tell the bastard. It was only a matter of time before he wouldn't be useful anymore, and then he'd kill him.

"Lord Herrick of the Hidden Lands hired me to bring your daughter to him. He showed his hand by telling me his plans."

The king's face paled. The queen gave him a wide-eyed look.

"The Hidden Lands," she whispered.

"That place is a myth." The king's voice warbled with uncertainty.

"No," Armond countered. "It was never a myth."

It had been his home until he had to leave, until the air itself had started making him sick, killing the crops and turning most of the realm into a wasteland. How others remained there, he didn't know. It was only a matter of time before the whole realm would be dead, when the curse killed it all.

"Why does he want her?"

"Something about a dragon's tooth."

The two monarchs exchanged a look. The king blanched again. Armond would have asked the king about his odd reaction when a knock sounded on the door. Armond tensed and stopped pacing. The two monarchs stared at the closed door with a mix of hope and terror in their eyes.

Armond approached the door peered through the peephole. He saw Stefan on the other side. He unlocked it, ushered him in and closed it with a snap.

"Did you find them?"

Stefan nodded. "She's in the mountains with that guy. Along with Freya and the other dragon-shifter Gunter stabbed." He held up a blood-stained obsidian blade.

"Where's Gunter?"

Stefan's face hardened. "Dead. Bastard killed him."

Anger flickered through him. Gunter was one of his best men. "And what about Herrick?"

"Word on the street is he's pissed," he said. "He hates you pulled one over on him."

"What does that mean?" the king demanded.

Armond shot him another warning look. He ushered Stefan into the next room out of earshot of the king and dropped his voice. "What's going on in Andonia?"

"Karl is serving as regent in your absence. The palace is locked down. It won't be long before the news media gets wind of it and makes it international news. It may have already hit the AP wire."

"That's what I'm counting on. The more people who know about it, the better."

Stefan looked at him as though he'd lost his mind. "Why?"

"Because then it will make it more difficult for Herrick to get his hands on the obsidian blade forges and control the country. That's what he wants and right now we control them," Armond said.

"You don't think Mia is going to turn herself over to you, do you?" Stefan asked.

He gave him a pointed look followed by a wolfish smile. "No, I don't. We're going to make a surprise visit."

Stefan returned his smile. "When do we move?"

"Soon. Get the team ready. And tell them…" A new idea bloomed. A hint of a smile pulled up the corners of Armond's lips. "Tell them to be prepared to shift."

The man had a glimmer of excitement in his eyes as he gave Armond a nod.

"I hope you know what you're doing." He flung the words over his shoulder as he walked away.

Armond did, too.

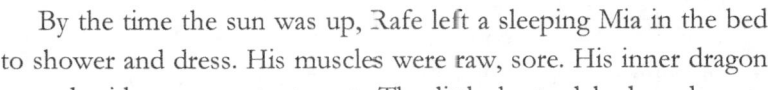

By the time the sun was up, Rafe left a sleeping Mia in the bed to shower and dress. His muscles were raw, sore. His inner dragon purred with pure contentment. The little bastard had made sure Rafe knew he was happy he'd mated with the princess.

He made his way to the kitchen. He was cooking breakfast when Freya made an appearance. She gave him a sheepish smile and flashed a little grin as she looked at him. He poured a cup of coffee and handed it to her.

"Sorry about earlier," he said.

"It's all right. I figured you and Mia…" She tried hard not to look at the quilt still on the floor as she pressed her lips together.

"Yes," he answered without a wave of guilt washing over him.

"I'm glad." She looked down into her cup, avoiding his gaze.

He gaped at her. "You are?"

"She needs someone like you. Someone strong and resourceful." Freya gave him a pointed look. "The men her parents paraded in front of her to marry haven't been very manly."

He almost laughed. "What does that mean?"

"It means they spend more money on clothes and personal care than Mia does. They are nothing more than perfumed, pompous aristocrats." She looked him over. "You aren't like that."

Far from it. He did enjoy living in luxury when it suited him, but he never was interested in fashion labels. One glance at his weathered hands showed he'd never had a manicure in his life, nor would he ever. But he was no fool either. He knew, as Mia did, they wouldn't be able to stay together, mated or not. She was a princess. He was far from royalty. Once he got Armond out of the way and she returned safely to Andonia she would forget him as he would forget her.

Or try to.

He knew with their bonding he would forever long for her with an ache so deep, it would cut to the marrow of his bones.

"I'm not good enough for her."

"Maybe you should let her decide that," Freya suggested. She took a sip of coffee.

Rafe turned the bacon, shoving away thoughts of the princess and a future with her. He changed the subject. "How is our patient?"

"Mostly healed." Jaxson sagged against the kitchen doorway with one arm clutched against his middle. Though he looked pale, he appeared to have recovered from the stab wound.

That was the thing about dragon blood. Even though the cut was deep and he had poison in his veins, he was feeling better and on the mend. The antidote was working its own magic.

"I'm certainly a lot better than I was." He gave a glance to Freya. "I had a good nurse."

She blushed and stared down into her mug, avoiding his gaze. Rafe glanced at Jaxson with question in his eyes but the man's expression gave away nothing.

"Glad you're feeling better. Don't push it," he said.

"Yes, don't push it," Freya agreed. "My turn in the shower. Hopefully Mia hasn't used all the hot water."

She headed out of the room. Jaxson pinpointed Rafe with a

look that said he knew what he'd been up to all night.

"You and the princess, huh?"

"Is it that obvious?"

"Aside from that," he nodded to the quilt still on the floor, "I can smell her all over you. You mated, didn't you?"

Rafe pulled bacon from the pan and plated it, remaining as casual as he could. "What if I did?"

His face broke into a wide smile. "I thought you were past your prime, you old dog. I feel like I should congratulate you."

"Don't." His mouth was set in a grim line as he put more bacon in the pan.

"Why not?"

"She's a princess and I'm a…" He paused, not wanting to voice his shame aloud.

"I know what you are. Does she?"

"She does."

"What does it matter?" Jaxson reached for a mug and poured coffee.

Rafe gave him a pointed look. "You and I both know what's going to happen when this is all over. She'll go back to her country, her kingdom, and it will be over."

A shadow flickered over Jaxson's face, as though a dark memory of his own haunted him. "And you'll be parted from your mate."

A glimmer of longing was in Jaxson's eyes. Rafe could see there was sympathy in his expression. It made him wonder. All dragon-shifters could scent if one of their kind was mated. That's how Jaxson knew Mia's scent was on him. He inhaled the man's scent as covertly as he could and caught a faint whiff of *her*. A faint scent of applewood and lavender.

He didn't know exactly who she was, but he knew for certain it wasn't Freya. That girl was merely a passing interest for Jaxson. No, there was someone else and that someone had to be the mate Jaxson had never mentioned.

"Neither of us deserve that fate. I'd like to say I tried to stop it

MICHELLE MILES

from happening, but my dragon was having none of it."

"Because you wanted her, and she wanted you. When that happens, nothing will stop the mating. You know this as well as I. It's part of our DNA." His voice cracked only a little before he got it under control.

It confirmed Rafe's suspicions. Jaxson was parted from his mate.

He sighed. "I know. She doesn't realize how difficult it will be for her. And there is the matter of her status."

"What of it?" Jaxson sounded as though it didn't matter.

"I don't have royal blood."

His lips thinned into a straight line. "This is a new century, Rafe. I don't think that matters now. Likely, she can marry whomever she pleases."

"I can't worry about that right now. We have bigger matters hanging over us."

"Yes," Jaxson agreed. "We have several issues we need to discuss."

Rafe plated more bacon and handed it to him. "But first you're going to tell me how you were stabbed."

Mia made an appearance then, her silver hair damp from her shower. She'd donned one of his shirts again along with a pair of jeans he'd bought. The shirt was so large on her, it hung down almost to mid-thigh. He tried not to like the way she looked in his clothes.

"I thought I smelled bacon and coffee." She offered a bright smile.

It was the happiest he'd seen her look since he met her. A warm radiance dusted her cheeks, that chill still gone from her. As though the afterglow of their night together lingered with her. She brushed by him as he threw more bacon in the pan and he caught a whiff of the soap she'd used.

"That stunt you two pulled on the highway caused a lot of problems." Jaxson took a slow sip of coffee, keeping his gaze on him over the rim of his cup, adeptly ignoring Rafe's demand to

180

know how he was injured.

"What stunt?" Mia gave her best innocent look.

Jaxson wasn't buying it. "You know what I mean. Freezing the highway, knocking the shadow dragon out of the sky with whatever magic you have." He narrowed his gaze. "What kind of magic do you have?"

"Mia is a cold-drake," Rafe said.

His eyes widened at the mention as he looked at her. Her face had gone still and quiet, her skin returning to that opalescent shimmer. Gone was the warm tones from their bed play. He gave an imperceptible shake of his head indicating he wanted Jaxson to keep quiet.

"A cold-drake, you say?" Jaxson said. "Very interesting."

"Why is that interesting?" Mia filched a piece of bacon as she passed by and headed out of the kitchen.

"No reason," Jaxson replied.

She stopped cold when she saw the quilt spread before the fire and the cocktail table shoved to one side of the room. Rafe kept his gaze on her back looking for any movement, any acknowledgement about what they'd done there. She took a deep breath and turned to face them, her expression a serious façade as though she hadn't a clue why the quilt was on the floor.

While holding her coffee cup in one hand, she lifted her other, palm upward. Concentration lines creased the corners of her eyes. A moment later, snowflakes danced above her palm.

"I have more control than I ever have."

"What changed?" His voice was rough.

She looked at him, her violet eyes darkening with emotion. "Something shifted inside me. Like something thawed from a deep freeze and gave me the control I've always needed."

A warm glow pulsed through him and his dragon emitted a satisfied hum in response. He wanted to shove the thing deep down, tell it to shut up, that it had nothing to do with this sudden change in Mia. But he knew that simply wasn't true. Since their mating, his beast had been silent and content, coiled into a lazy knot deep inside him.

But with Mia's snowflakes dancing in her palm, it awoke the sleeping beast inside him and begged for attention. He blew out a heated breath, melting her snowflakes instantly. In a playful gesture, she stuck out her tongue at him. He laughed.

"I thought cold-drakes were extinct," Jaxson said.

Annoyance flashed across her face before she got it under control. "We are not."

"Clearly." Jaxson bowed his head. "My apologies, your highness. I meant no offense."

She closed her palm. "None taken."

"Now about your stab wound—" Rafe started.

"Right. It was Drakana," Jaxson said. "I was doing a little recon at Logan's request."

Rafe stared at him, surprised to hear that. Logan hadn't mentioned it on the phone. Nor had Rafe mentioned an injured Jaxson had appeared on his cabin doorstep. "What kind of recon?"

"He asked me to check out someone named Armond."

Mia sucked in a sharp breath. "What about Armond?"

"Maybe we should all sit down before I tell the story." He motioned to the small dining table.

Freya returned, her hair damp and her coffee cup emptied. She filled it and turned to the them, all with solemn looks on their faces.

"What's happened?" she asked.

"I'll finish cooking breakfast, then we can all talk." Rafe reached into the refrigerator for the eggs.

"You know something," Mia said to Jaxson.

Silence descended as Rafe cracked eggs into a bowl and whipped them. Jaxson refilled his coffee cup, emptying the pot. Freya moved to the princess's side.

"I know something," Jaxson said at last.

"Tell me." Mia used her best princess tone.

Rafe said, "We'll discuss over breakfast."

"No, now." Fire flashed in her violet eyes.

They stared each other down while Rafe cooked eggs. He wasn't backing down. "Over breakfast. Freya, would you make another pot of coffee?"

"Rafe—"

"Patience, princess. We're not going anywhere."

Mia huffed out a heated breath and headed for the dining table while Freya scurried into the kitchen and set about making more coffee. Her ire burned through her as she plopped down in one of the chairs and waited, her hands clenched in her lap.

The oven dinged. Rafe pulled out a sheet of biscuits. He scooped the eggs onto the platter with the bacon and walked the heaping plate to the dining table, setting it in the middle. He returned to the kitchen to deal with the biscuits, putting them all in a bowl while speaking to Freya in a soft tone she couldn't hear.

She wanted to be angry with him, but her stomach rumbled so loud she was sure everyone in the house could hear.

Freya carried plates and silverware to the table, Rafe on her heels with butter, jelly and honey. With a calm exterior, he sat at the table across from her. Freya passed out plates while Jaxson took a seat. Mia couldn't take it any longer.

"Are we just going to sit here and pretend everything is situation normal and the world isn't falling down around our ears?" She blurted out the words as she watched Rafe scoop eggs and bacon onto his plate with a maddening calm.

Jaxson filled his, refusing to make eye contact with her. Freya prepared a plate and handed it to her. Mia scowled at the plate but took it anyway.

"Tell us what you know, Jax, before the princess pops a vein," Rafe said.

She shot him a glare.

"Armond is Drakana," Jaxson said around a mouthful of bacon.

"We know that already," Mia said on a huff.

"Then do you know he is one of the leaders?" he asked.

Mia stared at him. Her mouth had gone dry. Her heart did a quick palpitation. "No."

"He infiltrated the palace with his men posing as palace guards while he managed to get a position as your personal security detail. That's how he was able to launch the attack and take over," he added.

Her world tilted. Freya's fork froze halfway to her mouth.

"What do you mean, take over?" Freya asked.

"And how do you know for sure?" Mia added.

"I've been in this realm working various security gigs for a while," he said. "I have reliable sources."

"Armond's men control the palace?" Rafe asked.

"Yes," he said with a nod. "I was tracking one of his men back to his hideout in the city when he attacked me. I fought back. Even managed to get some information out of him before he stabbed me and I had to kill him."

Mia winced.

"What did you learn?" Rafe asked.

Jaxson cut her a glance, then looked back at Rafe. He swallowed hard. "Lord Herrick hired him to deliver the princess to him because he wants to harvest one of her dragon teeth."

Mia's fork slipped from her grip and clattered against her plate. Every muscle in her body froze as she stared, wide-eyed, at Rafe. He'd mentioned something about a dragon's tooth to Logan on the phone earlier.

"One of my dragon teeth," she repeated, slowly. "Why?"

Her question was directed to Rafe, who cleared his throat. "You are of the Gildhara bloodline, Mia."

Hot pinpricks tingled the back of her neck. "What does that mean?"

"It means," Jaxson drawled, "that you are from an ancient powerful bloodline that once ruled the Hidden Lands. That power still runs through your veins. And because of that, one of your teeth can infuse power into objects."

The blood drained from her head as she looked at Rafe. His face had blanched. *He knew.*

"You son of a bitch," she breathed the words in a plume of frost.

"Mia—"

She shoved back from the table and stood with such violence all the dishes rattled. Her hands clamped into tight fists. "You son of a bitch! You knew about this all along, didn't you?"

The temperature in the room plunged as frost formed on her exposed skin. Her blood turned to ice. Dark pinpricks of light danced in her vision. She felt as though she'd just been gutted.

"Why did Logan ask you to get a dragon's tooth, Rafe?"

His mouth thinned into a white line. She could see his mind working to come up with an answer. An answer she'd accept? A lie? She pushed against his thoughts but he deflected her, keeping her out.

"*Why?*"

Hoarfrost spread across the table, freezing the plates of freshly cooked food. Freya's eyes were wide and round as she looked between them and got to her feet.

"Your highness, your temper," she warned.

She snapped a glare at the girl. Freya bit her lip and sank back into her chair, silent. When Rafe didn't answer, Mia turned her fury on Jaxson.

"Why does this Herrick person want it?"

Jaxson's throat bobbed. "He plans to forge obsidian blades with power from the tooth to make them into super weapons." He cut a glance at Rafe. "He's going to use the weapons to wage war on Logan and the Hidden Lands."

The temperature dropped again as they all glanced at each other.

"He wants me and my kingdom." She turned back to Rafe, the rage shuddering through her. Snowflakes danced around her head. "And you and Logan knew about this."

"No," Rafe said. "I didn't."

"Explain to me why you were talking about a dragon's tooth." She folded her arms over her chest.

Rafe expelled a breath of defeat and sat back in the chair. "Logan has the Blood Stone, Mia."

And with those words, her life shattered all over again.

❦ 21 ❧

"**Y**ou lied to me."

Rafe could not stand the disappointment that flooded her face, the way she looked at him as though he were the enemy. He'd lied to her by omission which made him a fuck. He looked at Freya and Jaxson.

"Could you two give us a minute?"

They didn't need any encouragement. Jaxson got to his feet and held his hand out to Freya. "Come on. Let's go for a walk."

As soon as the door closed behind them, Mia said, "All this time Logan's had the Blood Stone. *My family's heirloom*. You knew I was searching for it and yet you kept it from me."

"You have every right to be angry with me—"

"Yes, I do," she agreed in a haughty tone. "When were you planning to tell me? Was our mating planned? Did you plan all of this?"

He held his hands up to silence her as she fired off question after question. "If you'll give me a chance, I'll explain everything."

Cold anger creased her face. "You've had ample time to explain to me since the moment you knew I was here looking for the Blood Stone. You brought me out here and for what? To get me alone, gain my trust, talk me into shifting and steal one of my teeth?"

"No." He rose, the frost crackling on the table and under his feet. "It's not like that. I would never do that to you."

He raked his hand through his hair, his breath pluming in front of him. Snowflakes still floated around her head, a sign of her ire.

The small dining room and part of the kitchen was coated in a thin layer of ice.

"I wanted to tell you many times," he said at last.

"But?" she demanded.

"But I never found the right words or the right time."

He moved from his side of the table toward her. She backed up a step and shook her head. "Stay away from me, you traitor."

Traitor. The word speared through him with such violence it made his inner dragon take notice. The beast uncoiled, sensed Mia's fury and her ice and wanted to counteract it. Now was not the time for his dragon to come out to play. He clenched his fists.

"The Blood Stone, a tooth from a Gildhara cold-drake and one other relic are the keys to breaking the curse on the Hidden Lands, Mia. That's why Logan wants it and why he wants to keep the Blood Stone."

"I don't give a shit about your Hidden Lands. I want my Blood Stone and the other royal gemstones back."

So that was that. She wasn't willing to help them or the Hidden Lands. Not that he had expected her to or that he was going to harvest one of her teeth, either.

"Take me back to the city." Her tone brooked no argument. Fire flashed in her eyes.

"No. It's not safe."

"Yes. I demand it. I'd rather take my chances with the Drakana and Armond than a filthy liar. I can find my parents on my own and get back the gems. I don't need your help."

Rafe shoved the chair out of the way and charged her, moving so fast she didn't have a chance to react. He pushed her against the wall, pressing his face close to hers. Her chill pulsed off her into him. His dragon reacted, too, coming alive and beating against his skull wanting out, wanting to warm her. He ignored it.

"Do you understand what they'll do you, princess?"

She searched his eyes and he could see she was trying to come up with an answer.

"They'll force you to shift and take what they want. Herrick will turn you over to Armond as his prize. Is that what you really want?"

She shook her head. "Not if I refuse to shift."

He almost laughed. How naïve she was. "You won't stand a chance against them. They have ways of making you shift whether you want to or not."

Fear flickered through her eyes. "You're just saying that to scare me."

"Am I? First, they'll give you a drug to keep you from resisting. Then they'll strip you down. When you're naked, they'll give you another drug to force your body into shifting. You won't get a say in the matter."

She swallowed hard.

"I'm nearly five hundred years old, princess. I've seen it all."

He moved away from her, back to the table where he picked up the ruined food and carried it to the kitchen. He left her there, ignoring her, letting everything he'd said sink into her. At last she stepped away from the table, walked to the front door of the cabin, and left.

Numb, Mia stepped out onto the small porch. Snowflakes followed her, like a halo around her head. Her mind reeled. Why hadn't he told her the truth before? Why did he keep it from her?

She half expected him to stop her from leaving but he hadn't. He'd let her go. She considered bolting into the woods, but where would she go? Where *could* she go?

Rafe was right. She didn't stand a chance on her own. She couldn't fight Armond alone. She wasn't strong enough. She wished Helmut was there to help her, protect her.

She needed time to think. She plopped down on the top step of the porch. Two sets of footsteps in the new fallen snow went from the cabin into the woods. Freya and Jaxson. She was glad they weren't here now. She didn't want to answer questions from her assistant and she didn't want to listen to anything Jaxson might have to say.

Mia ran her hands through her tangled hair. What was she going to do now? All this time she felt like she could trust Rafe and now that trust had been shattered. She had believed he wanted to protect her, keep her safe. He'd lied to her. He knew Logan had the Blood Stone. Knew and refused to tell her. Knew he wanted one of her dragon teeth. How was her tooth and the Blood Stone connected?

Jaxson and Freya were on the edge of the woods, making their way back. They paused when they saw her sitting alone on the porch. She got to her feet.

"Well, the cabin is still standing. That's a good sign," Jaxson said with a quirk of a smile.

Mia glared at him, unamused by his quip. "Is it true?"

"Is what true?"

"Everything you said," she clarified.

"Yes, your highness. It's all true. And there's more I didn't get to tell you."

Her mouth went dry. "More?"

"Armond *did* save your parents from certain death upon landing in Sydney. If he hadn't intercepted their plane in Singapore, they'd be killed in Australia at the hands of Lord Herrick's men," he said. "At least now there's a chance we can get them back safely."

"We?"

"Logan, me, Rafe. Whether you like it or not, we're the only ones that can help you." He started to brush by her, paused. "For the record, Rafe is one of the best dragons I know. If he was ordered to take your tooth, he wouldn't have done it. I doubt he ever had plans to do it."

She lifted a brow. "What makes you think so?"

"Because he still lives by the knight's code."

He strode into the cabin. Freya followed, but Mia caught her arm and stopped her.

"What do you think?" she asked the girl.

Surprise flickered over her face. "You want to know what I think?"

Mia huffed out an annoyed breath. "Yes, by the gods, I do. Would Rafe do something like that to me?"

She considered for a long moment as she chose her words. "I think, your highness, that if the way Rafe looks at you is any indication, then no, he wouldn't do that to you."

"How does he look at me?" she whispered.

"Like you're the only woman in the world he sees." She tugged her arm free and continued inside.

Mia stared out at the woods, clutching her elbows, trying to make sense of everything. Most of the last few days had been a nightmare. The only thing that wasn't was Rafe.

And yet the fact remained he lied to her. She had one more day before she had to contact Armond. She had hoped it would be spent with Rafe, naked and in his arms. Not harboring anger and disgust.

The door opened and he stepped out, as if thinking about him summoned him. She knew it was him by his scent. The door closed with a soft snick. He made no move to step around her, to touch her.

"Mia, I'm sorry."

She closed her eyes, a shuddering breath expelled in a plume of frost. "Do you honestly think an apology is all it's going to take for me to forgive you? It's not that simple."

Silence stretched, then he said, "That day you landed on my roof, Logan came to me. He wanted me to find you. He'd arranged for us to meet at the state dinner the following night."

The state dinner that never happened because of the kidnap attempt, which had gone awry. She opened her eyes and stared out at the snow-tipped trees, aware of the chill in the air but immune to it.

"He offered to release me from exile if I could bring him your tooth. When you landed on my roof, it changed everything."

Yes, everything about her life changed in that one moment.

He continued, "Logan only sees a way to break the curse on our ailing realm."

Finally, she turned to face him. "And what do you see?"

He stroked a hand down her cheek, his knuckles brushing her skin in a light touch. "A beautiful, strong woman. My woman. My mate."

At those words, her dragon and the magic in her blood stirred deep within. It didn't change the fact he'd lied to her.

"But, Rafe—"

"I should have told you, yes. You're right. I was wrong to keep it from you." He reached for her, grasping her by the upper arms and pulling her closer with a gentle tug. "You *are* of the Gildhara bloodline. A descendant of Ienir the Great. The Hidden Lands belongs to you, too."

"That's not reason enough for me to willingly give up one of my teeth for a place I've never heard of or seen, or an ancestor I never knew existed."

His eyes searched hers. She could see the pain and regret and guilt lingering there in those silvery eyes. Even sense his own feral beast simmering under the surface wanting to repair the rift between them. It was almost enough to forgive him.

"If there's another way to save the Hidden Lands, I'll find it. I swear to you. I won't let anyone do that to you."

He slipped a wicked looking folding knife from his pocket. With a flick of his wrist, he opened it. Before she could say anything, he sliced open his palm then squeezed his hand into a tight fist. Blood dripped to the wood planks with soft plops.

"I swear by my own blood."

Her stomach twisted in a tight knot as she watched the blood drip from his enclosed hand to the porch. He meant it. Had sworn a blood oath to prove it to her. She placed her hand on top of his fist.

"And if you fail and don't bring Logan my tooth?" She was afraid of the answer almost as much as she was to ask the question. But she had to know.

"I suspect I'll live in exile until the end of my days."

Hearing him say it sent a jolt of pain through her. He'd risk his freedom, his only way to return to his homeland, to keep her safe. How could she ever accept that? Or repay him?

And what did that mean for the two of them? Would he return to Andonia with her, as her mate? There were consequences of her actions with him. Their mating would come as a shock to her parents. He hadn't been approved as a suitable royal suitor.

Would living in exile with her be so terrible? She wanted to ask, to find out what his true feelings were for her. She could, perhaps, get past the lying. But she didn't know if there was a possibility of a future with him.

She swallowed the sudden lump in her throat. Hot tears burned the backs of her eyes. She blinked them away and somehow managed to maintain control.

"We better see to that hand of yours."

She motioned to the door, stepping around him. As he followed her inside, her stomach was still in a tight knot. She suspected it would never quite go away.

◆ 22 ◆

After Rafe bandaged his hand, the four of them sat at the now-thawed kitchen table and formed a plan of action. Jaxson had rebuilt the fire. It warmed the small cabin. A fresh pot of coffee brewed. If this had been any other time, they could have enjoyed the coziness of the small cabin. With Armond's threat looming over them it made it impossible.

Rafe's hand throbbed as a reminder of his blood oath he'd sworn to her. Logan would be furious when he discovered it, but it was the only way to break his word to his friend. His dragon was restless, stirring deep inside him in a way he hadn't felt in a century or two, as if it was spoiling for a fight. And maybe it was. It had been too long since he'd shifted.

When Rafe first arrived in the human realm, his dragon had been bloodthirsty. It had taken a lot of self-control for him to get it under control. Everything he'd left behind in the Hidden Lands had felt unfinished. He hadn't been able to go back and right his wrongs. His dragon hated that and hated him for it. Almost as though it were a separate, thinking entity inside him. There were days when he'd come to the mountains, shift into dragon form and roam the skies high above. That was before technology took over the world. Before cameras were everywhere and every Joe Schmo had a cell phone in their hand.

He did not want to admit to the things he'd done in dragon form in those early days of exile to anyone. He had forgotten the code, his honor. Over time, though, he regained his sense of self. Now that he was faced with an impossible dilemma, his dragon's indignation was roused.

"It's less than twenty-four hours before Mia has to contact Armond again," Rafe said. "We need to figure out a plan to keep her out of his hands and get back the king and queen."

"Armond has them hidden somewhere in Brooklyn. I didn't have a chance to find out exactly where before I was stabbed," Jaxson said.

Rafe was familiar with the area. "That doesn't narrow it down much."

"I didn't have time to investigate further." Jaxson sounded apologetic. Rafe waved it away.

Mia chewed on her lower lip. "How do we know Armond isn't bluffing?"

"What do you mean?" Rafe asked.

"He didn't give us proof he has my parents," she said. "He could be lying to get me to come to him. It could be his ploy to finally get what he wants. Me."

"If he's bluffing, it's one hell of a gamble," Jaxson pointed out.

"Do you think he'd do something like that?" Rafe asked.

"No. I don't know." She sighed. "I've only known him a short time. He was supposed to be my retiring bodyguard's replacement. I didn't think he'd be capable of attempted kidnapping, so I suppose anything is possible."

Rafe could see the wheels turning in her head. "Do you have an idea?"

She nodded. "Yes. We call his bluff."

Everyone stilled as they looked at her. Rafe shook his head. "No. It's too risky."

"How?" Jaxson ignored him.

"We stay right here." She pointed at the table. "And call him back. Tell him we're back in the city and demand proof he has my parents."

"I don't think that's such a good idea, your highness." Freya spoke for the first time.

"Why not?" she demanded.

"Because if he does have them, he could make good on his threat and kill them," Rafe said. "Are you willing to risk that?"

She chewed her lower lip again as she looked at him. He knew the worry gnawing at her. "What do you think we should do?"

"We call him," Rafe said. "Make a plan to meet him somewhere. Central Park, maybe. Demand he bring your parents and offer to exchange their lives for yours." When she stared to object, he held up his hand. "Jaxson and I ambush him and take him out before he can get his hands on you."

"Ambush them with what? Our good looks?" Jaxson said.

Rafe gave him a deadpan look. "I have a few tricks up my sleeve."

Mia's eyes widened. He could tell she wanted to ask questions but refrained. He wasn't sure how much longer he could keep his dragon at bay. He'd have to shift, and soon, to assuage the restless feeling. If Armond could shift into his shadow dragon, perhaps it was time he met Rafe's own inner beast.

"Great. When are you going to share them?" Jaxson asked.

"Soon enough." He glanced around at the group. "Let's call Armond and plan to meet in the city."

The slam of a car door outside made them all jump. Mia's eyes went to the door. Rafe and Jaxson immediately got to their feet. Rafe charged to the nearby window and peered out. Several cars had pulled into the narrow drive. Men exited carrying handguns and rifles. Drakana, no doubt. He swore under his breath as he turned back to the three of them.

"Mia, you and Freya go to the bedroom. Barricade yourselves inside. Don't come out no matter what you hear out here. Jaxson, you're with me."

She got to her feet, her hands shaking. "Why? What's happening?"

He met her gaze keeping his voice steady. "They found us."

She knew who "they" were. She and Freya hurried to the bedroom. When he heard the door close with a snap, he turned to Jaxson.

"Do you think he followed me here?"

"It's possible," Rafe said. "Armond is determined to get her back. It was only a matter of time before he found us."

He took a deep breath, nodded. "So, what's your plan?"

"I have no weapons here," Rafe said. He met the man's level gaze. "But we both have dragon magic."

Jaxson lifted a brow. "Isn't that a little risky?"

"We're not in the city but yeah, it's still risky. There are others here on the mountain. Humans. They wouldn't understand what they're seeing."

"We proceed with caution." Jaxson gave him a nod. "Got it."

With his keen dragon hearing, there were more car doors. Rafe was smart enough to realize the cabin was likely surrounded by Armond's men. The man had yet to make an appearance but Rafe was certain he wouldn't let someone else touch his prize.

The living room windows exploded in a shower of glass. They ducked as it rained down around them.

"That didn't take long," Jaxson said. "He must be desperate."

A flash-bang so powerful, both of them lost their footing. Rafe was on the ground, his ears ringing. It sounded as though he was in a tunnel. Smoke filled the room, pouring out of the broken windows stinging his eyes and throat.

The door splintered and caved in. The next thing he knew, there was a gun pointed at his head.

How arrogant he was to think he and Jaxson could fight off so many armed Drakana with dragon magic. They never had a chance.

"Where is she?" A deep voice rumbled over him.

Rafe decided to play dumb. He squinted up through the smoke and haze at the man standing next to him. He recognized Armond.

"Who?"

Without warning, he cocked him in the side of the head with the butt of the gun. Stars burst through his vision as his head exploded in pain. The dragon inside him came alive and did not take kindly to the assault. Rafe did all he could to push the beast back down, down, down.

It growled at him. A deep, dark menacing growl of warning.

"You know who," Armond replied.

"I thought you were going to give her a chance to turn herself over to you."

As casually as he could, Rafe took a cursory glance of the living room. The men had Jaxson at gunpoint, too.

Armond snorted his response. Rafe lifted his head and glared up at Armond, his dragon magic surging through his veins, warming him from the inside out. He lifted his palm encased in a ring of flame as he got to his feet and wrapped his fingers around the man's neck. Armond's eyes were wide as he stared through the flames—flames that were not as hot as they could be because Rafe controlled the heat. Then a smile creased his face.

"Too late to be a hero," Armond said with a sickly smile.

A loud explosion rocked the back of the small cabin followed by a familiar sound. The sound of a dragon.

The bedroom...Mia.

The female screams ripped through the cabin. He shoved Armond away, releasing him. He would burn down the entire cabin to save Mia if he had to. But Armond and his men were retreating. They'd got what they came for.

"You made that too easy, my friend." He gave Rafe a jaunty salute as the scurried out the broken door.

"Rafe, the women."

Jaxson hurried to the bedroom, Rafe on his heels. At the doorway, they both halted. There was a gaping hole where the window had once been. Tattered remains of curtains billowed in the cold breeze. The bed had been destroyed as well as most of the furniture. It looked like a war zone. Only one thing could have done that—a full size dragon.

Jaxson swore under his breath. A cold numbness set in as Rafe clenched his hands into fists.

In an effort to protect Mia, he'd done the absolute worst thing. He'd left her alone and unguarded and given Armond and his men the chance they needed to take her. He thought it had been the right thing to do.

But he was wrong.

Memories punched through his gut as he stared at the destroyed room, his hands balled into tight fists at his side as his gut twisted into a knot. All he could think about was the princess and queen he once failed to save. He failed again. He failed Mia.

"We'll get them back," Jaxson said.

His inner dragon pounded against his skull with a deafening roar. It was not happy and spoiling to get out of his skin. Rafe tried to push it back down but it was having none of it. It wanted *out* and *out now* and it would do whatever it took to get its way.

Princess. Mine. Protect.

His dragon spoke in a demanding, booming voice inside his head. It was a voice he had not heard in ages. Not since the last time he'd let the beast out. His hands started to shake. His heartbeat raced, making him lightheaded.

Dizziness swept through him. Black dots swam before his eyes. He knew what the dragon inside was doing just as he knew he couldn't stop it. His skin heated from palm to shoulder and then spread through his chest. The beast uncurled, ready to push its way into the world, splintering what little control Rafe had left. The leash he'd put into place shredded into a thousand pieces and disappeared in a puff of smoke.

"Rafe?"

He spun to face Jaxson, his breath see-sawing in and out. "I can't control it, Jax. Whatever happens..."

Alarm creased his features. He reached for his friend but Rafe shook his head and backed away.

"What do you mean? What's happening?"

Before he could answer, a feral scream exploded from his lungs. His hands fisted his shirt and ripped it in half and then he was lost to the beast within him.

For the first time in over a century, Rafe shifted.

Jaxson watched his friend shift from man to beast in a matter of seconds, his heart in his throat. Rafe had just broken one of the unwritten rules of being in the human society. He snatched his cell phone and dialed Logan.

When he answered, Jaxson said, "We have a major problem."

❧ 23 ❧

Mia's wrists were bound in front of her, a gag over her mouth. After the dragon destroyed the bedroom, she and Freya were herded into the back of the black SUV. More of Armond's men piled in. They drove at breakneck speed from the cabin. Each one had a starburst tattooed on their inner wrists. *Drakana.* Armond's men were *Drakana.*

Not that she didn't know. Knowing was one thing. Seeing it made it all the more real.

As they drove away, she got a glimpse of the nearly destroyed cabin and it made her heart hurt. They didn't stand a chance when the wall of the cabin was completely destroyed by the dragon. Six armed men invaded what was left of the bedroom. Worry gnawed at her for Rafe and Jaxson. They were still in there when all hell broke loose and she and Freya were captured.

They left the mountains behind and returned to the city. They had all been naïve to think Armond would happily sit by and wait for Mia to come to him. She had been nothing but a sitting duck at the cabin. Even without the necklace, he was still able to find her. Perhaps the men had followed Jaxson as they had before when he brought Freya to them. The worst thing that could happen, did. Now she was in enemy hands.

The men herded her and Freya out of the car into a ramshackle warehouse somewhere in Brooklyn. The fenced off brown brick two-story building looked like it had seen better days. They entered through the loading dock. It hosted drab concrete floors and garish fluorescent lighting that emitted a yellowish glow. The stale air was oppressive as they entered. The cavernous empty space was big enough for...her breath caught. She knew what they meant to do to her. She scanned the place, looking for a way out, but saw no options.

They walked across the empty warehouse through a doorway into a hallway that led to a set of metal stairs heading up to the second level. At the top of the stairs, they entered a loft-like space. It was clear this had once been someone's apartment. One wall of windows overlooked the streets and the buildings across the street. Not a great view. Here the place was sectioned off in what looked like more apartments.

They were taken to one that smelled like stale cigarettes with a faint undertone of body odor. A mattress stood on end against the far wall, the headboard and footboard were broken down and looked as though it had been through a war. One of the men dragged in two chairs behind them and ordered them to sit. With their wrists still bound, they tied them to the chairs. They left, but Mia knew men were positioned outside the door as guards.

Freya sniffled, trying hard to keep back the fear and the tears. Mia glanced at her.

"We're going to be okay," Mia whispered, sounding more sure than she felt.

"How do you now that? They have you, your highness. The warehouse is big enough for—"

"I know," she said, cutting her off. "But I have to believe Rafe will find a way to us. He swore a blood oath to protect me. He won't abandon us."

The girl sniffed again. "I hope you're right."

"I know I'm right."

Even as she said it, a bit of doubt crept into her mind. She had to keep it at bay. Had to trust Rafe would come for her and Freya.

From the time they were captured to now, Mia managed to keep her dragon magic in control and contained. She thought she might need it later so she didn't want to expend any of it. She could feel the full force of it churning inside her, wanting out. Her skin was paler than usual, colder than normal. It was a strain to keep the magic controlled and contained.

The door to their room opened. A slash of bright light from the hallway beamed inside. Three men entered, one of them Armond. He paused in front of her, looking down at her with malcontent. She stiffened, peering back up at him determined not to let him intimidate her.

Despite her desperate attempt to keep her magic in check, snowflakes drifted from her skin.

"Princess Mia, I'm glad to see you found your way to me at last." His breath plumed as he spoke. One of his men untied her from the chair.

She took a deep breath through her nose and swallowed hard. Pulling back the magic was difficult because she had always allowed it to run rampant. But since her mating with Rafe, she thought of him, of his warmth, his inner fire and pulled it back into herself, regaining some of that control.

She narrowed her eyes. "You didn't give me a choice."

"You didn't give *me* a choice. I had to find a way to retrieve you since you escaped me more than once."

Every muscle in her body tightened as the anger surged through her. Her magic stirred, fluttering like butterfly wings inside her, against her skull. "You got what you wanted. Let's get on with this."

"With this?" He lifted an eyebrow. "Whatever do you mean?"

"I know your men control the palace. I know you want me for your bride. Get on with it."

Surprise flickered over his features before it was replaced with a wan smile. "You flatter me that you want to marry so quickly. I'm afraid we have some unfinished business first."

He grabbed her arm and hauled her to her feet. She wanted to protest but knew it would do no good. She let him drag her out of the room, his two men following. They left Freya behind.

"What about Freya?" Her voice shook when she asked.

"I have other plans for Freya."

"If you mean to kill her—"

"Plans that do not concern you."

She flinched at his curt tone.

They headed back down the long hallway to the loft area. There, in a circle of light, her parents were bound to chairs, their wrists shackled in irons. The sight made her weak in the knees. She faltered but Armond's vice grip on her upper arm kept her on her feet. He gave her a shove toward the king and queen.

Tears of relief and terror sprang to her mother's eyes. Her father could not hide his relief even as he turned his glare to Armond.

"I'll give you a moment to enjoy your family reunion," Armond said.

He and the others moved to the other side of the room. It didn't offer much privacy but Mia would take what she could get. She fell to her knees to the worn carpet between them, a choking sob shuddering out of her with her wrists still bound, she couldn't reach out to them.

"Papa. Mama. I'm so sorry."

"Do not apologize, Mia," her father said. "It is I who hired Armond. I'm the only one to blame just as I'm to blame for Helmut's death."

"No, Papa. You aren't. It was my fault. If it hadn't been for me wanting to get back the Blood Stone, none of this would have happened."

"The Blood Stone? Mia, you thought you could get back the Blood Stone and the jewels?" he asked.

"I had a solid lead that led to New York City." A sob hitched in her throat. "I thought…"

"None of that matters now," he said, his tone soothing.

Her mother started crying, silent tears rolling down her cheeks. She knew, as they all did, their lives would never be the same after this experience.

"Armond's men took over the palace," Mia whispered.

He was silent a moment as he looked down at her with

something she couldn't read in his eyes. She felt like she'd failed him and her mother and the kingdom. She had failed everyone.

"We will get back the kingdom," her father said, sounding strong and sure.

Armond returned with his henchmen and another man she didn't know.

"Family reunion over. We have business." He glanced from Mia to the king of Andonia. "This is Lord Herrick."

He motioned to the man standing on his left. His oily black hair was slicked back from his high forehead accenting his hawk-like nose, pointed chin and thin lips. He wore an immaculate designer suit and shoes as though he were dressed for Wall Street or a high-ranking official job. Herrick stepped forward and paused next to Mia, gazing down at her with a sickly smile.

"It's a pleasure to meet you at last, your highness."

His unnatural cordial tone sent a chill up her spine.

"Stay away from my daughter." Her father's words were laced with such anger and hatred, she glanced at him in surprise.

"I'm afraid I cannot. Her dragon form has something I need very much."

"You want my dragon's tooth," she said.

He gave her a pleased smile. "That's right."

She straightened her back, sitting upright with her knees folded under her. She tilted her head back up to him in defiance. "You can't have it."

"Mia—" her father began.

"I will take what I need from you and then decide whether or not to kill you," Herrick said.

"You told me she was mine after you finished with her," Armond snapped.

"I belong to no man." Mia flung the words at them as she glared at them both.

Armond tipped his head to the side as he regarded her with a cool demeanor. "I thought you were ready to wed me, princess."

"By the gods, you will not!" her father shouted.

One of the henchmen smacked the king in the side of the head with the butt of his gun. Her mother screamed. Mia cried out as she watched her father's head loll against his shoulders. Blood dripped down the side of his face but he was still conscious.

"Next time, your father won't be so lucky." Herrick turned to her, folding his arms over his chest. "Do you wish to cooperate?"

She stifled a whimper and bit her bottom lip. Her magic quivered inside her, begging to be unleashed. She managed to hold tight to it, keeping it contained. She needed to build it up more and knew she had to stall. She tilted her head back a little and looked down her nose at him.

"I'll give you want you want if you promise to release my parents."

His brows lifted to his hairline in utter shock. "You wish to negotiate with me? I don't think so." He laughed at her.

Snowflakes drifted off her skin. Snowflakes she could no longer control. Frost formed around her body, leaving a ring of ice around her. She could hear her mother's hitched sobs and her father suck in a sharp breath.

Control. She needed to find control. She needed to keep herself in check.

Herrick moved to stand in front of her, then squatted down to her level. He grasped her chin in his hand. When she tried to jerk it away, he gripped her so tight, his fingers dug into her flesh. He tilted her head one way then the other, examining her features and looking her over with a critical eye.

"So beautiful. So perfect. So exactly what I need. You'll cooperate, won't you?"

Mia knew her skin was cold to the touch and knew it had to be burning his fingers, yet he didn't even flinch. She managed to force one word through her lips. "Or?"

His eyes narrowed into slits. "Do you wish to test me?"

She sucked in a breath through her nose, held it in her lungs for a count of three and parted her lips ever so slightly, as though exhaling from a cigarette. Her crystalized breath erupted from deep within her lungs, breathing cold smoke right into his face. He jerked back, releasing her chin. Frost coated his eyebrows, eyelashes and his cheeks. His face turned red.

"Bitch."

Her father surged forward, but the restraints held him in check. Mia climbed to her feet, her wrists still bound in front of her, her hands fisted. She could feel the magic pounding through her now. It was a winter storm ready to be unleashed.

"You will release my parents or I will freeze you and your men."

Herrick swiped his hand over his face, wiping away the frost. Amusement danced in his eyes. He didn't take her serious. "And if I don't?"

She hesitated, remembering the things Rafe had told her. His words echoed in her head.

First, they'll give you a drug to keep you from resisting. Then they'll strip you down. When you're naked, they'll give you another drug to force your body into shifting.

No, she would not let them to do that to her. She would rather die fighting back, than allow them to have their way with her to get whatever they wanted.

She uncurled her fingers and concentrated hard on the bindings around her wrists. The rope iced over. She gave it a swift yank and broke it as though it was nothing more than paper. Ice crystals tinkled to the floor. Herrick watched, wide-eyed, as she lifted her hands, palms upward. Flakes of snow lifted from her skin and danced in the air hovering over her hands.

"Do you wish to test me, Lord Herrick? Perhaps you wish to see what I can really do, what I'm capable of before you'll believe my threats are real." Her voice was far calmer than she thought possible as she looked at the simpering man across from her. "Perhaps you think I'm a weak child with no backbone. Perhaps you, Lord Herrick, are wrong."

She flung her hands at him. Shards of ice streamed from her palms toward him but he ducked before the deadly icicles pierced him. One landed in the heart of one of his men who went down clutching the melting weapon, his eyes wide and full of fear and shock.

"Mia!"

It was her mother's screech that rang in her ear but she ignored it.

A roar rumbled the entire building and suddenly she knew...*knew*...Rafe had come for her and he was not in human form. Her heartbeat quickened at the very thought. He had come for her as he promised he would in his blood oath.

Everyone in the warehouse apartment immediately lifted their gaze to the ceiling, as though they could see through it to the dragon flying overhead. Another screech that rattled the rafters. Oh, how she wished she could see him. She wondered what his dragon form looked like. If it was even half as magnificent as his human form. Powerful. Awesome.

Something heavy and large landed on the roof, making all the windows rattle and the walls shudder under the weight of the beast. Herrick barked something to his men. Armond grasped her by the upper arm. He started to drag her away, was saying something in her ear but she couldn't hear him. She was too focused on what was happening outside and knew her mate was there. Her blood sang with the cheerful happiness that he was *there* right outside the building and her own dragon flapped into a hysterical response against her skull, wanting out. *Needing* out.

She had an uncontrollable need to shift but she tamped it down. Way, way down. Good thing too because a second later, the entire ceiling caved in and Rafe's dragon head poke inside, tendrils of smoke curling out of his enormous nostrils.

Boy, did he look pissed.

And breathtaking.

He was huge. His scales changed color from orange to red to yellow reminding her of flickering firelight. Every now and then, she could catch bright blue undertones, as though he burned bright and hot. His wings spanned behind him, the opaque membranes the color of sunshine. He perched on the edge of the building and leaned in, his yellowed claws inches from the nearest Drakana's head. He looked poised and ready to swipe the man off his feet as though he were nothing more than a plaything.

He was her flame to her ice. He was warmth to her cold.

Everyone froze. Armond's hand tightened around her arm, his fingers digging into muscle and bone. A crystallized breath shuddered from between her lips, pluming in front of her. Rafe turned his dragon head and looked at her, his silvery eyes meeting hers. Her heart thumped in response, but the cold did not thaw inside. It built and built and built to a pressure inside her ready to burst.

Snowflakes drifted off her skin. Armond sucked in a sharp breath and snatched his hand away, holding his wrist. His fingers were encased in ice and had turned blue.

She pinned him with a stare. "He came for me," she said in her best haughty tone. "And now you'll pay."

As though in answer, Rafe roared. Drakana scattered like cockroaches fleeing from a bright light.

A shriek from her mother made Mia whirl around. Herrick's henchmen had hauled her parents from their chairs. One had a gun pointed at her father's head. Another held a knife to her mother's throat.

"Let them go," Mia said.

Ice coated her skin and the floor underneath her feet. Knowing her mate was close made her dragon want out. But shifting was what Herrick and his men wanted her to do.

"You give me what I want, I'll give you want you want. That's how it works, princess," Herrick said.

"Don't do it, Mia. You know what he wants—" her father started.

"Shut him up," Herrick demanded.

One of the men pulled out an obsidian blade and stabbed her father. He sucked in a sharp breath and clutched his side. Blood welled and stained his shirt. A scream ripped from her mother.

"No! Papa!"

Her father had been stabbed with a poisoned blade.

"You bastard," she seethed.

She started to bolt toward him, but Armond grabbed her again, pulling her to his chest and wrapping powerful arms around her, holding her tight. Overhead, Rafe roared again, rattling what was left of the walls and rafters. Herrick gave him a sideways glance, but didn't seem intimidated by him at all.

"Now, princess, you will do as I ask or you father will surely die without the proper medical attention. He only has a few hours with the poison from the obsidian blade making its way through his system. You can save him, though. All you have to do is shift into your dragon form so we can take what we need from you," Herrick said. "Then his healing can begin."

Mia couldn't respond. White hot rage flooded though her. It was taking all her concentration to control her magic and keep from shifting.

Don't do it, Mia.

It was her father's voice in her head. She met his gaze and he gave her an imperceptible nod.

Should I let you die? she asked.

They're going to kill me anyway, no matter what you do. If you shift and give them what they want, they will kill you, too.

What am I supposed to do?

She was faced with an impossible choice. She could not, under any circumstances, let these men kill her parents. They were her everything, her whole world. She glanced at Rafe who clung to the edge of the destroyed building, waiting, watching. Together, they were fire and ice. If they couldn't save her parents, who could?

As if in response to her thoughts, a low growl rumbled from him, his snout inches from Armond. He puffed out a plume of heated smoke from his nostrils. The warm breath cascaded over her, warming her. It sent her dragon into a tizzy.

Armond flinched, his arms loosening enough for her to wiggle free, turn and kick him in the balls as hard as she could. In that instant, all hell broke loose.

Armond doubled over with a grunt of pain. Herrick barked orders to have the king and queen removed. The henchmen dragged them away. Two men charged her but she let her dragon magic flow into her, encasing her body in a fine sheen of frost, though she could not feel it. She held up her hands and threw shards of ice daggers at them. They had no choice but to duck out of the way.

Armond tackled her from behind, knocking her to the dirty floor. He covered her with his body, grinding into her and shoving her face to the ground. He pinned one of her arms between the two of them. It sent Rafe's dragon into hysterics. She could hear the *whump-whump* of his wings as he took flight and then a bark of a howl.

Mia closed her eyes and let the magic burst through her, coating her body in a shield of ice. She felt rather than saw the burst of flame from Rafe's dragon as he belched blue-white fire all over Armond. He screamed and leaped off her. Thankfully, her shield of ice protected her from Rafe's blaze.

She climbed to her feet and spun around to see Armond's singed clothes and skin. Smoke curled from the ends of his hair. She could see blackened pieces of skin along his arms. The smell of burned flesh permeated the already odorous air. She tried hard not to gag.

Armond stumbled backward, pain and agony in his eyes.

"Enough of this," Herrick said. "Princess, we need your tooth. We have your kingdom, you father is dying, so there is no reason not to give us what we want."

She cut a glance to her father who gave her a stiff shake of his head. She lifted her chin a little higher. "*Never.*"

"Very well, then. You leave me with no other choice, princess. Armond, if you will."

Armond pulled out a gun and shot her.

⚜ 24 ⚜

Searing pain pulsed through her left shoulder as Mia stumbled backward. She pressed her hand against the wound. Warm sticky blood coated her fingers when she pulled it away.

The moment Armond pulled the trigger, Rafe's dragon howled. He turned his giant head on the man and snarled, steam coming out of his nose surrounding the men. Armond took a step backward, away from the giant beast as Rafe leaned closer, his mouth parting enough for smoke to spill out of it in a curling steam. She could see the flicker of blue-white flame deep inside his mouth.

"Rafe, no," she said on a gasp.

He turned his head, looked at her and blinked those silvery dragon eyes. She reached for him, placed a cold hand on his nose and let him warm her. It seemed to calm him. Her own dragon stilled deep inside her.

"I'm all right. He's not worth it," she whispered. Her frosty breath turned to a hiss.

"Armond, do something with that thing." Herrick indicated Rafe. Then to one of his men, "Bring the princess and the other girl."

Someone clamped a hand around Mia's arm and dragged her away. Freya. They were going after Freya. Several men left to retrieve her.

Mia craned her neck to see Rafe growl at the men, baring his sharp teeth before taking flight, the *whump-whump* of wings beating the air. Her heart stuttered in her chest. There was no way he would leave her alone. He would find another way to get to her. She was sure of it.

With Rafe gone, Armond and Herrick fell in step behind them down the long hallway, down the metal stairs and into the cavernous, echoing warehouse. This is where they had brought her parents, their wrists still bound in irons. Blood, now drying, streaked down the side of her father's face and his shirt had a large bloodstain where he'd been stabbed. A few minutes later, the others joined them with Freya in tow. The girl's eyes were wide with fright as she looked at Mia, then across the expanse of empty warehouse at the bound king and queen.

Her father was going to die if he didn't get help soon. Sweat beaded his forehead. Already he looked pale and weak, much like what Jaxson looked like when he arrived at the cabin. The only person she knew that could help him was Rafe.

Herrick accelerated and lengthened his stride, reaching one of his men who held a silver case that looked suspiciously like a medical case. He took it from the man and dropped to his knees, placing it on the floor and flipping open the locks. When he opened the lid, he pulled out a syringe and held it up for her to see.

Cold dread pulsed through her as she looked at it and knew. Knew everything Rafe told her before was true. Knew he was going to do something horrible to her in front of her parents, Freya, and all these men. Knew they intended to inject her, strip her bare and force her to shift.

Herrick looked at one of his other men and gave a nod. The man came forward holding a pair of primitive shackles like the ones around her parents' wrists.

"Do you know what those are, your highness?"

She bit down hard on her lip to keep from answering. Herrick moved toward her, halting in front of her still holding that syringe. Armond grasped her wrist and held it out for the first one to slide around her wrist and click closed with a twist of a strange lock.

"Iron shackles perfect for suppressing magic. All kinds of magic." Herrick gave her a quiet smile. "Even yours."

The second one clamped around her other wrist.

It was as though a switch turned off inside her. Her cold-drake power blinked out as though someone snuffed out a candle wick with their fingers. Her heart rammed hard against her chest as Herrick tapped a thumbnail against the syringe in a tap, tap, tap.

Freya whimpered. Herrick shot her a warning look. She pressed her lips together until they were a thin line, but the fear remained in her eyes.

"Since you won't willingly help me, princess, I will have to resort to Plan B."

Armond moved to stand next to her parents, holding the gun on them. She thought for sure Herrick was going to plunge the needle in the crook of her arm but he didn't. He merely gave her an oily smile as he turned toward her parents and walked slow steps toward her father.

Her father.

The reigning monarch of Andonia.

Oh, gods.

Her father was too weak to move, to fight against Herrick as his men picked him up from the floor and held him in place. Mia could only watch with sickly horror as he shoved up the sleeve of her father's shirt and stuck the needle in his arm. Her mother shrieked as Herrick pumped the yellow serum into him.

Mia whimpered, wishing she could conjure that icy wind deep inside her but she couldn't. She couldn't bring it to the surface no matter how hard she tried. The iron shackles kept her from wielding it.

"It will only burn for a moment," Herrick said to the king, his voice calm and cold. "Once the serum has made its way through your system, you will not be able to disobey." He looked at Mia over his shoulder, that same oily smile still on his lips. "He will do whatever I wish. I will have complete control over him. And though the king is not as powerful as you, your highness, he'll do. His tooth will provide me with what I need."

A sob hitched in Mia's throat. Tears blurred her vision as she looked at her mother, her father. She could hear Freya's whimper turn into crying.

"Once I have the tooth, I will go to Andonia and forge powerful weapons from the obsidian glass. After that, it will only be a matter of time before I get my hands on the Blood Stone. Then, my reign of the Hidden Lands as High King can begin."

Logan would be in danger since he had the Blood Stone. Mia didn't think he would give it up to Herrick.

Her shoulders sagged in defeat. She had failed. This horrible, ugly man did his best to destroy her, her parents, her kingdom. She clenched her fists, the shackles rattling.

Rafe. Where was Rafe?

Herrick squatted down in front of her father.

"Now, your majesty, you will shift into your dragon form."

Her father nodded in compliance. He reached for the buttons on his dress shirt and started to undo them one by one, the shackles around his wrists clinking. Burning anger clotted in Mia's throat. She was powerless and could do nothing to help or save her father.

The door of the warehouse blew open. Her father's hands halted and all eyes flew to the three hulking forms entering the warehouse, each with a gun in hand. Rafe stood in the center once again in his human form wearing clothes she didn't recognize. Rage and fury pulsed off him in heat waves hot enough she could feel it. She nearly cried out in relief when she saw him. Freya sucked in a sharp breath.

Jaxson and another man who could only be Logan flanked him. Standing shoulder to shoulder, they were like a wall of dragon-shifter muscle ready to tear apart the Drakana in the room.

"Let them go. Let them all go," Rafe demanded.

Her gaze flickered from Rafe to Herrick and back again. Nobody moved as silence descended on the warehouse. Mia's breath pooled in her chest as she held it.

All hell broke loose. Herrick pulled a gun and shouted something in a language she didn't know. More Drakana poured down from the apartment, all armed.

"Mia, duck," Rafe shouted.

She didn't hesitate as she flattened herself on the cold concrete floor. Gunfire erupted all around them. In the openness of the warehouse, men dropped like flies. Others ducked for cover while they returned fire. Most of them dispersed, doing a disappearing act. The next thing she knew, Rafe stood over her, between her and Herrick and the others.

Her parents. She had to get to them.

She glanced up long enough to see Armond jerk her father to his feet and drag him away. One of Herrick's men grabbed Freya and hauled her behind him. They disappeared through a doorway and down the long hallway. Watching it happen was like being gutted from neck to navel.

"He took my father and Freya." Her voice hitched.

"I'm on it."

Jaxson sprinted by, Logan on his heels. Rafe took out the remaining Drakana, then kneeled down next to her. He brushed hair back from her face.

"Are you all right? Your shoulder—"

He reached for her but she batted his hand away.

"They took him." She could not stop her chin from quivering.

"The bastard shot you."

"I'm fine. Rafe, they took my father and Freya."

"Logan and Jaxson will get them both back. Let's get you out of these." He lifted her shackled wrists.

"How?"

Rafe examined them briefly, then twisted the odd lock. First one, then the other and the offending shackles were off. She snatched them out of his hand before he could say anything and hurled them as hard and far as she could in the warehouse. They landed with a clang against the floor somewhere in the distance.

As soon as the offending iron shackles were off, the magic flooded through her. Her skin turned cold once again, ice in her veins. And her inner dragon begged for release, desperate for blood. *Eye for an eye.*

Mia hurried to her mother, ignoring the fluttering of her dragon. She pushed it back down into the recesses of her mind. It wasn't the time or the place for her to shift into dragon form. When she reached her mother, she knelt in front of her.

"Mama, are you all right?"

Her mother blinked, as though she had a difficult time focusing on her. Mia placed a cold hand on her mother's cheek, meeting her gaze.

"We have to get him back, Mia."

Rafe was at her side a second later. The queen's gaze flickered up to him, then to Mia. The princess could swear there was knowing deep in her eyes.

"We will, Mama."

"What did they do to him?" Rafe asked.

"He injected my father with something. Some kind of serum to make him shift. And…" she paused, met his gaze. "He was stabbed with an obsidian blade."

He swore under his breath. "There's not much time. I'm going after them."

"I'm coming with you," Mia said.

"No. Stay here with your mother."

Mia dragged her lower lip through her teeth in annoyance, trying to come up with a retort. But he was right. She couldn't leave her mother alone.

"I'm coming, too," her mother said.

"Your majesty, I don't think that's a good idea," Rafe said.

"Who are you, young man, to tell me what I can and can't do? He is my husband and my king and I'm coming."

Rafe blinked surprise at her mother' haughty queenly tone. He pressed his lips together. Under any other circumstances, she would have thought it hilarious.

"All right. Stay behind me. I don't need you two getting hurt, too." He removed the empty clip from his gun and replaced it with a full one, cocking the 9mm.

They headed for the darkness where Herrick and Armond disappeared with her father in tow. She only hoped they weren't too late.

❦ 25 ❧

Mia and her mother followed Rafe down the long hallway, following the sound of voices and Freya's crying. There was another empty warehouse by the loading dock, still big enough for a large dragon. A cold breeze blew in, kissing her exposed arms. Rafe felt it too and turned to look at her, question in his eyes.

"It wasn't me," she said. "It's through there." She pointed toward the loading dock.

He nodded, holding his gun at the ready. As they headed down the narrow hallway, they heard a sickening crack followed by a muffed wail. Mia's heart was in her throat. Rafe pressed them against the wall, pushing them behind him as he peered around the edge of the open door. He pressed back against the wall.

"The loading dock doors are open. They made him shift," he said, his voice low. "The poison in his veins from the obsidian blade wouldn't allow him to do it without help."

Her stomach turned, a sickly knot forming in the pit. Damn Armond.

"Freya?" Mia asked.

"She's with them."

She wrapped her hand around his rock-hard upper arm. "You have to do something."

He turned toward her. "Stay here. Both of you."

"But—"

"Let me handle this." His eyes were hard steel as he said, "I need you to stay here. I need you to stay safe."

Her heart did a little tumble as she gave a nod. "All right."

A breath of silence passed between them. He kissed her, hard and fast, before he disappeared around through the open door.

She licked her lips, tasting a hint of him. She flattened her back against the wall and realized her mother peered at her, her purple eyes so much like her own assessing her with amusement and curiosity.

"Who is he?" her mother asked.

"Not now, Mama."

"He kissed you, Mia."

Her eyes fluttered closed for a moment as she relished the feeling of his mouth on hers. "Yes, he did."

"I think I have a right to know who the strange man is kissing my daughter."

Mother first. Queen second. Mia sighed through her nose. "I think we have bigger things to worry about than a man kissing me, Mama."

Her mother's lips thinned as she glanced from Mia to where Rafe had disappeared. "Quite right."

She crowded closer to Mia and shivered. She slipped an arm around her mother's shoulders. Mia knew Rafe would do everything in his power to save him. Even so, it didn't stop the worry from gnawing at her raw gut.

Rafe kept to the shadows on silent feet, keeping his eyes trained on the giant silvery dragon. Freya saw him, but quickly averted her gaze so as not to give away his presence. Herrick and Armond acted fast, knowing the serum was short-lived so they could get what they wanted.

He could hear a murmur of voices and sharp commands. The dragon's tail thumped as if in pain against the floor, making the walls and ceiling shudder. He pressed against the wall, halting to scan the room. They had the dragon's mouth opened, holding it open with chains. Likely iron chains to keep his magic at bay.

Armond stood in front of him, Herrick next to him as he gave orders. And then Rafe spied his friends. Both of them captured, both of them bound and gagged. Freya, her pale face tear-stained, was held at gunpoint by one of the Drakana.

Fuck all.

It was up to him and he only had one clip. Though he was a good shot, there was no way he could take out all the men at once. He needed something more, something bigger. He needed a distraction so he could get to Logan and Jaxson. He put the gun in the waistband of his pants at the small of his back.

Shifting earlier had only sated his dragon momentarily, but he couldn't let it out again. Finding Mia, making sure she was okay calmed his inner beast, but even so. He wanted more, needed more. He wanted blood.

No shifting, he told the beast.

No fun, it replied.

If he couldn't give him the shifting, perhaps he could give his inner beast something else.

A wail of pain rumbled from the giant followed by a crack. Armond and his men were extracting a tooth from the king's dragon but having some difficulty. Another crack, another mournful wail. He had to act. An idea formed.

He reached for the gun and removed the clip, taking one of the bullets out of the chamber, then pocketed it. Replacing the clip, he put the gun at the small of his back once again. Holding his hands loosely at his side, he recalled the flame and let it dance along the fingers of both hands. Taking a deep breath, he stepped out of the shadows and made his presence known.

"Get away from him, you son of a bitch."

Armond's head snapped up in surprise.

"Keep going," Herrick ordered. "Armond, deal with him."

He pointed at Rafe without so much as a nod in his direction. He was solely focused on the men continuing to work to get the tooth out of the king's dragon form. Another crack. Another wail.

"Even if you get the tooth, you don't know where the Blood

Stone is."

"The Blood Stone is in Andonia. I currently control the country and the palace," Herrick said, his tone arrogant.

"No, it isn't."

"What do you mean?" Herrick turned his glittering dark eyes on Rafe.

"Exactly what you think. It's not in Andonia."

Herrick made a low command. The workers continued on as he moved around them and gave Rafe his full attention. "And you know where it is, I suppose?"

Rafe gave Logan a sideways glance. His friend's eyes were hard, gleaming with warning and anger. Rafe wasn't going to give up the location of the Blood Stone—he didn't know it himself—but he was going to give Herrick a false lead.

"It was sold on the black market," Rafe said. "To the vamps."

Herrick remained still as he stared him down. He could see the wheels turning in his head as he decided his next move. Nearby, Logan's shoulders relaxed as though he guessed Rafe's plan.

"And you know this for certain?" Suspicion laced Herrick's tone.

"I do." Another glance at Logan. He could see a smirk in his friend's eyes. "Find Dominic of the *Signori Della Notte* and you'll find the stone. He has a place in the Meatpacking District."

One final crack and the tooth came free. Blood spilled from the open dragon's mouth as he moaned in pain. Herrick said something to Armond he couldn't hear, then fled. Ran right out of the warehouse following the thieves who took the tooth.

Rafe pulled the bullet from his pocket and threw it toward the fleeing man. With his flames igniting once more, he sent a shot of blue-white fire toward the bullet. It exploded only a hairsbreadth away from Herrick. He tumbled to the ground, rolled and popped back onto his feet, unscathed.

Damn it.

Meanwhile, Armond pulled a gun and started shooting. Rafe dove out of the way, toward Jaxson and Logan. He landed on the cold hard floor and skidded the rest of the way, coming to a halt in front of them. Logan was already working the ropes around his wrists. Rafe pulled his pocket knife and sliced through them.

Just as he did, Logan jerked the gag off his mouth and shouted, "Behind you."

Armond was on him before Rafe could react. He tackled him from behind, knocking him face first into the ground. His chin cracked against the floor, the pocket knife skittered from his hand. Logan snatched it up and freed Jaxson.

Then the two were on Armond, dragging him off Rafe and getting control of the gun. As Rafe climbed to his feet, pain throbbing through his jaw.

Standing beside her father in a ring of ice, watery tears in her eyes, was Mia.

She heard the noise, the mournful wails and knew what was happening. She didn't have to see it. She dragged her mother behind her, telling her to stay out of harm's way.

She saw them break the tooth and yank it from her father's mouth, and ran. The coward ran away. She tried to stop them, but it was too late. They'd disappeared before she had a chance to use her magic or help Rafe.

In dragon form, her father slumped to the ground, his eyes heavy. Dark red blood stained his moon-colored scales. His breathing was labored, cold steam puffing out of his nostrils as she placed a hand on the side of his face.

"They'll pay for this," she whispered, her breath pluming in white between them.

"Mia." Rafe's calm voice echoed in the warehouse.

She glanced his way, saw Logan and Jaxson holding Armond between them. Saw Rafe standing there with blue-white flames encircling his fingers. Saw a white-faced Freya watching her with wide, baleful eyes.

Her mother shrieked and ran to them. She came to a jarring halt next to Mia and fell to her knees in front of her father. She pressed her hands on his snout, tears cascading down her face.

"You have to shift back, my love. So we can heal you."

He snuffed out an icy breath as if to say it was too late for him. A lump formed in Mia's throat. She looked to Rafe. He could read the question in her eyes and shook his head slowly.

The queen looked up at her, then to Rafe. Her voice warbled with more unshed tears when she spoke. "There must be something we can do. Some way to reverse the damage."

"The poison from the blade?" Mia's voice trailed away.

"I don't have the antidote here," Rafe said. "Even if I did, I couldn't give it to him in dragon form."

"After being stabbed and forced to shift, he's too weak to shift back," Logan added.

Her mother buried her face in her father's scales, her wracking sobs ripping Mia's heart. Helpless. The last time she felt this helpless was when she was lost and alone on the run from Armond. Before Rafe found her.

"We just watch him die?" she asked.

They didn't respond because she already had the answer. She sat on the ground next to her mother. Freya joined them, falling to her knees next to Mia. The three of them sat there, keeping a short vigil as they watched her father, the King of Andonia in his dragon form, take his last breath.

Her father was dead. The king was dead.

It was the most painful, awful thing she had ever experienced in her life. Freya reached for her, clasped her hand in hers and squeezed. Her mother covered her face with her hands, muffling her mournful sobs. Mia's heart cracked and broke, her life forever altered. Her mother's life forever altered. Andonia's future forever altered.

All because of one man. Because of one selfish, power-hungry man.

"My condolences, your highness."

Armond's voice snapped through her, made the dragon magic inside her come alive, made the cold of her power burn through her veins. Mia unfolded her form from the floor in a slow methodical movement and came to her feet. He stood between Jaxson and Logan still, blood dripping from his nose onto his chin.

Mia glared at him. Snowflakes drifted around her head. Her dragon magic had built up again inside her, pulsing with a wicked beat through her. She was damned tired of Armond and everything he had done to her, her parents, her kingdom.

She let the magic flow like an icy river through her. Her skin turned blue and a cold breath shuddered out of her, pluming in the air around her. She faintly heard the crack of ice on the floor beneath her feet, knew it spread outward from where she stood toward the men across from her.

"All my life, I've kept my magic in check," she said, her words a frigid plume of smoke. "All my life, I've kept it on a tight rein, keeping it from exploding from me like I've so long wanted to do."

She uncurled her fingers and lifted her hands, palm upward. Snowflakes danced in her open hands. Ice crystals formed on her nose and eyelashes. It was part of her, who she was, who she would always be. She had, at last, embraced her inner heritage, her magic. The ring of ice under her feet continued to spread outward, coating the floor, the walls. The temperature dropped to freezing.

Colder.

Colder still.

"I will no longer rein in my magic."

Freya gasped. Her mother called her name. Mia ignored them both.

Panicked fear filled his wide eyes as he watched her advance, one slow step after another. As though she were picking her way across a frozen pond. He wiggled in between Logan and Jaxson but they held firm. Until the ice reached them and started to crawl up their legs.

Rafe made a gesture to his friends who released the man and stepped away, out of her line of vision. Good. Then there would be no collateral damage.

"Princess Mia—" Armond began.

"No more speaking. *You did this.* You did all of this. You kidnapped me and my parents. You took over my kingdom. And for what? Power?" A shiver coursed through her but not from the cold, from the rage. The pure rage flowing through her with her magic. She shook her head. "You'll no longer hurt me, my parents, or my people."

Mia's eyes drifted closed and she sucked in a deep, deep breath. She blew it out, releasing the magic. Sleet and snow shot from her fingertips, pelting Armond with such force he cried out in agony. He had nowhere to go, nowhere to hide. She did not stop the onslaught as she released more and more of her magic. A bright flash of light exploded from her chest, ripping a startled scream from her throat as her back arched and she emptied every bit of her magic she'd been storing for years.

And then it was over. Drained, her shoulder throbbing in white-hot pain, she crumpled to the floor in a heap. She had forgotten about the gunshot until that moment, when she went down and crashed against the floor.

Rafe was at her side a second later, scooping her into his arms and cradling her against his chest. His warmth cascaded over her, pushing back the cold and chasing away the winter shadows once more. Balance. He was her balance. She had never realized it until that moment how much she needed him. How much she wanted him. How much she loved him.

"Is he dead?" Her voice was an icy whisper.

"Yes," Rafe said.

"Good. That's good." Her breath still plumed as she spoke. Her eyes fluttered closed and the darkness overtook her.

❧ 26 ❧

Rafe held the unconscious princess in his arms, still crouched on the floor. When she had expended her magic, her human form gave out. He launched toward her but not soon enough to catch her before she smacked the floor.

He glanced up at Logan and Jaxson, who remained in place, surrounded by a sheen of ice. The queen stood with her hands clenched into fists at her sides. Freya's cheeks were damp with tears as she stood next to the queen, quiet sobs making her small body shudder.

"Is my daughter...?" Her voice was timid in the quiet.

Rafe met her gaze. "She's unconscious but alive."

The woman blew out a breath as she closed her eyes in relief. "Thank the gods. That has only happened once before, when Mia was a child. The release of power nearly killed her and nearly killed her governess. It's why we refused to let her use it as she grew older."

Rafe looked from the queen to the sleeping princess in his arms. He understood now why she was not allowed to release the magic inside her, why she never learned to control it.

"We should have taught her better, I suppose. Show her how to control it but I feared she would do something she'd regret. Or that she would die from expending all that magic."

He had no words of comfort for the queen. There was nothing to be done about it now. Mia was drained of magic and energy, as evidenced by her boneless body in his arms. She killed Armond. Perhaps she may come to regret that someday but the man had pushed her to the breaking point. Rafe could not fault her for that.

"We need to get out of here, but the floor is still coated in ice," Logan said.

Holding her against him, Rafe extended one hand. His blue-white heat flickered out from his fingers with enough power to melt the ice and turn it to water. Cradling her, he got to his feet.

"Your majesty, we should leave," he said.

She gave a longing look to her dragon husband, placed a hand on the side of his elongated face. "I can't leave him."

"We have to—" Jaxson started, but Rafe shot him a warning look that had him snapping his mouth closed.

"What can we do?" Rafe asked.

"I must contact the embassy. There will be someone there to help," she said.

"We can't go there." Freya's voice was timid as she replied. The queen gave her a questioning look. "The embassy is overrun with Drakana."

The queen's face blanched. She looked from the girl to Rafe and his men. Jaxson gave a confirming nod.

"It's true, your majesty. I saw it myself. There's no one there to help you."

Anger flickered over her features before she got it under control and took a deep breath. "And the kingdom has been taken over by these...these...degenerates as well."

"Perhaps I can be of assistance," Logan offered. "I still have contacts in the Hidden Lands."

Her gaze slid to him and she looked him up and down. "And you are?"

"Chief Magistrate Logan Blake, your majesty. Chief of the Council of Five."

"Aragath, in the Amber region." She gave him a nod of understanding and it was clear she was very familiar with the Hidden Lands. "It's true then? The Hidden Lands still exist?"

"They do, your majesty," Logan said. "I'm impressed you know my region."

"Of course, I know it. We both did." She sniffed and gave him a queenly look down her nose. "The original cold-drakes were from the region north of that. We left generations ago because the land was dying and the climate changed. We didn't think we could survive, and so my ancestors migrated before it was too late."

"The land is cursed. A curse I intend to break. Herrick wants that, too. That's why he stole the tooth," Logan said.

"What does the tooth have to do with breaking the curse?"

"Combined with the Blood Stone and one other relic, the Ancient texts state there is a way to break it with a blood ritual."

"I see." She glanced back at her husband, a flicker of anguish over her face. "I would appreciate your assistance, if you will, Chief Magistrate."

"I will do anything I can for you, your majesty," Logan bowed his head in reverence.

She gave him a nod, then gave Rafe a sidelong glance. "As for you. You're my daughter's mate?"

Heat lashed through him as he kept his face as impassive as possible. He hadn't wanted her to find out this way. But, then, she would have been able to smell it on him, on Mia. He could only nod.

"I bid you to get back my husband's stolen tooth. Do whatever it takes, but make sure that man does not keep it," she said.

Rafe gave her another nod. "As you wish, your majesty. I know where to find it, I think."

Logan chuckled. "Do you think Herrick will fall for it?"

"If he's as desperate to recover the Blood Stone as I think he is, yes."

His friend couldn't hide the smile that spread over his face. "You know you sent him into a trap, right?"

"I do."

"What does that mean?" the queen asked.

"It means, your majesty, the man I sent Herrick to find is a vampire mafia boss who dislikes dragon-shifters. He won't be happy to see him," Rafe said.

"No, but luckily, I managed to save Dominic's life with the Blood Stone. Perhaps I can ask for a favor?" Logan lifted a brow in amused question.

Rafe gave his friend a broad grin. "Perhaps you can."

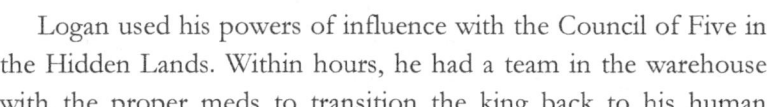

Logan used his powers of influence with the Council of Five in the Hidden Lands. Within hours, he had a team in the warehouse with the proper meds to transition the king back to his human form so he could be moved.

Then Logan made a phone call to Dominic of the *Signori Della Notte* and gave him a heads up that one Lord Herrick of the Hidden Lands and his Drakana would come knocking. The vamp chuckled and agreed to hold them until Rafe and Jaxson arrived.

It had pained him, but Rafe left a still unconscious Mia, as well as Freya and the queen, in Logan's care. He intended to take them back to his home on the Upper West Side to make sure they were safe. In the meantime, Logan was already working on getting the kingdom of Andonia back under control of the monarchs with the help of his Council of Five. He called in every favor he had to get people to Andonia to reclaim the territory.

But Rafe couldn't think about any of that. He had to focus on the task at hand and that was getting to Herrick and making him pay for what he did to the king. The tooth, if he still had it, would come second.

He and Jaxson needed a quick way to get out of Brooklyn and back to the Meatpacking District. At this time of day, the subway would be jammed. Traffic would be a nightmare. The only other way for him to get there with any sort of speed would be to shift.

"You all right?"

He and Jaxson jogged down the corner and came to a halt.

"Fine," Rafe said, his voice tight.

"What are you thinking?"

"That it's going to take too damn long to get back."

"We can't shift here." Jaxson's voice was low and strained as he gave a sidelong glance at the destroyed roof of the warehouse.

Rafe turned to him. "What do you suggest?"

As they looked at each other, Rafe could see his mind working. His mouth spread in a wide grin. "I have another idea."

Jaxson had this amazing way to open and close portals at will. That was why he was able to move around the city so quickly and efficiently. Rafe was in awe and a little envious. In all his long life, he hadn't been able to do that.

They made it back to the Meatpacking District in a flash, bypassing the rush hour traffic and stepping out onto Horatio Street. Rafe took off, his long strides eating up the pavement as he headed for the building where the vamps resided.

Jaxson stayed right with him as they made their way to the door. Niko, the vamp boss's right-hand man, buzzed them in and told them to take the private elevator to the third floor. The doors swished open to an apartment richly decorated with antique furnishings. It looked like something out of a vintage catalogue with the heavy draperies, the yards of velvet and silk and brocade, the silver, bronze and gold accents everywhere.

Niko and Dominic waited for them both in the posh living space. Both wore immaculate suits, both had skin the color of ashes.

"Welcome, dragon." Dominic's unnerving grin showed off fangs. "I assume you've come to retrieve this?" He waved to a cloth-covered lump on the low oak cocktail table.

Jaxson stepped to the table and flipped back the edge of the cloth. It revealed the blood-stained dragon tooth. Rafe gave him a nod and he covered it back up.

"By all means, take the offending thing. We have no use for it here," Domenic said.

Jaxson scooped it off the table, cradling it in the crook of his arm as though it were a newborn babe.

"Where's Lord Herrick?" Rafe asked.

Dominic steepled his long, slender fingers in front of him. He tapped the tips of his pointed nails together. "You will be disappointed to know the dragon got away."

Anger pulsed through him but he kept his temper in check. There was no reason to piss off the head of the most powerful vampire mafia. "How?"

"He was quite the coward, wasn't he, Niko?" His second nodded. "He and his Drakana, as you call them, showed up intending to invade my home. I did not take kindly to that."

Jaxson's throat bobbed as he swallowed hard. Rafe stilled and refrained from glancing around the room. The exterior of the building showed no signs there had been an altercation.

"Where is he?" Rafe's tone was cautious.

"When he realized who he was dealing with, he left his men and the tooth and disappeared." Dominic paused, a smile tugging at the corner of his mouth. "Like the coward he is."

Rafe wasn't sure if he wanted to know what Dominic had done to his men. He remained silent, trying to decide what to say next.

"Where are his men then?" Jaxson asked.

Dominic chuckled. "I'm glad you asked. Since your friend, Logan, took out my synthetic blood plant, it has caused us a hardship. We've had difficulty staying fed."

He paused. Rafe's head pounded with a sudden throb of anxiety. He and Jaxson exchanged a glance.

"And what does that mean?" Rafe asked.

Niko said, a smile in his voice, "If you see this Lord Herrick, dragon, tell him *Signori Della Notte* thanks him for the generous donation of blood slaves."

❧ 27 ❧

There was nothing else to be done. As they exited the building, Jaxson handed Rafe the tooth.

"What are you going to do?" he asked.

Rafe knew what he meant, knew this was a defining moment for him. He could hand over the tooth to Logan and get his release from exile. Or he could return the tooth to the queen as he'd promised. His mouth was dry and it was hard to swallow.

Things had drastically changed in that dilapidated warehouse in Brooklyn. He had been prepared to defend Mia's life with his own. Had intended to sacrifice himself for her if he had to, if it meant keeping Herrick away from her, stopping him from forcing her to shift.

He had never expected it to be the king, never expected their lives to be in such peril. Part of him blamed himself for not foreseeing what could have happened with her parents. He thought Armond and Herrick only wanted to use them to get to Mia, not use them to steal the tooth.

He glanced down at the covered tooth in his hands.

"I'll think of something," Rafe said. Though he wasn't sure what that something was.

"I don't envy you the decision you have to make." Jaxson clapped him on the shoulder. "Good luck."

"Thanks."

They parted ways on Horatio Street. Jaxson returned to wherever his haunt was, while Rafe knew he had to face Logan, Bree, Mia and the queen. He wished he could talk to Mia first, alone. But he knew the second he stepped foot in Logan's Upper West Side apartment, he would demand the tooth.

It *had* been their bargain from the start. But things had changed. He had never expected to have feelings for or mate with Mia.

His mind spun as he grabbed a cab and headed to W 57th Street. When he arrived, he couldn't ignore the jangle of nerves as he stepped into the lobby of the posh, ultra-modern glass and steel building. A swift ride up the elevator and then he was at their door on the twentieth floor.

He took a deep breath and knocked. Minutes later, the door whisked open. A pregnant and glowing Bree stood on the other side. She smiled so bright her green eyes twinkled. She hugged him before he could step foot in the door.

"Nice to see you, too, Bree," he muttered, patting her on the back.

"Your princess is lovely," she whispered. Still beaming, she stepped back and waved him inside.

The apartment was light and bright with a full wall of windows and a glass door leading onto the terrace. A thick, colorful rug covered the hardwood floors and the furniture was contemporary in light colors. The elongated living room gave way to the dining room where an oversized wood table with chunky legs was adorned with a crocheted table runner, surrounded by matching chairs.

The Queen of Andonia was nowhere in sight. Neither was the princess or Freya.

"She's resting. Her mother and Freya are with her," Bree said, as though reading his mind.

Logan exited one of the bedrooms and halted in the middle of the living room, Bree between them. He peered at Rafe with wide eyes, then glanced at the cradle in his arms.

"You got it." It wasn't a question.

Rafe only nodded.

"And Herrick?" he asked.

"Wasn't there," Rafe said.

"I see."

"He got away," Rafe added. "I don't know where he went."

"And his Drakana?"

Rafe swallowed hard. "Dominic is using them as blood slaves."

"Oh, dear," Bree breathed.

There was a beat of silence before Logan snickered. "Serves them all right."

"You don't intend to do anything about it?" Rafe asked.

"Why should I?" Logan walked into the small kitchen and removed two highball glasses from the cabinet. "Dominic and I have agreed to stay out of each other's way."

"Even if it means our own kind are his blood slaves?" Rafe's hands tightened on the tooth he still held.

"Drakana are not *our* kind, Rafe. They are traitors to our bloodlines. You know that as well as I do."

Rafe knew. He didn't like it, but he knew. Dragon blood went through their veins, but long ago, they started hunting the shifters and killing them.

"Any word about Andonia?" He didn't want to argue with Logan about the Drakana or the vampires.

"I called in as many favors as I could. I'm waiting to hear." Logan splashed amber liquid into each glass. "Armond had several of his men working inside the palace. The story leaked about the missing royal family to the Associated Press. It should have hit the wires over there already. Since the people are loyal to the reigning family, they will not take kindly to a usurper of the throne. They will do what it takes to get the invaders out and quickly."

Logan handed him a glass. Rafe juggled the tooth, tucking it into his elbow and taking the drink. He downed it in one gulp. He friend sipped his drink, eying the tooth.

"May I see it?"

Rafe nodded, extending it to him. Bree moved toward the low sofa and eased her body down keeping a watchful eye on both of them. Like a mother hen. She must have known, or sensed, this discussion about the tooth was coming.

Logan put his glass down and reached for the tooth, taking it from Rafe as though it were a fragile thing. He flipped the cloth aside and stared down at the white enamel, cracked and blood-stained.

Before Logan could say anything, Rafe heard himself saying, "You can't have it."

Bree sucked in a low breath through her nose. Tension suddenly filled the air. Logan didn't move a muscle as he lifted his gaze from the tooth to Rafe's.

"You know I need this to complete the ritual." Logan's voice was quiet.

"I know what you need it for and I said you can't have it. It doesn't belong to you. It belongs to the Queen of Andonia."

Logan lifted his head and stared at him, his tawny eyes sparking. Rafe could see the torrent of irritation and didn't care. He decided, at that moment, he didn't give a *fuck* Logan needed the tooth to break the curse on the Hidden Lands.

"This tooth is one of the missing pieces. I thought you understood that."

"I understood just fine," Rafe retorted.

"That's not what we agreed to. I agreed to release you from exile if you brought me the cold-drake tooth."

"No. You agreed to release me from exile if I brought you *Mia's* cold-drake tooth. That isn't Mia's. It's the king's and you can't have it." Rafe pointed at it.

Logan clenched his jaw and shoved it back into Rafe's hands. "You broke the agreement."

"I don't care. It doesn't matter."

As he said it, a pang of guilt, sorrow, longing, and disgust warred within him. Since Logan asked him to do this, promising him he'd release him, Rafe had looked forward to returning to the Hidden Lands. To stepping foot once again onto his homeland soil. A homeland he hadn't seen in a very long time.

But, deep down, he knew this was the right thing to do. He knew returning the king's tooth to the queen, to Mia, was what he *should* do. Not hand it over to Logan for some ritual that may not break the curse.

And anyway, they were still missing a dragon scale from a fire-drake. Who the hell knew where they could get one of those?

"If it doesn't matter, then you can stay exiled."

Logan's heated words seared through him like a hot knife through butter.

"Fine," he said through tight lips.

Bree witnessed the whole thing, her green eyes wide and rimmed in tears. Rafe could see them wobbling at the edges of her lashes, threatening to fall. He didn't wait for any other replies as he turned on his heel and stalked to the second bedroom, where, he guessed, the queen and the princess were.

"Rafe—"

"Let him go, Logan." Bree's calm voice stopped him from coming after him.

He made a mental note to thank her later for that. If there ever was a later.

Rafe turned the knob and pushed open the door, pausing in the doorway when he saw Mia's still unconscious form on the bed. Someone had bandaged her shoulder and tucked her underneath the crisp sheets. Her skin color had returned to the normal iridescence he had come to love. Her silver hair was splayed about her head in what looked like a halo. Pale color tinged high in her cheekbones, indicating she was slowly recovering. And yet she slept on.

The queen sat in a small club chair, flipping through a magazine to pass the time. Freya perched on the end of the bed. When they saw him in the doorway, they jumped to their feet.

"You found it." The queen breathed the words on a sigh of relief. "Thank the gods."

"I'll give you some privacy." Freya slipped out the door and closed it behind her.

The queen crossed the room to him as he extended the tooth to her. She took it, unwrapping it and gazing down at it. She ran loving fingers over it.

"I know it must seem silly to be so desperate to have it back."

The back of his throat clotted at her wistful tone. "Not at all, your majesty."

"But I know what sort of power this has." She lifted her eyes to his. "Do you?"

Rafe swallowed hard. "Only a little. That it infuses power."

"Yes," she nodded. "I read the ancient lore once in an old dusty book in our palace library. That the tooth of a dragon—a cold-drake—could be ground down to dust and used with other dragon relics or items. But the tooth had to be from a powerful cold-drake. One that could create a snowstorm so strong, it could plunge the land into another ice age." A small smile graced her lips as she glanced to the still sleeping princess. "Mia has such power," she paused, took a deep breath, "so, too, did her father. It was why he forbid Mia from using her magic."

She sighed. "Thank you for returning it."

"You're welcome."

"Would you like to sit with her for a while?" She motioned to Mia.

Rafe considered it. He wanted to. He really did. But he couldn't stay here with Logan's death glares pinning him. He had to leave, to get back to his own place and see what destruction had befallen it after they'd fled for the cabin.

"I can't." He tried not to let his voice crack, but was unsuccessful. He turned to the door, grabbed the knob.

"You and your friend argued," she said, her words stopping him. "I heard you."

"Yes." He didn't turn around as he said it and kept his hand tight around the knob.

"About the tooth?" she asked.

This time he looked at her over his shoulder. "Yes."

He whisked open the door and was gone.

∽ 28 ∾

Mia awoke in a strange bed with a raging headache, a bone-chilling body ache, and her mouth as dry as sand. She pried her eyes open and found her mother standing over her, a smile of relief on her haggard face. There were purple shadows under her eyes. She looked like she hadn't slept in days.

"Nice to see you awake," her mother said, still smiling. "How do you feel?"

Her only response was a croak, her throat scratchy from nonuse. Her mother reached for a glass of water and held it out to her.

"Here. Drink."

Mia took it and drank, draining the glass of the cool liquid. It slid down her throat, soothing it. She handed her mother the empty glass.

She shivered, gooseflesh rising on her arms. For the first time in her entire life, she was cold. It was a new experience for her and she wasn't quite sure what to make of it. She pulled the covers back up to her chin and burrowed deeper into the thick blankets. Her shoulder throbbed from where Armond had shot her, the bandage tight on her skin underneath the oversized T-shirt.

"How long?" she rasped.

"Four days."

Her eyes flew wide as she looked up at her mother. "Four?"

The queen nodded.

"Freya?" Mia asked

"She's fine. She's in the other room." She perched on the edge of the bed. The mattress sighed with her slight weight. "You gave us quite a fright, you know. So much so, Logan sent for one of his healers. After we explained what happened, he said your recovery time would vary but you *would* recover and that's all that mattered to me."

She gave Mia a faint smile.

Mia glanced around the modern room with the white-washed walls, the wall of windows covered with gauzy curtains. Sunlight peeked through, casting an elongated shadow on the hardwood floors and the shiny white dresser with silver knobs.

She didn't know this place. It wasn't Rafe's apartment, so, where was she? The last thing she remembered she had emptied the well of her magic right into Armond and fainted. She vaguely recalled asking Rafe—where was he? —if Armond was dead.

"What happened?" Her voice still sounded like sandpaper.

"What do you remember?" Her mother's cool hand landed on her forehead, then pressed against each cheek. "Your body temperature isn't as cold as it was before. That's a good sign."

"I remember." She licked her dry, cracked lips. "I remember Armond and the warehouse. And Papa." She gasped, her eyes suddenly filling with tears. "Papa."

"You emptied your magic, dear, and killed Armond. He can never hurt you or us again."

Mia squeezed her eyes shut as the wave of emotion went through her. She couldn't decide what to feel knowing she was the one responsible for his death. He had caused her so much pain and anguish, didn't he deserve to die? Didn't he deserve to meet his end with her magic?

"That's why you slept for four days," her mother continued. "The healer said you'd expended all your energy and would need the rest to recuperate. I'm glad you came to, though. I was starting to worry."

That worry was etched all over her face and Mia hated she'd been the one who put it there. Despite that, she was glad Armond was dead.

"Where's Rafe?" she asked.

Her mother's smile faltered. "Not here."

Mia met her mother's gaze, those eyes like her own peering back with a hint of sadness. "Where is he?"

The queen swallowed, her throat bobbling. "We haven't seen him since the first day."

Mia's stomach clenched as she stared at her mother, trying to decide what, exactly, that meant. She didn't know who "we" was and she wasn't sure what "the first day" meant either. She wanted to ask more questions, so many more questions, but she was tired. Too tired. It was an effort to talk, to keep her eyes open at all.

The door opened and a blonde woman poked her head inside. When she saw Mia was awake, a bright smile lit her brilliant green eyes. She moved into the room. Mia could see the swell of her pregnant belly.

"She's awake!" the woman exclaimed.

"Just now, yes." Her mother got to her feet. "Mia, this is Bree, she's the Chief Magistrate's wife."

Mia blinked her confusion. She had no idea who Bree was or this Chief Magistrate.

"He prefers you call him Logan, your majesty," Bree said with a smile. Then she turned that brilliance on Mia. "I'm glad to see you're awake, princess. We've been worried about you."

As she spoke, a tall man entered the room. Silver accented the temples of his black hair. He carried a red and white medical bag as he moved into the room and looked her over.

"Ah, good. She's up and around at last," the man said.

"This is Ivan. He's the healer that's been taking care of you," Bree said.

"It's time to check that bandage."

Her mother stepped aside as Ivan moved to the edge of the bed. He pulled down a corner of the blankets. He gave her a pointed look, his lips thinning. She read his face and knew what he wanted, so she pulled aside the neck of the oversized shirt, letting it drape down her shoulder.

He peeled up the corner of the bandage enough to see underneath it, then gave it a swift yank. She yelped from the momentary sting.

"Good as new," he said, smiling. He crumpled the bandage in his hand.

Mia glanced down to see a pink scar where she'd been shot and nothing more.

"It took longer than normal for you to heal since you were so drained," Ivan said. He looked up at her mother. "Now that she's awake, she'll make a full recovery in no time."

"That's wonderful news," Bree beamed.

"You'll no longer need my services," the healer said. "I'll be on my way."

He headed for the door and Bree followed him, closing it softly behind her. That left Mia alone with her mother once again. She pushed to a sitting position in the bed, blowing out a breath. Even that small effort made her tired. Her mother was there, helping prop her up on the pillows. As Mia got situated, she saw it. The dragon tooth shrouded in a cloth on top of the dresser.

Something went cold and still inside her as she looked at it and bit her lip to keep from crying. Her mother followed her gaze, walked over to it and uncovered it. Mia stared at the blood-stained tooth, her heart in her throat.

"You got it back." Her voice was nothing more than an icy whisper.

"Rafe got it back." Her mother placed the cover back over it. "Quite the honorable man to return it to me when he could have given it to Logan. I admire that."

Mia still stared at it, though. "Where is Papa?"

She perched on the side of the bed once more, reaching for Mia's hand and squeezing it. "He has been returned to his human form, with the help of Logan's healers. His body is being prepared for burial and will return with us to Andonia."

"And the tooth? What of it?"

The queen took a deep breath as she searched for the right

words. "That is something I wish to talk to you about, Mia. We have a decision to make." She dragged her lower lip through her teeth.

"About?"

"The tooth. You and your father are of the Gildhara bloodline. You have powerful cold-drake magic that flows through you. Just as he did. The men who took his tooth knew that, too." She paused, swallowed hard. "I have talked with Logan much over these last few days about the Hidden Lands."

The Hidden Lands. The realm that was cursed. Rafe had told her stories of the realm lost to him. She recalled him speaking about Ienir the Great and the Dragon's Breath hiding the Whispering Mountains from all other realms.

"We should have told you of your heritage long ago. But we...I...didn't have the courage. I was afraid I would lose you." Her mother squeezed her hand again, as if in apology. "They would have taken your tooth had it not been your father's."

"Why do they want it?" Her voice was scratchy, the words difficult to say.

"Because it is part of a ritual that can break the curse in the Hidden Lands." Another pause, as though she were struggling to find the right words.

Mia huffed out a breath. "What is it you wish to say, Mama?"

"If the curse is broken, we can return to our homeland."

It wasn't her homeland, was it? Andonia was. It was the only home she had ever known. Not the Hidden Lands.

But she thought about the stories Rafe told her, how those stories had moved her, sparked something deep inside her that made her want to see that place she had never heard of until then.

She thought of Rafe and wondered if he had been released from exile. If he had, would he be there?

She hadn't heard his mind. She reached out through the mating bond to see if she could find him. She sensed him there, somewhere far off. He was nothing more than a flicker.

"What are you saying, Mama? You wish to give the tooth to

Logan?"

Her gaze turned to her mother's, meeting it and holding it. She could see the uncertainty there, could sense the decision she wanted to make but was fearful of Mia's response. Finally, her mother took in a deep breath and expelled it through her nose.

"With the death of your father, you are queen. You will ascend the throne and you will rule. You should know, though, there were many nights your father looked to the heavens and wished he could go back to the Hidden Lands. I believe if he were to choose what to do with the tooth, he would give it to Logan to help break the curse." She rose from the bed. "I will let you decide, though."

Her mother left her alone in the room. Mia sagged back into the pillows and stared at the covered tooth on the dresser. She had no idea what she was going to do. She closed her eyes and drifted to sleep.

Mia wasn't sure how long she was out. When she awoke, her neck and back were stiff from sleeping in an awkward position. She pushed the blankets off and swung her legs to the side of the bed, sitting there for a moment while she gathered the energy to stand.

As she paused, she glanced over at the shrouded tooth. If there was a chance Rafe had been released from exile, if Logan could break the curse on the Hidden Lands...

Her mouth still dry, she swallowed hard. Then shoved out of bed and stood. The oversized shirt fell to her knees. Her legs and feet were bare. She wasn't sure if she had the energy to walk after being in bed for so long, but she gave it a try. One tentative step, then another, and she made it to the dresser.

She uncovered the tooth, stared down at it, ran her fingers over the cold enamel. Sucking in a breath, she covered it back up and scooped it off the dresser. Decision made, she turned toward the door.

~ 29 ~

Mia, Freya and her mother spent another week in the Blake's apartment before they were ready to leave. Logan, his men, and the Andonia armed forces liberated the country along with the obsidian blade forges. Andonia forces regained control of the city, while the newswires had gone crazy with the headlines of the hostage take-over, the formerly missing royal family, the now-dead king. Mia was not looking forward to restoring order or the coronation or even ruling the country alone.

"Thank you for everything," her mother was saying to Bree as they stood on the threshold of the doorway to their apartment.

A car waited for them downstairs to take them to the airport. Despite all her inquiries, no one could tell her where Rafe had gone. According to Bree, he and Logan had a falling out over everything that had happened while Mia was unconscious and trying to recover from her magic dump.

From the details she could gather, it seemed as though Rafe had not been released from exile, which meant he must still be in the city. She had to find him. She had to see him one last time before the got on that plane. She could not leave with things left unsaid between them. Freya and Bree said their goodbyes.

"Please let us know if we can help you with anything else," Bree said. She hugged the queen, who patted her rounded belly.

"I should like to know when your son is born," the queen said.

"I'll be sure to send you a birth announcement." Bree smiled a brilliant smile.

Her mother reached around the woman to shake Logan's hand.

"And good luck to you, Logan. I do hope everything works out for you."

"As do I, your majesty."

"Mia, it's been a pleasure." Bree reached for her, hugging her.

But all Mia could think about was getting to Rafe, finding him. She had decided last night she was going to ask him to return to Andonia with her. She couldn't bear the thought of leaving him behind. She needed him, even if she had realized it far too late. It went beyond their mating. With his absence, it was as though she had a gaping hole in her heart. Only he could fill it.

"Thank you for all you did for me and my family," Mia said, sounding stiffer than she had intended. She gave Logan a nod of thanks and goodbye.

He reached for her hand, shook it, holding it a moment. "Thank you, your majesty, for trusting me with your father's dragon tooth."

"Good luck breaking the curse," was all she could think to say.

She, her mother and Freya left the apartment and headed downstairs to the waiting car. This time, it would not be like when they arrived in the city. They would all ride in the car with the bullet-proof glass together.

Mia was last to the car and she paused to talk to the driver. She handed him a slip of paper. "Can you stop at this address in Times Square before going to the airport?"

He unfolded it, then gave her a questioning look.

"Well, can you?" she demanded.

He gave a nod. Mia got in the backseat and he closed the door after her. She made no attempt at polite conversation with her mother or Freya. Silence stretched between them as the car made its way through the traffic toward Midtown. When they pulled up to the building, her mother folded her arms and gave her a pointed look.

"Why are we stopping here?" her mother wanted to know.

"Wait here," Mia said and got out of the car before she could reply.

She bounded through the front of the building and into the lobby, heading for the bank of elevators. Her heart was in her throat, her nerves shot as she punched the button and the doors closed.

She talked to Bree about Rafe. It had taken some doing, but she at last coerced Bree to give her his address. It had cut her deep he hadn't come back to see her, to talk to her. But Bree explained the rift between him and Logan was large and it would take some doing for them to repair it. Logan had refused to release him from exile because he hadn't held up his end of the bargain. Rafe refused to turn over the dragon's tooth and instead had given it to the queen.

It was a mess.

Not one that Mia could fix between him and Logan but she could at least see Rafe one last time. She didn't know if he'd agree to come with her. She hoped so, since their mating bond had been so strong between them. She could feel the warm ember glow even now pulsing there, deep down in the place where her winter shadows lived.

Her mother knew they were mated and gave her hell about it when they were preparing for their return trip. She had ignored the endless questions and the disapproval from her for picking someone not of royal blood. Mia didn't care. She was mated to Rafe—for life—and she would always cherish that, whether or not they were together.

How do you intend to carry on the royal bloodline, Mia? Her mother had asked.

I'm sure Rafe would be willing to procreate with me, Mama.

Her mother didn't like that response and scowled at her.

Nowhere is it written I have to marry someone of royal blood. To press her point, she added, *Mother.*

And again, her mother scowled but let the topic die. Mia knew it wasn't the last she would hear about it. It was only the beginning.

The elevator dinged and the doors whooshed open. She took a deep breath and stepped out. The walk down the hall to his door was the longest of her life. At his apartment, she knocked and waited.

Holding her breath.

Several agonizing moments later, the door opened and there he was. Standing on the other side of the door looking as though he hadn't shaved in days. His cheeks and chin sported the stubbled growth. His face looked haggard as though he hadn't slept in days. But when he saw her standing there, a light came into his silvery eyes.

"Mia. What are you doing here?"

She blew out that breath. "Can I come in?"

He stepped aside. She breezed into the apartment and paused in the middle of the living area. The blinds were open to the floor-to-ceiling windows letting the morning light come in. It left slashes of sunlight on the contemporary furnishings. Mia knew it was the last time she would see this place.

Behind her, he shut the door and didn't move. She could see his reflection in the windows. He stood ramrod straight, peering at her. She couldn't read the expression on his face and turned at last to face him.

"I only have a few moments. My mother and Freya are waiting in a car downstairs."

She thought she saw his shoulders sag. "You're returning to Andonia."

It wasn't a question but she answered as though it were. "Yes. Our plane leaves shortly. We are returning with my father. He will lay in state for a short period before the funeral."

He closed the gap between them with slow steps. "Safe travels, princess."

"Queen, actually. With the death of my father, I am queen."

Surprise flickered across his face as it drained of color.

"The royal line went to me upon his death. I am to be officially crowned after my country mourns properly for its king." She met his gaze, those silvery eyes that she had come to love.

"You have my condolences and my congratulations, your

majesty."

Mia waved it away. "I didn't come here for that."

"Why are you here?"

She took a deep breath. There was no other way to say it than to just say it. "I've come to ask if you would return with me to Andonia."

Rafe stared at her. He swallowed hard, his throat bobbing. "Why?"

"I thought it obvious."

"You wish me to be the queen's consort? I'm not of royal blood. I can't rule as king," he said.

"My father gave my mother title of queen. I could give you—"

"No."

Her throat tightened as she snapped her mouth closed, her ire rising. "Then as the queen's consort and mate."

He shook his head. "You don't want me to do that."

A sudden hot fear pulsed through her. He was turning her down? "I wouldn't have asked if I didn't want that. We are mated—"

"Mated, yes. But I'm still in exile. I would bring disgrace and dishonor to your family. I can't go with you."

She hated tears stung the backs of her eyes. "Your exile doesn't matter to me. I never cared about that."

"But I do," he said quietly. "I have always cared about that." He reached for her then, placed his warm hands around her waist and pulled her to him. "Mated for life, yes, but I can't be who you want me to be."

"I want you to be with me always. Isn't that enough?"

There was more she wanted to say, to tell him, but the words stuck in her throat.

He gave her a small smile and brushed the pad of his thumb across her cheek, catching the one tear that had slipped from her eye.

"Be safe."

He kissed her, a soft slow kiss, and released her. He turned to the door and opened it.

He was letting her go and she hated him for it. Hated him for not saying yes. It took several minutes for her to force her feet to move. As she walked to the door, she halted, looked at him once last time.

"If you asked me, I would give up my crown. I would stay."

"I can't ask you to do that." He brushed his hand over her cheek. "You love your people too much to leave. I think we both know that."

Her chest tightened, her gut burning with the sorrow and pain of walking away from him. But she did. She walked out the door, out of the apartment building and got back in the car.

She never looked back.

❧ 30 ❧

Spring came, releasing winter's brutal hold on the city. It was a welcome reprieve.

Since Mia left months ago, Rafe spent most of his nights at Bar Inferno watching the crowds and occasionally playing bouncer when things got out of hand. It was the only way he could keep thoughts of her out of his head. He had been an idiot for turning her down. He should have packed his bags and gone with her to Andonia. Instead, he chose to remain in New York City.

In exile. Alone.

He was pathetic.

The pulse of their mating bond was an ever-present reminder of her. Her winter shadows lingered deep inside. Every now and then, his inner beast would emit a baleful moan. He knew she experienced something similar and hated he had done that to her.

News of the king's death had reached the masses. He watched every report and read every online article he could to keep up with what was happening there. It had been easy, too, since there was such a fascination with the royals. He watched the news coverage of the king's funeral and Mia's official coronation as queen.

She had looked radiant in a gown of gold satin and lace as she was crowned. Even in the photos, he could see her luminescent skin glowing. But there was something sad in those purple eyes.

It was a particularly brilliant spring day when he decided to pick up lunch at the bar. He'd called in his order ahead and walked the few blocks from his apartment. When he arrived, Meg was behind the bar talking to Bree who perched on one of the stools bouncing a drooling baby Elijah on one knee. The baby had black fuzzy hair and brilliant emerald eyes and held a baby rattle in his pudgy little hand.

He scanned the bar for Logan but didn't find him. It had been months since he'd seen him despite Bree's efforts to get the two to talk to each other.

"Hey, Rafe." Meg poured a ginger ale for Bree and slid it to her. "Your order isn't ready it. Want anything while you wait?"

"I'm good, thanks."

Bree gave him a sidelong glance. "You're looking haggard."

He ran a hand over his stubbled chin. He hadn't bothered to shave in days. He bent to kiss her cheek. "And you're looking radiant, as usual." The baby gurgled at him, holding out the drool covered rattle.

"You're just saying that," she teased. "There's something I want to show you." She slid off the stool and propped the baby on her hip. She gave him a nod to follow her.

Rafe didn't argue. He followed her past the bar and stairs to the private office that was once her father. She now occupied it when she was working. She pushed open the door and led him inside.

Logan sat at the desk. When they entered, he shot to his feet.

"What's he doing here?"

"Here's how this is going to work." Bree ignored him and gave them both the hairy eyeball. "You two are going to talk. Logan, I believe you have something to give Rafe." They both started to protest but she held up a hand. "I don't want to hear any excuses. I'm going to leave the room. There better not be any fists flying. I expect you both to kiss and make up. You have ten minutes."

Silence as they stared at each other, then Bree. She scowled at both of them.

"I mean it." Her voice was sharp as a tack and sounded like a stern mother.

She stepped through the door and closed it with a snap behind her, sealing them both inside. Rafe waited for Logan to speak first. He sank to the chair behind the desk and motioned for Rafe to sit across from him.

Fine. He'd sit, but under duress.

"You have something for me?" Rafe skipped the pleasantries.

Logan opened the top drawer on the desk and pulled out a velvet drawstring bag. He laid it on the desk between them.

"What's that?" Rafe asked.

"It's the stolen Andonia royal gemstones." Logan's tone was flat. "I thought you'd like to return them to the queen."

Rafe stared blankly at him. What the hell was he talking about? "The queen is in Andonia."

"Yes, she is." He nodded agreement.

He barked a laugh. "I'm not going to Andonia."

"Yes, you are." Logan swallowed hard, his throat bobbing. "Because you're in love with the queen of Andonia. And you're going to return those gemstones. I expect you to come back never."

Rafe blinked, his mind blank. He had no words, no sharp retort. No nothing.

"She's your mate. I can only imagine the pain you both experience by being separated," Logan added. "Besides, Meg is tired of seeing your forlorn face in here all the time."

"I have responsibilities here."

"Bullshit," Logan said. "Go to her, Rafe."

He stared at the velvet pouch, then met his friend's gaze. "She doesn't deserve me."

"She does. Because you're a knight. A good, decent, noble man. I've seen the news. I know she's been pining for you since her return to her country. I've also been in contact with her mother. She begged me to talk to you, to ask you to come to Andonia. Now you have a reason." He nodded to the pouch.

Rafe stared at the pouch of stones. "How did you get them? I thought that investigator had them."

"I called Shi'Ann Jones and talked to her. She agreed to let me have them back on the condition you would personally deliver them." He opened the desk drawer again and pulled out an envelope, then slid it across the desk to him. "That's a one-way ticket to Andonia. Don't come back."

Rafe stared at the envelope, his heart beating a wicked tattoo.

"Return the stones, Rafe, with my apologies I have to keep the Blood Stone a little while longer. I'll return it once the curse is broken. Then you can bring your mate to the Hidden Lands so she can see what she helped save, gods willing."

His mouth went dry as his gaze flickered back up to Logan. "I don't understand."

Logan heaved a sigh. "I'm telling you I'm releasing you from exile. Bree told me I was being an ass. She also pointed out I was wrong asking you to bring me the tooth from the princess in the first place. As much as I hate to admit it, my lovely wife is right."

"You never told her what you were up to, did you?"

He didn't hide the shame on his face. "No, I didn't. When the time is right for you to return to the Hidden Lands, a portal will be ready for you both."

Emotion clotted his throat as he looked at his friend.

"Go. Your queen is waiting for you." Logan reached across the desk and shoved the envelope and the velvet pouch toward him.

Taking a deep breath, Rafe snatched up the pouch and the envelope.

He was going to Andonia.

✺ Epilogue ✺

It was a warm spring night and the Queen of Andonia's feet throbbed from much dancing and reveling and merrymaking. She collapsed in a most un-queenly like fashion in a chair of the high table and watched as the revelers twirled and danced and celebrated, smiles on every flushed face. On one side of the banquet hall, the buffet tables were still set up. Several people mingled there with plates and drinks in their hands. The queen mother had long since retired but Mia wasn't ready to call it a night. Her assistant, Freya, danced with a tall, broad-shouldered gentleman. She looked gorgeous in a satin gown of deep blue. She looked even more gorgeous when she blushed in his arms while they danced. It made Mia smile.

When she returned to Andonia and reclaimed the country, when she buried her father and watched her mother sob, when she was crowned queen, she had decided her first order of business was to celebrate the birth of spring with a flower festival. The very one she'd created talking to Rafe. And so, the first annual Flower Festival of Andonia was born.

Mia had never quite released the idea when she came up with it that night in the mountains. The more she thought about it, the more she wanted it to happen. She issued a royal decree the first week of spring every year would be a week-long celebration of new life in her country and everyone who could make it to the capital was invited to the festivities. There were vendors in the streets selling their wares that was everything flower-related, food vendors, maypoles, girls with flower wreaths in their hair, ending with a masquerade ball—flower themed, of course—on the seventh night of the celebration.

She had loved every second of it. She and her mother made a point to visit every food vendor and every florist in the city with good cheer. The people loved her for it. They lined the streets cheering, waving flags and hoping the newly crowned queen would stop for a picture or a handshake. And she did—quite a bit, much to the dismay of her new security detail.

When she returned to Andonia, she began interviewing for a new head of security. Linus was her personal bodyguard and shadow and followed her everywhere. He was an older gent with salt-and-pepper hair and had been in the military and served in the Secret Service for a few years before going into the private sector. He had come highly recommended and qualified.

And his family had migrated from the Hidden Lands to the human realm six centuries prior. She had liked him on the spot. He had proven to be an asset, one that she came to depend upon. Knowing he was always there, unobtrusive but in the background gave her peace of mind.

He stood behind her chair now. Though he tended to blend into the shadows, she knew he was there.

"Have you eaten, Linus?" She didn't turn to look at him.

"Yes, your majesty."

"Had a drink?" she queried.

"No, your majesty."

"Then go and bring me back some champagne," she said with a smile.

"Yes, your majesty."

He wasn't a talkative sort, nor did he once look at her legs. She liked that about him. She heard his footsteps fade from behind her and knew he had gone to fetch her a flute of champagne. But as she sat there at the high table watching the dancing, happy crowd, she saw a man enter the grand ballroom on the other side.

Tall, broad-shouldered, wearing a tux with a pink poppy in the lapel and a gold mask covering his face, revealing only those silvery eyes.

Every bone in her body turned to ice as she gaped at him. He stood there, alone, scanning the crowd looking for someone.

Looking for her.

She hadn't thought of him in weeks. In fact, she hadn't felt the mating bond as strong over the course of the week-long celebration, mostly because she had ignored it and threw herself into her duties and events.

Now, with him standing across the crowded ballroom, that mating bond flared bright deep inside her. Her inner dragon took notice, too, and banged against her skull. She watched him scan the room and then his gaze landed on her.

Time froze. Her heart quickened. Her breath caught. The temperature plummeted. Snowflakes danced around her head.

She thought she would never see him again and yet, there he was. Standing at the edge of the ballroom, looking at her.

Linus returned with a flute of chilled champagne. He held it in front of her. She snatched it, downed it in one gulp, and handed him back the empty glass as she got to her feet. She reined in her magic. Containing it with Rafe so close was easier than it had been in months.

"Stay here," she ordered.

Her bodyguard didn't protest as she stepped into the dancing fray and made her way across the dancefloor, the voluminous skirts of her crimson gown swishing as she walked on slippered feet to the man who had both captured and destroyed her heart.

Rafe kept his eyes on her as she made her way to him, paused in front of him. He bowed low.

"Your majesty."

"Dance with me," she said.

He reached for her, took her in his arms and swept her onto the dancefloor into a waltz that led them from one side to the other. They danced in silence, each gazing at the other. She had forgotten how damn handsome he was. And clean-shaven. He'd shaved off all that stubble. And he smelled good, too, with a clean, spicy scent that made all her body parts stand up and take notice. With him so near, those winter shadows deep inside her were gone in a puff of smoke.

"What are you doing here?" she asked at last.

"Isn't that obvious?" Rafe replied.

"No," she said flatly. She needed an explanation, damn it.

"I came to see you."

She peered up at him through her lashes. "What took you so long?"

His hand tightened on her waist. There was another unspoken question on her lips, one she didn't dare ask. Was his arrival here because Logan had released him from exile?

"I have something that belongs to your family."

He deftly stepped around the question. Her heart skipped a beat. She had completely forgotten about the reason why she wanted to go to New York City in the first place—the stolen gemstones.

"And what is that?" Her voice was a raspy whisper.

"Perhaps we could go someplace less public so I can show you," he suggested.

The dance ended and they halted. Without saying anything, she took him by the hand and led him from the ballroom to French doors on the other side. She pushed one open and exited onto the veranda. The spring air was fragrant with the blooms from the royal gardens below. Moonlight splashed in a blue-white veil across the stone railing, illuminating in a pale glow that reminded her much of the night they spent in the mountains, walking and talking. She gripped the cool railing as she gazed out over the darkened topiaries of the garden.

"How did you get here?" she asked.

"In a plane." He slipped off the mask, dropping it on the handrail.

She shot him a heated glance. "That's not what I meant."

He chuckled. "I know what you meant."

He reached into the breast pocket of his tux jacket and brought out a small velvet pouch. One she recognized immediately. One that had a gold drawstring and the family crest embroidered on it. Before she could take it from him, Linus burst from the doors onto the veranda, his eyes wide.

"Majesty?" he inquired in a polite tone.

"I'm quite safe, Linus," she said. "This is Rafe. The one I told you about."

Her bodyguard looked Rafe up and down. "Are you sure?"

"Yes," she said with a nod. "I'll be in momentarily."

"I'll be right inside the door." He gave Rafe a pointed look. "Watching."

She rolled her eyes as he went back inside, closing the door. But she knew he hovered there. Indeed, watching and listening.

"Who was that?" Rafe asked.

"My new personal bodyguard. He's former Secret Service. He's good. Unobtrusive. And he's not interested in a coup."

"That's a plus," Rafe said with a nod. "You told him about me?"

"I mentioned if you ever showed up, I'm to be informed immediately."

He gave her a wary look. "Why is that?"

A demure smile crossed her lips. "I wanted to torture you."

"And I deserve that." His hand tightened on the pouch. "Can you forgive me?"

"That remains to be seen."

He handed her the pouch. "This belongs to you, princess."

She slipped it from his hand. "It's queen now."

"You'll always be princess to me."

Her heart skipped as she pulled open the drawstring bag and peered down inside at the glittering stones. The lost jewels of Andonia. They had, at last, been returned.

"Thank you for returning them."

"Logan wanted me to send his apologies about the Blood Stone. He has to keep it a little while longer, but he promises he'll return it to you."

"When the curse is broken." She tucked the velvet bag in the pocket of her gown.

"Yes, when the curse is broken."

"And will it be?" She looked up at him through her lashes, through the ridiculous mask she wore with peacock feathers.

"I hope so. I'd like to see the Hidden Lands again."

Questions swirled in her head as she tried to decide how to ask them.

"I've been released from exile," he said, anticipating what he knew she'd ask.

She smiled. "I'm happy for you."

"It doesn't matter, though," he said.

She lifted a brow. "Why not?"

"Because what I want isn't in the Hidden Lands."

Her heart clawed its way to her throat. "What do you want?"

"I thought that obvious."

"Nothing is obvious with you," she said, deadpan.

He took her hands in his, kissed her palms. With a gentle tug, he pulled her closer. "Then let me make it obvious. I couldn't stop thinking about you. You're everything I want. Everything I'll ever want."

"But the Hidden Lands—"

"It's not my home anymore. My home is with you wherever you are." He pressed is hand against her heart. "I should have said yes when you asked me to come with you."

Tears filled her eyes. "You're here now."

"Yes," he said. "I'm never leaving, unless you want me to."

"I thought you didn't want to be the queen's consort."

"I'll be whatever my queen wishes to be but a duke sounds pretty good."

"I'm sure that can be arranged. I *am* queen, after all. And now your queen commands you to stop talking and kiss her."

Rafe slipped the mask off her face and placed it aside on the handrail next to his. He ran his fingers through her long silvery hair. "As you wish, your majesty."

His mouth met hers and as he kissed her, their mating bond strengthened. His sweet kiss deepened into a demanding caress. Her pulse quickened when his firm mouth commanded a response. A response she gave him with her whole heart. When he tired of her mouth, he placed feather light kisses along her jaw and down her neck. There were no more winter shadows in her soul. He had chased away her chill.

"Don't you dare leave me again." Her fingers dug into the shoulders of his tux as her heart pounded a wild beat.

"Or?" His warm breath lingered on her skin.

"Or off with your head."

He chuckled, the laugh rumbling through his broad chest, and pulled her closer. His arms tightened around her waist as he looked down at her. Moonlight danced in his silver eyes. "Never. I will never leave you. I love you. Forever. Always."

"Forever. Always. You are mine and I am yours."

"Yes, my queen."

"I love you back." She stood on tiptoe and whispered it against his lips.

"That's a damn good thing."

As he kissed her again, Mia's heart was full. Her mate came home to her. It was the only thing that mattered. The only thing that made her happy. They'd figure out the rest of the details in the morning after she let him have his way with her.

Though he didn't know it yet, she was going to help him and Logan break the curse on the Hidden Lands. She was going home.

They all were.

Also by Michelle Miles

Age of Wizards (Epic Fantasy)
In the Tower of the Wizard King
On the Hunt for the Wizard King

**Dragon Protectors
(Paranormal Shifter Romance)**
Desiring the Dragon Lord
Seducing the Dragon Knight
Tempting Her Dragon Bodyguard
Dragon Protectors Book Collection (Books 1-3)

Dream Walker (Urban Fantasy)
Call of the Dark
Blood and Bone
Flame and Fury
Smoke and Ashes
Light of the World
Dream Walker Collection (Books 1-5)

Dream Walker: Origins (Fantasy)
Provenance

Enchanted Realms (Fantasy Romance)
Once Upon a Midnight Clear
Once Upon True Love's Kiss
Once Upon an Enchanted Kiss

Five Towers (YA Fantasy)
The Sorcerer's Daughter

Highland Destiny
(Fantasy Historical Romance)
Desiring the Highland Laird (Coming 2025)
Loving the Highland Warrior (Coming 2025)
Captivating the Highland Rogue (Coming 2026)

Ransom & Fortune Adventure
(Time Travel Action/Adventure)
Highland Fling, Vol 1
Dead of Winter, Vol 2
The Citadel, Vol 3
Lord of the Underworld, Vol 4

Guardians of Atlantis (Fantasy Romance)
Tempting Eden
Seducing Eve
Ravishing Helene
Guardians of Atlantis Box Set

Realm of Honor (Fantasy Romance)
One Knight Only
Only for a Knight
A Knight to Remember
A Knight Like No Other
Shadows of the Knight
Realm of Honor Collection (Books 1-5)

Shorts and Anthologies
A Dance Among the Faeries, Short Story
Eorwulf, Short Story
The Soul of Sharah, Short Story
Flights of Fantasy: A Collection of Short Stories

Watch for more at www.michellemiles.net

Did you love *Seducing the Dragon Knight?*

Pick up the third book in the Dragon Protectors series, **Tempting Her Dragon Bodyguard**, on sale now at your favorite retailer.

Praise for Tempting Her Dragon Bodyguard

"I loved reading this book and hope there are more to come."
—*5 stars, Amazon Reviewer*

"Book three in the Dragon Protectors series a well written story that kept me turning pages. I had to know what was going to happen." —*5 stars, Amazon Reviewer*

"...a captivating storyline..." —*4 stars, Amazon Reviewer*

He'll do whatever it takes to keep her safe.

Dragon Lord Jaxson Lane has spent a lonely existence drifting through the human realm with no real purpose. With the Hidden Lands cursed and his clans dying, his friend and ally, Logan, discovers the Drakana's sinister plot to use a blood ritual in the hopes it will heal their ailing world. The key to that blood ritual is Zahra, the only remaining noblewoman of the ancient Fire-Drakes and a woman Jaxson once loved now promised to another. Seeing Zahra again rekindles the fire burning within him and one kiss is all it takes to drive her back into his arms, even though he tries to resist her. Now with the Drakana after Zahra as their target, Jaxson will keep her safe by any means necessary.

Lady Zahra Veritor's betrothal to the son of one of the Council of Five leaders is not a happy one. The only man she's ever loved has been absent from her life for years until a chance encounter brings them together once again. When her life is suddenly in danger, Jax is the only man she can turn to for help…and the only man she's ever loved. As he protects her from the men who want to sacrifice her, tempting him back into her arms becomes her mission. But their game of seduction is cut short when she is captured. Now her only chance of survival lies with the only man she can truly trust—her dragon bodyguard.

Read more at www.michellemiles.net

About the Author

Michelle Miles believes in fairy tales, true love and magic. She is the award-winning author of the epic fantasy, IN THE TOWER OF THE WIZARD KING, as well as the fantasy romance series, REALM OF HONOR, featuring knights and their ladies fair, and the paranormal dragon-shifter romance series, DRAGON PROTECTORS.

In her spare time, she enjoys listening to music, reading, cross-stitching and watching movies. Even though she's a native Texan, she loves castles, dragons, fairies and elves and is an avid Game of Thrones fan. She can be found online at Facebook, Twitter, Instagram, Pinterest, and Goodreads.